TO THE END

Kenneth D. Reece

The characters and events in this book are fictitious. Any similarity to real persons, living or dead, is coincidental and not intended by the author.

To The End. Copyright © 2015 Kenneth Reece

First published in the United States of America by Reece's Publishing.

All rights reserved. In accordance with the U.S Copyright Act of 1976, the scanning, uploading, and electronic sharing of any part of this book without the permission of the publisher constitute unlawful piracy and theft of the author's intellectual property. If you would like to use material from the book (other than for review purposes), prior written permission must be obtained by contacting the publisher. Thank you for your support of the author's rights.

The publisher is not responsible for websites (or their content) that are not owned by the publisher.

Acknowledgments

I would like to thank several people for their support:

My mentor for priceless guidance

My mother & uncle for their endless support

My father for brainstorming with me

and last but not least

My friends for their continuous support through

countless barbs & jabs

This One Is For You

Grandma

Prologue

I'm one of a kind. I've lived a long time, with who knows how much more time to live. I've seen it all, from the most gruesome battles to all Seven Wonders of the World. I've been residing in the shadows, hidden from the world up until recently. Now, here I am, with this beautiful reporter, here to get my life story for what is going to have to be a T.V. mini-series.

"Before we begin I would like to thank you for agreeing to this interview, Mr. Silver." She looked around and added, "This is quite an extravagant home you have." She then sized me up, "Don't you think you might have overdressed?"

Sierra Morning, the country's most renowned deliverer of news. If there's a story that could potentially be the year's biggest, she'll be the first on the scene to investigate. She's beautifully commanding, the kind of person that makes you straighten your back when she enters a room. As a child, her father put her through multiple martial arts and other combat classes. Last year she sent some muggers to the hospital with baton injuries. Just over thirty, Sierra causes heads to turn as she captivates you with her soft brown eyes that compliment her flowing brown hair. Despite her gorgeous appearance and medium build, Sierra Morning is not to be taken lightly.

"Thank you for noticing. One could say I dress to impress regardless of my whereabouts." I never know who I might bump into and I always make sure to make the best possible first impression. At the moment I was wearing a navy blue suit vest over top of a popped white collared shirt with dark blue jeans and loafers.

I gestured to the couch, "Please take a seat, and you can call me Danny." After a narrow-eyed look of disapproval it was evident she wanted to keep things formal. "You and your cameraman buddy can make yourselves at home. This interview is going to take a long time." After Sierra took a seat, the cameraman set up, "This is going to be the story of your life, and probably the century. Would you like some coffee Si- I mean Miss Morning?" I think I could see a smile slowly creeping onto her face; then we made eye contact and she quickly wiped it away.

"No thank you." Sierra placed her bag on her lap. "And somehow I doubt that this will be the story of my life. I have reported on a lot of breaking news that would make anyone else's career." What she said was true; she had written and published many stories that would have satisfied any other reporter, but not her. She set out her personal recorder and laid out her notepad.

I walked to the thermos on the counter to pour coffee for two as I replied, "Oh I know, I carefully chose the reporter that would bring me into the public eye. I did some of my own research and I must say, you have had an impressive career." She stopped going through her bag to take in what I had just said. "You began your career in L.A.; as a lowly newspaper columnist and speedily rose to the top as an investigative reporter. Once you quickly learned everything there is to know over there, you came to The Big Apple for a new challenge." I looked over my shoulder to see a surprised and slightly violated look fall upon her face.

"Sounds like you have looked into my life a bit, but we are here for you, Mr. Silver. You seem to be the one with the extraordinary life." She paused when she saw me sit a filled-to-the-brim coffee cup on the table in front of her and then continued, "Thank you." She raised a finger to her cameraman and a green light on the camera flicked to life. "I would like to thank you again Mr. Silver, for meeting with me for this story." I nodded and let her continue. "Rumor has it you've lived longer than most, and hid it from the world. After World War II you decided to stop hiding and let more and more people find out you existed as time went on, receiving hardly any recognition, and until now you have not agreed to an interview." Sierra had an inquisitive look on her face, as if to question why.

"You forgot the part about being a crazy rich business man." I don't think she thought that was funny, she didn't smile, or break the lock she had on my eyes. I steadily returned her gaze as I announced, "I'm also a genius. I'm sure you have my school records in your mess of papers there somewhere. I used my real name in school." That broke her stare, as she shuffled through her archive of information. She pulled out a few papers to read.

"You've graduated at the top of your class from a lot of schools. Most remarkably, Harvard medical and business schools. Care to explain how you managed that?" Raising her eyebrows, Sierra looked back up at me and crossed her arms, as a mother would when questioning her child.

"There's nothing to explain. When you've lived as long as I have, you learn everything as it's discovered. It's much easier than learning it in the time given at a school. As far as business goes, I guess I sort of always had a knack for it." Even though I've lived for hundreds of years I'm still far from knowing everything. I'm still learning new things all the time.

"Do you own or run any businesses yourself?"

I took a sip of my coffee, "As a matter of fact I'm the founder of four Fortune 500 companies and I still own them." Sierra took note of what I was saying. "Due to the sensitive nature and private methods in which I have remained in control of these companies, I cannot reveal which ones they are or what it is they do."

"Are you sure there is nothing that you can share about these four companies?"

I smiled, "All I can tell you is that as of right now they are among the top three-hundred on the Fortune 500 list." I turned and looked into the camera, "To anyone out there that might try to find out which ones they are, I have taken many precautions, so that you can't and you won't."

Sierra unfolded her arms and rested her elbows on her knees. She was intrigued, "It takes a long time for anyone to achieve such accomplishments. Answer me this, the big question everyone wants to know: when and where were you born exactly?"

Sierra clearly wanted to know this more than anything else. Her body showed an intense eagerness as she awaited my answer. "I was born in New York, I'll tell you when, if you agree to a date with me." I watched as Sierra leaned back with wide eyes and began laughing aloud, as if I had actually said something funny.

"You have got to be joking." Without even turning her head, she pointed at her cameraman and demanded, "Delete that from the footage. You are joking right?" The expression on her face was a mixture of flattery and shock, as her eyes pierced mine.

I set my mug down on the table, looked right into her eyes, with a straight face and firmly answered her question, "No, I'm not joking."

Sierra seemed to ponder the thought of a date. There was an unmistakable glint of desire in her eyes as she replied, "Hmm. Alright, tell me when you were born and I might consider having lunch." I was satisfied with a maybe. "Besides, aren't you a little old for me?"

"It's fine. I don't mind dating younger women." She smiled at that. "I was born in 1669." Sierra's smile vanished into awe as her even eyes quickly widened and the cameraman's jaw dropped.

I looked at both of their astonished faces, "Why the wide eyes and the gaping mouth? What did you think this interview was for?" I smiled and looked right at Sierra, "So how about that date?"

Her face returned to normal. "It's just that it's not often you meet someone nearly three-hundred and fifty years old. We'll get back to the date later." Sierra leaned forward once more. "But first, tell me, who are you?"

Chapter One

It took one thirty-minute episode a week for six weeks to fit the whole interview on T.V. I'm relieved to have finally told my story to the world, though a larger part of it than I had expected wasn't ready for someone like me. I've received hate mail, angry phone calls, and people have even gathered outside my front gate spewing nonsense. One night Joey, my butler, chased off someone who broke in after they left a message on the foyer wall that suggested that I go back into hiding and figure out a way to kill myself. I swear if I ever get a hold of them I'm going to break their hands.

On the brighter side of things, I finally convinced Sierra to go to lunch with me a week after the interview, and we've been seeing each other whenever her work permits. I've received requests from freak science organizations that want to "study" me; I think that's a positive. The President even requested a private sit down with me, but I've had my fair share of dealings with presidents and I prefer keeping my distance from them anymore. Some group of psychos has started a website claiming that I'm some sort of "higher" being from "the great beyond." I mean come on, pick up a Bible and learn it.

Some people call me egotistical, but I like to know how the world sees me. It's recently become common for people to say "I don't care what other people think of me" which is ignorant for somebody to think. Even if they're wrong, you should always listen to your critics and use what they say to improve yourself. You can always be better. The trick is not letting what your critics say bother you.

Afterwards I was mailed a copy of the unedited version of the interview. I was in the home theater preparing the video when someone started ringing my doorbell. I shouted out to my butler, "Hey Joey, can you get the door?" Joey's been taking care of my house since eighty-two and he's become a good friend of mine. Though he has a few more grays than he would like, he's proven more than capable of being my bodyguard/partner in action when a situation calls for it.

Howard Brixton, my best and oldest friend had arrived, as planned. He didn't want me watching the interview without him. "Thanks Joe. Where's Danny?" Before Joey could even get a syllable out, "Ay Danny, where you at!?"

As I approached the top of the foyer stairs, I shouted back, "Keep it down! I'm right here." I started down the stairs to greet him.

"Well if you didn't live in a mansion you could answer your own door 'n it wouldn't be so hard to find you." Howey turned and looked around the foyer at the walls and the ceiling. "Steppin' into this place is always the same for me. It's like a home out of a movie or somethin'. Look at all this art, and you can't tell when the walls meet the ceiling. I hate the size of this place, but I do love what you've done with it." We said hello our usual way, with a simple handshake.

"Thanks and sorry if I try to enjoy life a bit with a big house. Deal with it." We began up the stairs then I stopped and turned, "Hey Joey, grab us a couple drinks and one for yourself, then join us in the theater." I continued up the stairs then shouted back, "I appreciate you Joey!"

Howey and I rounded the corner at the top of the stairs. "So Howey," I turned and gave my friend a concerned look. "How's the job been treating you?"

Howey answered as if his career were something as normal as a store clerk. "You know, same thing, different day; always havin' to deal with people that piss you off." Howey was making light of it, but I really wanted to know how he was doing.

Howey and I took a left at the end of the hallway into the home theater. "Howey, come on man. What's goin' on in the office?"

Howey remained silent until we sat down at the front of the theater. "Now you make it sound like I'm an accountant. Like I already told you, it's been the same thing every day. More potential terrorist attacks that I help put a stop to that the nation doesn't even know they're being saved from. Also I've been providin' oversight for black ops' in hostile countries. Not to mention intercepted transmissions between enemy nations. Nothin' unusual."

Howey and I met on the job back when I had been working for an above top-secret, un-named U.S. government black ops' agency. Howey became the youngest to be recruited at age twenty-three back in eighty-two. He was born and raised in Brooklyn New York where his parents were murdered during a home robbery when he was fifteen. Howey shot and killed the intruder with his father's gun in self-defense. With no siblings or any other family to look after him, he got a job and began to support himself, forced to grow up at a young age. Having no ties to the outside world is the only way to get recruited by The Agency, and so he did. Howey would be smarter than me if he was as old and it's his brains that kept him his position within The Agency.

"There hasn't been anythin' new bein' said about you if that's what you're really askin' me." Howey knew exactly what I was thinking. "Not since the threat came in from that terrorist cell making America an enemy for, and I quote, 'harboring a threat to humanity'. We haven't learned a single thing about them. Not even what they call themselves." Twenty-four hours after the broadcast of my final episode an unnamed and unheard of terrorist group sent an encrypted transmission directly into the Pentagon. This terrorist cell made it clear that they wanted my head on a spike and they've branded my country an enemy until they get their hands on me.

"What about that other thing I asked for you to look into?"

Howey looked down at me, "Really man? You don't have to be secretive in your own home. Say what you mean, but no. The geeks back at headquarters haven't discovered anythin' unusual with that blood sample you gave me. Don't worry though. I'll make sure we find somethin' out." Howey chuckled then continued, "They don't even know where the blood is from. I told them my team found a strange breed of chimpanzee."

"Thanks man. I really appreciate you doing this for me. Keep me posted on anything you find out; on the terror group too. I don't want to be the reason for a terrorist attack." Joey came back with our drinks. "Thanks Joey."

"Don't be so full of yourself. You're nothin' special." Howey took the remote and started the interview. "Now stop talkin' so I can watch your interview." I laughed at him then we quieted to watch "The Life of Daniel Silver."

***

"Tell me what you're living arrangements were like, the places you've been to, and the things you've seen." Sierra picked up her pen to begin writing down in her second notepad.

I laughed and told her, "The list of places and things I have *not* seen would be much shorter than what I have seen." I grabbed a throw pillow and wedged it between the couch and the back of my head. "I've lived on every continent at one time or another. Even Antarctica you ask? Yes, even Antarctica. I've seen everything from the most nightmarish things you could ever imagine, to the most heavenly beautiful things you can't even fathom."

"Can you describe any specific things or events you've witnessed?"

I've witnessed such gruesome and grim things that I wasn't about to share. "I've served in the Revolutionary War, Civil War, World War One, World War Two, and the Vietnam War. The Civil War was the worst as I'm sure you can imagine. I always thought that there should be a metal awarded to those who've served in all the major wars in American history. I was a prisoner of war in Vietnam. Being as I can't die, you can't imagine what that was like." I've been through worse so that wasn't difficult for me to talk about, but viewers won't know that. Joey and Howey know more of what I've been through than anyone else.

"I'm so sorry to hear that." Sierra slightly lowered her head, seemingly out of respect. "On behalf of America, I would like to thank you for your services and sacrifices." Little did she know, she knew nothing of my sacrifices. None I regret of course. "Let's move away from the horrors and how about you tell us about the beauty you've seen."

"Other than the one sitting right in front of me?" Sierra blushed and broke eye contact to look at her notepad.

This was a topic I always loved talking about. "I've seen new life being brought into this world and old life peacefully leaving." I closed my eyes to visualize the things as I was recalling them. "I've seen the sun rise over Niagara Falls and the sun set behind the ocean as schools of dolphins jumped out of the water. I've seen lions and gorillas defend their young from would-be predators. Once I was in the Appalachian Mountains as it was snowing during the sunrise, and I saw the sunlight reflect off of every little snowflake as each slowly fell to the ground. That's only a few breath-taking things I've seen." I could remember each thing as I was saying it. I opened my eyes to see a beautiful smile on Sierra's face.

"That sounds wonderful. I'll have to witness those things for myself one day." Sierra turned a page in her notebook to write more. "Why don't you tell me about your personal life over the years? Any family? Children? Wives?" This is the hardest part of my past to talk about and Sierra must have seen that on my face. "If you wouldn't like to talk about it, we can come back to that later."

I forced an uneasy smile, "Thank you, but it's okay. I've been married five times. Two of those marriages resulted in children. Two found out I couldn't die. One tried telling the public about me so I had to leave. The other that found out didn't, instead she loved me more for it. Together we decided not to have kids. And as far as they go..." I wanted to continue, but I couldn't and when Sierra saw that, she was generous enough to change the line of questioning.

Sierra had a sympathetic look on her face. "Let's talk about the cultures you've been a part of. Are there any other languages you can speak?" She smiled to get me to reflect it back to her, but it didn't work.

I took a deep breath and moved on, "I can speak all major languages: Spanish, French, German, Russian, Mandarin, Japanese, and obviously English. I learned Mandarin while studying martial arts in China, and I learned Japanese while living with the samurai in Japan.

Sierra seemed impressed. "Oh, so you're a martial artist. Are you also saying you're a samurai?"

"I'm definitely not a samurai. I do practice martial arts and I am familiar with the way of the samurai. I've trained with traditional martial artists and traditional samurai. Definitely two of the coolest things I've ever done."

"I've seen movies like 'The Last Samurai' and 'Ninja Assassin', so I can't help but wonder, how was the training?"

I thought it funny that she even asked. "It was brutal, like voluntary suffering." Sierra didn't seem to understand. "Everyone I met was born into that culture, so they didn't really have the option to leave. I went to their villages because I wanted to learn. Hollywood always exaggerates their stories for the viewer's entertainment, but in my case, they sold the story a bit short. Movies depict ruthless training, especially 'Ninja Assassin'. The training was that difficult and then some. I made my sensei aware of my ability, so he showed no restraint in my training. I would have died many times if not for my-". I searched for the right word, "- uniqueness. After it was all over, I was glad to have done it and now I can say I have. The knowledge and training I received have proven extremely vital in certain situations throughout my life."

"Are you saying it would be unwise for somebody to sneak up on, or attack you?"

"My training had conditioned me to instinctively attack anyone who would have snuck up on me with lethal force, so about hundred years ago I might have accidently killed somebody for sneaking up on me. Over the years I have learned to exercise restraint when necessary, but to answer your question, yes 'it would be extremely unwise to sneak up on, or attack me."

"I am happy to hear that what you went through was not for nothing. Well we have reached the end of the interview." Sierra clicked her pen and closed her notebook. "I'm not convinced you've been totally forthcoming. I believe you intentionally left chunks out of your life."

"You may be right. You may be wrong. You might find out if you were to meet with me in a formal setting one evening for a meal." I smiled and waited for Sierra's response.

Sierra smiled and stood. "We'll see."

Chapter Two

The date was September fourteenth, half past seven in the morning when the alarm on my phone started played Guns N' Roses' rendition of "Knockin' On Heaven's Door". I think the song is kind of ironic. If I had a theme song for my life, that would be it. I do have a butler that could wake me each morning, but I prefer waking up to the sounds of Slash lightly stringing along on his guitar.

As usual, Joey's timing was impeccable, he had set my breakfast on my nightstand just minutes prior. Joey re-entered my room and opened the curtains. "Good morning sir. I fixed you eggs, bacon, sausage, and poured you a glass of orange juice." The sunlight shined brightly onto my face giving me the warmth that made me happy to be alive. I reached for my coffee to not find it in its usual spot. "You need to hurry. Your coffee is on the table in the foyer. Your clothes are hanging in your bathroom."

Joey is not only my butler, but also a jack of all trades when it comes to running my life. "Thank you, but what's with the rush?" I leaned up against the headboard and began stuffing my mouth just as Joey advised.

"Miss Morning called at 6:42 and requested that I send you to meet her for coffee at 8:45. I would have woken you earlier if you hadn't stayed up late talking with Mr. Brixton. I'll pull the car around then wait for you downstairs."

"Hingks Oey." As I took my last bite of egg I hurried into the shower and Joey left my room.

***

The streets were abnormally clogged with traffic for this time of day. "Thanks Joey. I'll take it from here on foot." I opened my door, or at least I attempted to. The street was gridlocked and I couldn't get out on either side. "Open the sunroof." I climbed through the roof and hopped across cars to get to the sidewalk. Judging from the car horns and the gestures, they didn't seem to like it.

Two minutes late and I was still a block away from the coffee house. I spotted a floral stand and traded a five-dollar bill for a lily, Sierra's favorite flower, as I passed by. I picked up my pace a bit until I reached the door. I walked inside and the place was packed, "Hey Sandra congrats on the newborn." Since I frequent the shop I know a lot of names and faces. Sandra smiled and waved.

The coffee shop waiter Kevin shouted at me from across the crowded room, "Hey Mr. Silver! You want your regular?" He had gotten used to my face and always knew what I wanted.

"Yes Please. How's the new place?" I recently helped Kevin move into a new apartment. He smiled and gave me a thumbs up then I waded through the crowd to get to Sierra's table.

"I'm sorry I'm late." As I bent down to say hello with a quick kiss. I snuck the lily into the side pocket of her purse for her to find later, then I sat down across from her.

"It's only three minutes. It's fine." I signaled with my hand to Kevin for a second coffee and Sierra explained the meeting, "My work has been making it hard for us to spend time with each other so, I just wanted us to sit down together when I got the opportunity."

I reached across the table and held one of her hands in mine. "Don't worry about it. I have plenty of time. I'm happy to spend however much of it as I can with you." Sierra smiled and the waiter brought us our coffee. "Besides, I'm having some renovations done at home and I like to keep an eye on the workers to make sure everything is perfect." I held my ceramic cup of steaming coffee in both hands allowing the heat to warm them. There's just something about the classic ceramic and the way it warms your hands, unlike the paper and foam cups that are becoming the fad.

"Can I stop by tonight after work and take a look?" Sierra added two sugars and some cream then drank her coffee.

I gave Sierra a mischievous smile, "I don't think so. You'll have to wait until it's finished. It should be done by tomorrow evening anyway, and then I'll show you. I'll come over to your place tonight. Do you know when you'll be home?"

"If everything goes well I should make it home by…" Sierra's phone started ringing. "It's one of my sources. I'll call you when I get the chance." Sierra leaned across the table and gave me a quick goodbye kiss. "See you at my place at ten tonight." Sierra rushed out to get back to work.

I murmured under my breath, "Yeah. See you tonight." I understood her job, sort of reminded me of how I used to be, but it didn't make it any easier not being with her. I finished off my coffee and put my money on the table.

Just as I stood, another man behind me stood, "Hello Mr. Silver." A man I hadn't noticed was sitting right behind me. Maybe I'm getting rusty, "That's a touching relationship you've got with Miss Morning."

This man was Russian in his late forties. I turned around to face him, "Well, you know my name and my girlfriend's name. It would only be fair if I knew yours."

"My name doesn't matter. What does matter is that I know who you are and what you've done. Not just what you admitted to in your interview. I know *all* about you. You took something very valuable away from me that cannot be returned nor replaced and I intend to make you suffer much more than I did." The man turned around and began walking towards the exit.

I quickly grabbed the man's arm and he stopped, but one of two other men who must have been his bodyguards grabbed my arm. I let go and the guard let go. "Make sure he doesn't follow me. Oh and Mr. Silver, I'll be sure to say hello to Miss Morning for you." The man put his phone to his ear then began walking away, but I couldn't let him get away. I've learned that it's better to stop someone after they've made a threat rather than wait to see if they actually carry it out. As he walked out I heard him say, "Do it." Whatever that means I don't know.

The two guards each stood shoulder to shoulder and watched me. I took out my phone to call Sierra. As I was entering my password, one of the men took my phone and stomped on it. He smiled and then I made up my mind. I stepped forward as both men raised an arm, like mirror images. All eyes were on us. I kicked one of them in the groin and punched the other in the throat, quick and clean. There were too many people here to let it draw out, and I didn't have time to waste. People gasped and some started to evacuate as I ran outside, but the mysterious Russian was nowhere to be seen.

I went back inside and took one of the guard's phones. I turned to Kevin, "Call 911 and tell them everything that happened here." He looked horrified and picked up the phone. I dialed Sierra's number to warn her. I whispered to myself as the phone rang, "Come on, come on, come on." Damn, no answer. "This is Danny. If you get this message, stop whatever you're doing and go straight to my house." What can I do? Howey! I used my newly acquired phone to dial Howey's personal number next, "Howey this is Danny. Can you hel…"

"Sorry Danny. Can't talk right now. We're slammed with chatter of bombings around the world right now."

"Wait what? What are you talking about?" I ran back outside and looked for a taxi. Waiting for Joey to come back around the block would take forever, "When did this happen?"

"The first one was about a minute ago, but there are more explosions that we don't know the locations of yet. At least a dozen, with a few in the U.S. It's bad Danny."

Across the street there was a ground shaking rumbling as chunks of brick, stone, and shards of glass came exploding out of the second story of the building. The force of the blast knocked me onto my back. Pain jolted through my spine but I quickly shut it out. I got back up to my feet and saw that the windows of the coffee shop had been blown out too. I moved my head on a swivel, first searching for a person that might have detonated it then immediately realizing that because there were others that all the bombs were probably remote detonated from a single location.

I heard Howey shouting on the phone next to me. I picked the phone back up, "Get a list of all the locations and get them to Joey. I have an idea of what's going on." This was worse than I could have imagined. If I'm right, then this man really does know all about me; I once lived in the building in front of me that had just been reduced to rubble. "One more thing, Howey: track Sierra's phone for me. I think she's in danger. Text me the address of where her phone is, and I'll call you back."

I searched for any wounded bystanders, anybody that could use my help. One of the cars caught in traffic had been crushed by a chunk of the building. I ran to the car, hopping over debris and heard a baby crying from within. I pried the driver side door open and found the driver slumped over the steering wheel with her head turned facing me. I checked for a pulse and she mumbled, "My baby." I tried to undo her seatbelt but she pushed my hand away, "My baby first."

I opened the back door and crawled inside to the far side to detach the baby's chair from the seat. I moved back to the lady and her breathing had become shallower. I pulled her out of the car and yelled for Kevin. He came running out, "Grab the baby and bring them inside." I carried the woman inside and he followed close behind. "Get something soft to prop her head on and a few rags." The woman was bleeding from a head wound. Kevin returned with a towel and slid it under her head, "Apply light pressure on the wound with the rag, just enough to slow the bleeding."

He did so just as the phone I had began ringing. "Hello?"

"Hey Danny I got your message. What's the matter? Did you hear that loud bang? And whose phone are you using?"

Too many questions but she was alright and she sounded calm. "I think you're in danger. Where are you?"

"Calm down. I'm fine. I'm just outside my sources apartment door."

"Trust me, leave and…"

I heard a door open on Sierra's end of the phone. "Who are you? You're not A-" I heard the phone drop to the floor followed by screams. "Three men! White with black clothes!" I heard struggling, a man yell, and more screams.

Someone picked up the phone, "I told you I would say hello."

Chapter Three

After the call ended I got a message from Howey with the address of where Sierra was when I called her. I was both furious at the situation and scared for her. I called Joey and started running down the sidewalk dodging and shoving pedestrians. "Hey Joey, stop what you're doing and meet me eight blocks north and four blocks east of the coffee shop with a small infiltration kit." I hung up and entered a full sprint.

***

I paced back and forth on the sidewalk outside a rundown apartment building for about thirty seconds before Joey rolled up in my black Maserati. He stepped out with the briefcase that held my gun and gloves. "Here you are sir. I will also accompany you." Joey opened up his coat to flash his own gun.

I turned around and walked into the building of Sierra's contact. "Sierra was taken to get to me and this is where she called me from."

We stopped at the front desk to ask for directions. "Did a woman come through here looking for directions to a room? It would have been no longer than ten minutes ago."

This kid looked like a stoner and reeked like one too, "Yeah I remember. How can I forget, she's hot. But I don't think I can trust you." I don't have time for this. I pointed my gun at the young man. "Whoa! Okay! Room 216!"

"Thank you for being so helpful." I put my gun away, and ran up the stairs.

When we reached the top of the stairs I stopped and turned to Joey, "When I get into the apartment, stay on the door." Joey nodded and we proceeded. 212, 214, found it, 216. As I noticed Sierra's shattered phone on the floor, I screwed the suppressor onto my gun. "Sierra said there were three white men wearing black."

With the gloves on my hands I attempted to turn the doorknob, but it was locked. I backed up, checked both ways down the hall, breathed in, and kicked the door down. There was a burst of splintered wood that accompanied the unhinging of the door. As Joey kept an eye on the hall, I quickly stepped into the seemingly vacant apartment with my gun up. I saw a female on the floor across the torn apart living room and I could tell was not Sierra, but I would check her after I cleared the place. I moved from the living room to the kitchen where a savory looking meal was sitting on the counter. I raised my gun and moved down the hall after hearing a crash from one of the two bedrooms. A man was lying still in the doorway of the room I was approaching. I saw that the man had a large shard of glass in the side of his neck. I heard some more noise from the room and stepped into the doorway.

Sierra was on the floor with a man standing over her. I shot twice from the doorway and the man dropped dead. Before I could check her condition, the third man, who must have been in the other room, wrapped his arm around my neck restraining me. I struggled to get loose, but this guy had me in a flawless head lock. Sierra was badly injured and tried to stand up to help, but I raised my hand for her to stop. Right before I broke free, the man behind me released and I heard him thump to the ground. I quickly twisted around and saw Joey down the hall holding his smoking gun. With much gratitude, I simply nodded in thanks.

I turned and rushed to Sierra's aid. I looked her over and saw she was pretty banged up. She opened her mouth and whispered something nearly inaudible. "'Allison'? Is that who's in the other room?" Sierra winced in pain as she nodded. "Don't talk anymore. I'll explain everything later." As I got my arms underneath her, "Joey, check Allison." I lifted Sierra in my arms and met Joey kneeling over the body on the floor in the living room. He looked at me and shook his head. I looked down at Sierra, but she had already passed out. "After we leave the area, call 911, anonymously of course."

Joey escorted us out as I carried Sierra. "Joey, hold on." Before we reached the door to the outside I stopped. "Take my gun and drive us to the hospital. Then go home, call Howey, tell him what just happened, and ask him to meet you." When we reached the car I sat in the backseat and laid Sierra's head in my lap. Joey came around to close my door and I put my hand on his shoulder. "Thanks again Joey, for having my back. I don't know what I'd do without you."

Chapter Four

After Sierra finished recovering in the hospital that evening I brought her home with me and put her in bed. I met with Howey in my lounge to discuss the day's events. "So you're tellin' me that some mysterious Russian threatened you and Sierra because, according to him, you took something from him that can't be returned?" I nodded in confirmation. "Then he blew up a bunch of random places around the world? That doesn't make much sense." Howey showed up at my place just an hour after I called him.

"Yeah, except for the random part. This guy chose those locations on purpose, and I think I know why. That's why I asked you to bring a list of the bomb sites." Howey sat looking at me in deep thought. "So did you bring it?"

"Yeah. Why do you think this guy is targeting you?" Howey handed me a folder with the papers inside.

"I'm not sure yet. My mind has been running through every possible scenario, but so far I only have one theory." I quickly glanced at the locations listed on each of the papers Howey brought for me. I was right.

"Is anything poppin' out to you?" I couldn't believe it. "Hey Danny you there? What is it?"

"These places are all residences, homes." I looked up at Howey and he shrugged. "Each one of these places has been a home of mine at one point or another since records of home owners have been kept."

"So you've lived in at least two different countries on every continent and one place in Antarctica." I nodded. "You have definitely lived a good life my friend." Howey leaned forward to ask a good question, "So this Russian, you did say he's Russian, has proven to know who you really are. Maybe while you were in Russia you did something to piss 'em off. And now he has some personal beef to settle with you. What's his next move?"

"You may be onto something, but it's worse than that Howey. Some of these places I've lived at while on the job for The Agency; it's not even on record." I wiped my hands down my face in aggravation. "To answer your question: I don't know. We need more answers."

"So this Russian not only knows where you've lived, but also where you've been on active duty for The Agency." I stood once I realized something was missing. "He might even know exactly what it was you were doing for The Agency."

I paced the room in thought. "That goes both ways, he may not know about The Agency or my connection to it. There was one place in Russia I lived at from after World War Two to 1966." I turned back to Howey and gestured to the papers. "That place is not one of the locations that was hit."

"Okay. So you're thinkin' it has somethin' to do with your assignment in Russia. What were you doing there and why didn't he blow it up? Maybe it has some sort of significance. He probably left the building standing because he knew it would turn us in his direction."

"Follow me Howey. I want to show you something." Howey got up and followed me out of the room. "I've been working on something that isn't quite finished yet, but it can be used for what we need."

"Where are we goin' Danny? What are you showin' me man?"

"Before I left The Agency I copied everything, and I mean everything, off of their systems onto an external hard drive and brought it here." When we entered the study Howey grabbed my shoulder.

"Dude, I don't need to warn you that that's a federal offense right? And if a judge wanted to, you could be charged with treason."

"Pssh, please. Committing treason is the very last thing on my to-do list. I mean, dying comes before treason. Besides, unless you tell anyone, my secret is safe." I continued into the library and over to the bookshelf.

I turned away from the shelf to face Howey. "Come on. You know I would never turn you in; no matter how many laws I know you've bent and broken." I have twisted, bent, and broken quite a few laws; Howey only knows about the ones from after we met though.

"I haven't shown this to anyone yet. Well, except for Joey of course. And like most of my things, you can't tell anyone about this." I turned back to the shelf and pulled a book.

"Really Danny? You've brought me down here to show me a book?" The bookshelf began to move along the wall revealing a hidden passage. "Ahhh, now a hidden passage is definitely more your style." When the shelf stopped moving the lights flickered on and the stairs became visible. "Did you seriously build a tunnel under your house?"

We began walking down the stairs into the tunnel. "Just stop talking until we reach the bottom." When we stepped into the darkness at the bottom of the stairs I flipped a switch on the stone wall. Suddenly the bookshelf closed behind us and the lights all around hummed to life revealing the massive cavern that had laid underneath my home.

Howey stood still in astonishment as he tried to understand the place he was in. "Holy s-"

"Come on, enough marveling. I have more to show you." I walked over to a set of computer screens on a platform in the middle of the cavern. "I've always had hidden places to lie low when I needed to hide and I just recently got around to building one here. I was inspired to build this place after watching a few movies."

I bought the property knowing that someday I could turn the cavern under the property into a small command center, training area, lodging place, pretty much anything I might need. After reading a few comic books and watching a few movies, I finally decided to start making the plans. I had a total of five metal platforms built along the cave walls. A platform for my workstation and computers, one with a large mat and wooden dummies for training, one with a small infirmary, another for storing stuff I don't want anyone knowing about, and lastly a platform that has an emergency exit that leads into the forest at the edge of my property.

Joey came in behind us and turned the computers on for me. "Sir, I didn't think you were allowing anyone down until it was finished."

"Special circumstances changed things up a bit. A Russian is targeting Sierra and me and the threat is very real. He's already proven to know who I am."

Howey finally rejoined me in front of the computers. "I have to ask Danny." I smiled and got ready for his obvious question. "Is this… the Bat Cave? If it is then this is the coolest thing I have ever seen. I've seen this place on paper and on screens, but it's even better in person."

"It inspired me, but no. This is not a Bat Cave, nor am I Batman. This is just where I do things that I would get in a lot of trouble for. If you really want to call it something, just call it a man cave."

"Really? Way too corny. A man cave is what a thirty-year-old momma's boy calls his room in the basement."

"Fine, just call it The Pit then." I patted my friend's back and sat in front of the computer monitors as I suggested we get started, "Now let's find out who this Russian is." I started typing on the keyboard.

"I lived in an apartment building in Moscow for The Agency and if your intel is right, that place is still standing. I was there to find a Communist group that had USSR loyalties and the capabilities to prevent its disbandment and make it an even larger threat to the world then it was before. I was to prevent any serious attacks and relay all intel I could find on their associates, contacts, informants, and suppliers." I pulled up the operation on the main screen. "I found the group of radical Communists and infiltrated their ranks. Of all the Communist groups that I found, this one had the most potential. These people had it all: handguns, machine guns, rocket launchers, armored trucks, a couple tanks, and a few ships, mostly kept in a warehouse hidden underground. They had politicians in their pockets, so until I came along, they were untouchable. I had become one of them and after a few years I worked my way up the chain of command and became third in charge."

Howey stopped analyzing the cavern to pitch in, "Hold on just a sec'. You don't need to explain the entire op. Who did you have complications with and how did the op end?"

"The leader, Anton Richtov, had-"

"Anton Richtov?!" Apparently Howey felt the need to interrupt me, again. "I've heard of him. That guy was linked to all kinds of shady stuff in the Eastern Hemisphere. The Agency could never move on him because we never could find any evidence of what he was doing. I heard that one day he was killed by his underling, but I would've never guessed that it was you over there."

"That's real great Howey. Can I continue now?" Howey motioned with his hand for me to go on. "Richtov had high expectations for me and probably thought of me as his successor, but because I wasn't there very long I remained third in charge. After a few years, The Agency said that they had all the info they needed and I was given permission to destroy their armory and eliminate Richtov. I never had the privilege of being shown the armory, and I could never find it. One day during a meeting in Richtov's office, I poisoned his vodka and he died within seconds of his first drink. The vodka was terrible by the way. The second in command, Dimitri Krinchov, never liked me and always waited for me to slip up. When he caught me over his boss's body, he could finally kill me, or so he thought. He attacked, we struggled, and I cut his arm off with a nearby sword mounted on the wall. I escaped through the window and went to the extraction point."

Howey stroked his chin in thought. "You let the only witness survive to hunt you down. Not very smart. You know better than that Danny."

"His arm was gone. He couldn't have survived. He would've bled out."

Joey was listening intently the whole time. "Sir if you don't mind." Joey's my friend, but he still acts like he needs permission to speak freely, so I waved him on. "I can tell when you are hiding something and you're leaving a large piece out of your story."

Howey looked at Joey and back at me. "Yeah, what he said. You can't hide any important details from us." I remained silent. "Danny, it's us and this is important."

I looked up at Howey. "I got married while I was in Moscow." Howey closed his eyes, faced down, and shook his head in disappointment. "Her name was Natasha. She was my last wife and I went to see her before I went to the extraction point. We were in love and I thought it would help my cover, which it did."

"You're the smartest person I've ever known, but that's the dumbest thing you've ever done since I've known you. Do you know what happened to her after you left? Krinchov might have followed you to her."

"I don't know what happened. I completely cut all ties with everyone I knew over there once I left." That's how you handle working for The Agency. "Besides, Krinchov was bleeding out. He was in no condition to chase me."

I never thought about it, but I guess there's a slight possibility he survived. I just realized, "He can't be the guy we're dealing with now, he would be too old. The Russian that I had the pleasure of meeting in the coffee shop, if I had to guess, is forty-nine and he definitely had two fully functional arms. The year was 1966 when I left, so the Russian was probably born that same year."

"So maybe the thing you took that can never be replaced is actually a person, and that person was Anton Richtov." Howey was just grasping at straws now. "Or better yet, this Russian is your son and he thinks you killed his mom, Natasha." Howey laughed at his own joke.

"Seriously dude, not even funny." Howey looked at me like a neglected child. "I don't think we're going to figure anything else out tonight." I got up out of my chair and put my hand on my friend's shoulders. "Thanks for your help you two." I turned to the computer monitors and shut them down. "We can pick this up when we find a new lead. Until then just keep an eye out." I headed to the exit of the cave back up into my house, "I need to check up on Sierra then I'm off to bed. You can look around a bit more if you want Howey. Good night." I reached the top of the stairs into the study, leaving the cool, hollow darkness of the cave behind me.

Chapter Five

I tried, but I couldn't get a wink of sleep. Not after all that happened yesterday. I spent the night reading Sierra's reports. I had just finished reading her final report from before she left Los Angeles. It was 6:49 in the morning when she found me sitting in the morning room. "I didn't realize you had witnessed and accomplished so much while in L.A."

Sierra sat down next to me and rested her head on my shoulder as I put my arm around her. "Yeah well you're not the only one that can pretend to be someone else for information. A lot of stuff I did isn't even on file due to the frowned-upon methods I used to acquire my information."

I wasn't sure what she meant by that, but I decided to save those questions for a later time. "I am so very sorry to have put you through this. Whatever is going on, I won't let anything else happen to you; not again."

Sierra remained silent at first then calmly and quietly spoke, "I know you've done some shady things in the past, probably a lot of shady things. I have no doubt that you'll do whatever you need to but, neither of us knows what it is that needs to be protected against." Sierra leaned up and looked at me with fear and confusion. "What have you done that's come back to haunt you and threaten me? Ever since the interview, I knew you were hiding things, and I told myself that I would wait for you to share, but now I think I deserve to know what secrets you're keeping. What are you keeping from me?"

I leaned back, closed my eyes, gave a deep exhale, and began, "I used to serve the country through a group called The Agency. It's a black ops unit founded and funded by myself to ensure no true connection to the U.S. government. This is necessary because The Agency operates outside of the law and the only oversight it receives is from the Cabinet voted, and President approved, Director of The Agency."

"I did things from recon for intelligence gathering to preemptively eliminating terrorists that threatened national and/or world security among other clandestine operations." I looked into Sierra's intense eyes. "I haven't done a single thing that I regret. Everything I did that one might say is wrong, was for the prevention of something evil. Many times I had to make a decision between two options where there was no good or right choice; just two bad ones." Sierra seemed to have been staring right through me and didn't respond. "Tell me what you're thinking."

She blinked a couple times then looked back at me. "I trust that what you did was justified and that you'll do what you can to fix whatever we're in. Are you done working for this 'Agency'? Or do you still travel around killing people?"

Joey brought us breakfast. "Thanks Joey." I looked back at Sierra. "You need to eat something. You haven't eaten since you passed out yesterday." She didn't break eye contact, waiting for me to continue my story. "I left The Agency after my last op in Moscow, and something I left behind is what I think has come back to face me now." I told Sierra about what happened in the coffee shop after she left.

"So I'm being targeted by a Russian to get back at you for something you did to him?" I gave Sierra a sad nod. "Is that why you called and knew to come find me?" I nodded again and she continued. "Did Howey and Joey work for The Agency too?"

Sierra began to eat her breakfast. "Joey never did, but Howey still does. Joey was in the Special Forces for the military and usually operated off the record. He was so good that at a young age I recruited him to run missions, and he was my subordinate for a few years. He always spoke of living a peaceful life and doing something simple, so I offered him a position as my butler/bodyguard once he became a bit old for field work. Howey used to work in the field too and now runs field ops. He helps me get classified info that I ask for and gives me information on things that may involve me."

Sierra polished off her orange juice then gave me a puzzled look, "What do you mean 'may involve' you?

"Howey's been using The Agency's resources to help me find out who and how I am. He might find something groundbreaking or nothing at all." It was difficult for me to share since the idea of learning anything new about myself could be a fool's quest, and she might see it that way.

Sierra looked at me with deep, compassionate eyes. "It doesn't matter why you are the way you are; just that you are and you need to make the best of it." She laid her head back on my shoulder. "If you ask me, it seems you've done a lot of good. I don't think anyone could make better use of an endless life. You've given your all for the safety of other people. Be thankful you're still alive and that you've been able to stop evil in this world. I don't think it matters, but I hope you find some answers." In that moment, Sierra made me hopeful and less interested in who I might be. "Now back to the issue at hand; why would this Russian come to you at the coffee shop and risk being caught? Why not just do what he wants and get it over with?"

I had been asking myself the same question and came up with only one answer, "This man is methodical, calculated, manipulative, fearless, and he wants us to fearfully anticipate what he might do next. He's so confident in himself; his goal was to warn us that something is coming, yet make us feel like we can't do anything to stop it. He wants to make me suffer like he did." Sierra held me a bit tighter after I profiled and revealed to her our hunter's motives. "Don't worry. We'll be fine. Joey isn't just my butler, he's also my bodyguard. Howey is finding out everything there is to know about the Russian. Last, but not least, there's me; I'll handle anything that comes our way."

Sierra kissed my cheek and changed the subject, "Honestly, so far, I'm enjoying the excitement. I like the mystery. You mentioned earlier, that you've prevented acts of evil." I could hear her question coming and I braced myself for it. "What did you do about 9/11 and the assassination of presidents Lincoln, Garfield, McKinley, or Kennedy?"

And there it was. Five questions actually. "I'll answer the 9/11 story for now and save the assassination stories for another time." I grabbed the blanket at the end of the couch and covered us. "Hey Joey, can you get us some coffee?" It was a long story. "You know about the two planes that hit the World Trade Center, the one that hit the Pentagon, and Flight 93 which, though not made official to the public, was targeting the Capitol Building. Though these events were beyond tragic, it could have been worse." Joey delivered and handed coffee mugs to Sierra and I.

"There was a fifth plane that was targeting the White House. I was on this plane with no knowledge of the hijacking about to take place. I was just on my way to D.C. for a meeting with President Bush. Something didn't feel right, and I was suspicious of something going awry on the plane. I was alert and watching everyone. When one man walked towards the front of the plane and our flight attendant stopped attending, I knew something was off. I got up and passed the curtain between the cabin and first class. A different man tried to send me back to my seat. He wasn't wearing a uniform and he wasn't speaking, probably because he didn't know English. I twisted his arm behind him, and choked him out, then tied him to the cabinets. I proceeded to the cabin where I found the pilots lying on the floor and the first man I saw before, piloting the plane. The hijacker thought I was his partner and spoke to me in Arabic, which only confused me more at the time. Before he could look at me I umm…" I looked down at Sierra and finished, "I broke his neck." I paused to drink my coffee and to let her say something, but she only waited for me to continue.

"I sat down to take control of the plane. I had only just put the headset on when a third man came from behind and began to choke me. I was too focused on piloting the plane to free myself from his grip and he broke my larynx. When I regained consciousness, I could see the White House far off in the distance and I could hear warnings from ground control telling us to leave the restricted airspace, or we would be shot down. I saw the hijacker piloting next to me. I quickly swung my forearm into the hijacker's throat then retook control of the plane. With the headset still on I yelled, 'Don't fire! Hijackers eliminated! Do not fire!' I piloted the plane out of the area and landed at the original destination. Over the next couple weeks, I debriefed for just about every U.S. agency you could possibly think of."

Now that I was finished with my story, Sierra only had one question, "Is that what happens? Instead of dying I mean." She set her cup down and leaned up. "Do you just black out and wake back up later?"

I chuckled a bit, "After all that, that's all you want to know? Yes, I just black out when anyone else would die."

"I don't mean to pry, but I've been wondering, and I'm sure you have too: is there any way for you to actually die?"

I narrowed my eyes and looked at her like I couldn't think why she would even ask. "I hope you don't plan on trying to kill me." I smiled and she reflected it then shook her head no. "I have some theories, but none that I'd care to test. I won't share any either." Sierra looked disappointed. I guess it was the reporter in her that wanted to know. I kissed Sierra on her cheek then got up, "Come on, we have a long day ahead of us."

We got up off the couch and my phone began ringing. I looked at the screen and saw Howey's name, "Start getting ready I'll catch up." Sierra smiled and left the room. "What's up Howey?"

"Hey man. After I left last night I gave some computer nerds the task of lookin' into this Russian guy, starting with where you met him. When I came in this mornin', they found some great stuff. Our Russian has a name: Boris Leskov. I know, it sounds badass."

"Alright what else do you have?"

"That's it, just a name. Sorry man."

"Thanks for the call. Let me know when you find anything else."

Chapter Six

After I washed up, I started thinking about Moscow again. My best guess would be that this Russian from the coffee shop, Boris Leskov, is the son of Dimitri Krinchov. His mother probably found Krinchov dead and raised her son to hate the person who did it; a classic terrorist origin story. After all, the sons of murdered men make the worst terrorists. I can speculate all I want but the fact of the matter is, we know pretty much nothing so far.

The ring of my phone interrupted my train of thought. It was Howey, hopefully with some good news. "What's up Howey?"

"Hey man I'm callin' bout Leskov. Turns out he's got a past full of illegal activity and he wasn't as discreet as he is now. He had been arrested many times for being involved with mobs, drugs, and prostitution rings, and it's not what you think. He put bad guys out of business. By himself he would go around killin' mobsters and drug dealers. He didn't give 'em quick deaths either. When Russian authorities would find the bodies, they had been brutalized. Leskov tortured his victims before he ended their suffering, most likely to get info and locations on their associates and contacts. He was never locked up because Leskov was smart enough to never leave any evidence. He was never even charged with anything because well, I don't know why. If I had to guess I'd say somebody, somebody with influence, was lookin' out for 'em. Not to mention the authorities weren't too eager about stoppin' Leskov since he was doing what they couldn't to get bad guys off the streets."

"Now we know Leskov's past and that he's a serious threat. Tell me about what he's up to now."

"That's the thing. After he brought down a whole drug ring by the age of thirty-two, he just disappeared. After a year and still no activity from the not-so-friendly neighborhood vigilante, mobsters and drug lords started reappearing all over. Leskov never reappeared to put them back out of business."

I started looking up Boris Leskov on my computer. "So are we at a dead end, or do you have anything else for me? Do you have anything on his parents or childhood?"

"I'm glad you asked. As a child, Leskov was seen with a Russian who had a pretty obvious prosthetic arm. I think it's safe to say it was Krinchov. Leskov was also seen with a woman more often than Krinchov. When asked, she said she was the nanny, and never gave her name. We couldn't find out who she was."

"Do you know why they had the attention for this information to be found out?"

"Sure do. Apparently Anton Richtov's death was a big deal. A lot of attention was drawn to Richtov and all of his known colleagues after his death. The media was naturally drawn to Krinchov since he lost his arm the same day you killed Richtov."

"Is Krinchov dead, or could he be pulling the strings and using Leskov?"

"Krinchov is dead, so he can't be doing anything. He was admitted to a hospital in Moscow back in ninety-eight. He died eight years ago. I have the hospital records right here on the screen. I don't know very much Russian, but I think this says something about a heart disease. Which means Leskov is doing this all on his own."

While listening to Howey, something about the info just clicked in my head. "Wait hold on. What year was it that Leskov disappeared?"

There was brief pause while Howey searched for the answer to my question. "1998. He disappeared in ninety-eight. What are you thinkin'?"

I added the new pieces of the puzzle before answering. If Leskov was thirty-two in ninety-eight that means I was right about him being forty-nine and, "Do you know what this means?!" I jumped up out of my seat waiting to reveal what I learned.

"I have a feeling you're about to tell me."

"Boris Leskov was born the same year I left Moscow back in sixty-six!"

"Not sure how that's going to help us, but I'll look into it. I'll also forward that info to the geeks downstairs and get back to you when they find something."

"Thanks a lot Howey. Keep looking for stuff and keep me updated. I'm going back to where Joey and I found Sierra to see if there's anything we missed."

"Will do. Stay safe."

After I hung up with Howey, I finished getting dressed and went to find Sierra, but bumped into Joey instead, "Oh hey. Do you know where Sierra is?"

"She was in the study when I last saw her." I started to pass Joey to make sure Sierra didn't find anything she wasn't supposed to. "Don't worry sir, she isn't snooping, so she won't find the cave."

Without warning Sierra crept up and wrapped her arm around me. "What cave?"

Her sudden appearance startled me, "Uh, nothing. I was just asking Joey where you were, then he went on about some cave." That was probably the worst excuse I've ever come up with and she didn't seem to buy it. I looked for Joey to back me up, but he had gone, just walked away from the conversation. "I'm going out and I want you to stay here with Joey."

"Haha, no. I, am coming with you. We finally have the time to do something fun together." Sierra didn't really leave any room for debate, but I didn't want her leaving the safety of my house. "Where are we going?"

"I'm not taking you with me. You're safer here with Joey than anywhere else." I turned away and prepared to leave.

Sierra followed me and went on, "I didn't ask you, and I don't want to stay cooped up here in your house. I want to help you." She grabbed my arm and forced me to turn around. "I can help." Sierra was determined to get her way. She manipulated every part of her face that made her beautiful and turned it into something so gorgeous that no man could turn away, "Plus it'll be fun."

I dropped my head in disappointment at myself then looked back up at her and put on a fake smile. "So that's how you always get the inside scoop." Sierra didn't let up. "Fine, but you have to do things my way."

Sierra's face returned to normal. "This'll be fun. Wait for me while I grab my coat." Sierra turned around and bumped into Joey holding her coat. "Oh, sorry Joey. Thank you."

Joey looked at me, "I knew she would win."

Sierra was smiling at me and Joey was waving goodbye. Sarcastically I smiled, "Thanks for the support, Joey. Alright Sierra, lets go."

***

We reached the floor of Sierra's old source's apartment. The local police and paramedics were at the door pulling a body out on a gurney. I rushed up to the paramedic, "Hold on. I need to check the body." I pulled the tarp up to look at the woman's face.

"Sir, step back, this is a crime scene." The officer stepped between me and the body and pushed me back.

"Take your hand off of me. I'm with the FBI." I flashed my badge to the officer and he stepped back. "What happened here? What happened to the female and three male bodies?"

The officer spoke up, "This woman and her partner were paramedics that were tasked with retrieving four bodies. They never returned, so an officer was sent to check on them. The only bodies here were the two paramedics."

Leskov must have sent some men to retrieve the bodies and the paramedics were just in the way. Another officer came out of the apartment holding Sierra by the arm. "I found this woman snooping around inside." Sierra didn't look happy, or guilty for being caught.

I flashed my FBI badge again, "Let her go, she's with me." The officer let Sierra go and she pushed herself away from him, then I grabbed her other arm. "I need you to get everyone out of there so I can look around before you compromise the crime scene anymore."

I pulled Sierra inside with me to look around. "What were you doing in here? How did you even get in?"

Sierra looked at my hand on her arm and waited for me to let go before she answered. "When you distracted the guard, I slipped inside, but another officer found me. You didn't need to grab me like that. Besides, what are you doing with an FBI badge? Have you ever even actually worked for the FBI?"

"First of all, my goal wasn't to distract the guard. Second, you should have waited for me; I knew what I was doing. Third…" I put on my mischievous smile. "I lifted it from a real FBI agent a long time ago. The funny part is that the current FBI shield is different from the one I have. Fourth of all, I'm one of the founders of the FBI, so technically I can't impersonate an FBI agent."

Sierra had a look of surprise similar to the one she had during the interview. "Are you serious? Are you really one of the founders?"

"Yup." I quickly scanned the room we were currently in. "Let's hurry up and take a look around before they call their supervisor and find out I'm not really an FBI agent." The only reason Leskov would have the bodies collected would be so that they can't be identified, or maybe there were clues on them he didn't want anyone to find.

"Hey Danny, in here." I was in the kitchen when Sierra called me into one of the bedrooms.

"Did you find something?" I stepped into the room and Sierra was kneeling on the floor holding something small. "What is that?" She tossed it to me to look at. "This is a pin." I analyzed the pin more closely, "It's black with a yellow design on it. It's too small to make out what it is. We'll have to take it back and put it under a microscope."

"That's what I noticed, but I can't think of what it could be. I don't think we'll find anything else. The Russians were thorough; all the blood from their bodies that was left on the floor is gone. Even my blood is gone."

I looked at her impressively, "I finally get to see your investigatory side in action. I like it."

Sierra stood and smiled mischievously, "Oh there's a lot more to see." I was surprised at first since it's not often she makes innuendos. She usually only does it when she's having fun.

We both looked down at the pin as if we would notice something we hadn't already, "Leskov must not want any outside parties interfering with his plans."

Sierra looked up at me, "Wait, did you just say Leskov? As in Boris Leskov?"

Not sure how she could possibly know that name, "Yeah how do you know that name?"

"I've only seen it on paper from when I was in San Pedro Sula for a piece I did on Jamie Juarez."

San Pedro Sula is one of the most dangerous cities in the world and just so happens to be the home of one of the most dangerous men in the world: Jamie Juarez. I blankly stared at Sierra, partially in disbelief and partly in lust. I had never been with a woman so daring, and I liked it. I blinked back to my senses, "This isn't the place to talk about this. We'll continue this conversation when we get back to my place."

We were on our way out until I peered around the corner at the apartment entrance. An officer walked back into the apartment and put his phone away. I turned around and stopped Sierra, "What's the holdup? Let's go."

"Sshhh. They know I'm not FBI and they're coming to arrest us. We need to run for the door and push the officers down out of the way. I'll push the first one then you get the second. Got it?"

Sierra smiled from ear to ear, "I knew this was going to be fun. I'm ready."

"Alright, on three." I turned my back to Sierra and faced the exit. I held my hand out to my side to signal her. Three, Two, One. I rushed forward and shoved the first officer onto the floor. At the same time, Sierra ran passed me and kicked the second officer between the legs, forcing him to tumble to the floor.

We ran outside the building and when I reached the sidewalk, I stopped, causing Sierra to bump into me. "Pay attention. Don't look suspicious." I signaled with a nod of my head, "There's another officer out here. Walk fast, but be nonchalant about it."

We were walking at a good pace away from the officer when, "Hey! You two! Stop!" The officer I shoved had caught up to us.

I put my hand on Sierra's back, "Go home. Run. I'll distract them." Sierra dashed away into the cluster of pedestrians. I waited a couple seconds then ran in the same direction. I crossed the street at the end of the block and waited. I watched the reflection in the store window in front of me. When the officer was close enough I spun around, stepped to my right, and threw my arm out to my side. The officer ran into my arm and crashed to the pavement, but the next officer was right behind him.

"Stop right there!" The officer aimed his gun at me and the crowd of pedestrians quickly dispersed. I had no choice. I put my hands on my head and got on my knees. The officer approached me with his gun still raised. When he got close enough, I quickly pushed his gun up with my left hand and took his handcuffs with my right. I cuffed the officer to the parking meter, and disassembled his gun in front of him to pick up later. "I'm sorry, but I'm in the middle of something." When I turned around, I sensed something was different about him.

I walked a block away from the scene then hailed a cab to get home.

Chapter Seven

I paid the taxi driver and opened the front door of my mansion. I stepped inside and only just closed the door when I saw Sierra run across the foyer and jump into my arms to claim my lips for a lasting, passionate kiss. She pulled back a second at a time to talk, "That was… fun. We… should do… that more… often."

I held Sierra for a few moments longer then I lifted her off of me, "Yes that was." For me it was like a walk in the park on a Monday. "We need to finish talking about how you know the name Boris Leskov. He's still after us; we don't have time for pleasure."

Sierra folded her arms, "Oh come on. You're no fun." She turned around and began to walk away, "What do you want to know?"

I followed Sierra down the hall and around the corner into the kitchen. "How do you know the name Boris Leskov for starters?"

She opened up the cupboard and took out the supplies for a sandwich, "Like I said back at the apartment, I only know him from what I've read on paper. I was in San Pedro Sula, Honduras investigating Jamie Juarez's empire." In short Jamie Juarez was the largest money manager in the world for the criminally inclined and he had enough foot soldiers on his payroll to rival an army.

"Hold on. You're meaning to tell me you went to one of the most dangerous cities in the world and met an infamous crime lord that could have killed you just for kicks?" Sierra simply nodded while working on her sandwich. "For an article?"

She stopped what she was doing and looked at me, "I've put myself in harm's way for a story many times. That's what makes me the best at what I do. I know how to handle myself in dangerous situations." Sierra continued on her sandwich, "You saw the man I killed back at the apartment. It isn't the first life I've had to take. I've killed once before."

I walked around the island we were standing on opposite sides of and put my hands on Sierra's shoulders, "Why haven't you told me this?"

"It was a long time ago and I've gotten past it. Why are you getting so worked up over me killing somebody now? You seem to have done it plenty of times." The butter knife she held began to shake in her hand.

"I was going to talk to you about it when I thought it had finally dawned on you. You never get over your first kill. Not even I have." I placed my hand underneath of Sierra's chin, "You know you can talk to me about it right, about anything?"

Tears began to form in her eyes, "It was when I… I was still living in L.A. I had just gotten out of the shower after working on a story for thirty-six hours straight." This is the first time I've ever seen Sierra in this state. "I was staying in an old apartment building and I heard the floor creak as it usually did. I put on my bathrobe and walked down the hall to see what it was. I flipped the switch to turn the lights on so I could see what was there, but they wouldn't turn on. I had kept a gun in one of the kitchen drawers for protection. For well, you know, the line of work I was in." Sierra must have been a rambler when she was nervous or scared.

"When I reached for it, it was gone and I was suddenly attacked from the side." She took a deep breath and I pulled her in for a hug, "He shoved me to the ground, sat on me, and clenched my neck in his hands." I could hear the fear in her voice still so long after this must've happened, "I reached for anything around me to use, but nothing was close enough for me to grab. I tried to push him off of me when I felt the gun in his pocket. I took it and he tried to take it back. We struggled until a shot went off." Sierra looked up at me, "He, or what used to be him, fell to the ground next to me, lifeless. I got up onto my feet as fast as humanly possible and shot him two more times. I sat on the couch huddled up under a blanket, as if it would have kept me safe or something, with the gun in my hand until the police arrived in response to the sound of gunshots. I behaved like a coward, I know."

"No, of course you didn't. Don't think like that." I kissed Sierra on the forehead. "Killing a person is never an easy thing to do. You did what you had to." I turned her around to face the counter and stood behind her, "Nobody can blame you for that. It's wasn't your fault." I put the knife back in her hands and helped her continue making the sandwich.

"I know it wasn't my fault. It's the fact that I took a life from a person's body. You see people every day doing normal things, but the first time you see one that is just an empty shell of the man that once inhabited it; lying on my living room floor." Sierra lifted her hands and looked at them, "And my hands being what did it…"

"It's okay now." I put my hands underneath of hers and webbed my fingers between hers, "You're hands are clean. You won't ever have to take a life again. I'll make sure of that."

Sierra turned around and pulled my head down to give me a kiss. She pulled back and looked me in the eyes, and I in hers, "I love you Daniel."

I wiped a tear from her cheek and smiled, "I love you too." It was the first time we said those three little words to each other and it wasn't awkward like you see in those T.V. shows either, it felt right; like it was time that we finally said it. I looked past Sierra and at the unfinished sandwich, "How about we finish that and go lie down and watch a movie; something to ease your mind?"

Sierra wiped her eyes and nodded, "That sounds nice."

I kissed her once more on the forehead, "I'll go get it set up."

That was our first conversation that was emotionally intense for either of us. I learned something about her that deeply affected her as a person and she felt comfortable enough to tell me herself. I really did love her and I have for a while; I'm just glad we finally said it to each other. And from what I can tell, we have a promising future ahead of us, but until Boris Leskov is dealt with Sierra and I can never truly have a life together.

Sierra had arrived in my room and was standing in my doorway, "Danny I was thinking." She looked around the room, "Where are you?"

I peeked my head around from behind the small stand that the DVD player sat on, "Yeah? What about?"

Sierra walked over and began browsing through the different movies I had set out for her to choose from, "I was thinking that we should pay a little surprise visit to Jamie Juarez tomorrow. Maybe he can give us some information on Boris Leskov."

"You know I've never watched a movie in here before?" I finished plugging in the final cord to the unused DVD player, "I wasn't sure if you would've wanted to go, so I didn't say anything, but I already asked Joey to make arrangements for just that." I repositioned the television and faced Sierra, "I would argue that you shouldn't come with me, but I know I would just be wasting my breath." Sierra smiled, "You do realize that it'll be very dangerous right?"

Sierra put the stack of movies down and held one, "In case you haven't figured out why I love my job so much yet I'll tell you; it's the mystery and occasional danger. The rush that comes with the danger is so exhilarating. And in case you've forgotten, I've been there and I've met Juarez. If I don't go with you he'll consider you a threat before you can even explain your unannounced visit and then lock you up once he realizes he can't kill you." She tilted her head in thought and sarcastically asked, "You kinda need me don't you?"

She had a point, "I'll admit you're right, he trusts you, so he won't see you as a hostile. You'll go as yourself, writing a story, and I'll be your assistant on the article. Assuming the trip goes smoothly I think we can actually have some fun. We'll need to leave early in the morning, so it would be smart to make sure we get plenty of sleep tonight."

"Sounds a bit like role-play to me. I'm glad you're starting to see things my way." Sierra looked at the movie she held, "How about a romantic comedy; Valentine's Day?" I took the movie and looked at it for a few seconds, "What are you waiting for? Are you just going to stand there or are you going to put it in?" I looked at Sierra, giving her a chance to clarify what she meant, "But if you still want to watch the movie, that's okay too." Seductively, Sierra walked over to my bed and laid down. After being with each other for as long as we have now she still catches me off guard with some of the things she says.

I didn't mind the occasional rom-com, so I opened up the case and put the movie in the DVD player, "Do you want anything like popcorn or a drink?" Sierra shook her head no and patted the empty space on the bed next to her. I walked over to the blinds to close them and laid down on the bed next to Sierra.

She wiggled as close to me as she could and rested her head on my chest, "On second thought, instead of watching a movie, how about you tell me a story?"

I thought for a moment about what I could tell her, "Hmmm, alright." I turned the television off just as the movie was beginning, "This story starts with my earliest memory. The story that starts with me waking up on an island and ends with my first friend's death…"

Chapter Eight

My first memory begins with me waking up on the shore of an island though at the time I hadn't known that yet. I didn't know my name, who I was, or how I had ended up in my current state. There were clouds all in the sky and in the distance there were flashes of lighting accompanied by the sounds of thunder. I stood up and turned my back to the ocean to face the mass of land I found myself stranded on. I ventured into the foliage and searched for anything whether it be people, a shed or house, or even an animal; any sign of life other than myself.

I wandered around for a few hours and as I was doing so I found myself being able to navigate through the small forest, as if I had always known how to. Not that I had been there before, or even if I'd know if I had, but in the sense that I knew what I was doing. I knew exactly what hour of the day it was, which direction was north, which plants were safe and which ones were unsafe. After a day stranded I came to realize that I was in fact stranded on a small island. I wasn't sure how, and I still don't; but I had the knowledge of how to build a raft among the other previously mentioned things. At two days in, I determined to build a raft all the while feeding off of edible bugs and berries. I would estimate that it was about nine months when I actually left the island on my raft with stockpiled bugs and berries for the journey.

After a few days of floating in the ocean, I spotted a shore line. It took a few hours after that to paddle my way to the shore. With about a day's supply of food left in a sack made of leaves I continued my adventure by going into the mountains of this newly discovered land. As I traveled for days I had long run out of my collected food and the plants and insects I found were unlike any I had ever seen before. Eventually the berries I had eaten began having a negative effect on my body. Soon after I began feeling sick, I could no longer stand, and as I was losing consciousness someone approached me.

***

When I awoke I found myself lying on a floor in a room with a view outside where I saw unfamiliar trees surrounding a courtyard that appeared to be being used as a training ground by strange looking people in strange attire. A woman was sitting on the floor next to me and when she saw that I had awoken she quickly arose and ran off. As I leaned up to examine the strange architecture and strange new setting I found myself in, a wet rag fell down from my forehead. I placed it in the bowl next to the low-sitting bed and took a sip of the hot tea that was sitting on the short table. As I stood to my feet an old man with a long, white, and very well groomed beard walked in from an adjoining room through a sliding door. The woman that was kneeling next to me was now standing behind him. He gestured to himself and said "Sensei".

    He began to walk out to the courtyard while I remained still until the woman opened her hand and waved me forward to follow. The Sensei gave me a tour of the village, all the while speaking to me in a different language. At the end of the tour he opened his arms, and gesturing to all of the surroundings, said "Nihon" which when translated into English means Japan.

    Next the woman led me back to where I awoke and brought me to realize that it was my living quarters. I spent the next few months learning their culture and, through much trial and error, their language and dialect. I came to find out early on that the village I was in, trained their men to be warriors that they called samurai. After I became able to communicate well enough to hold a conversation they explained to me that when they found me my heart had stopped, yet there I was living and breathing. I requested to be trained in the way of the samurai. It was through rigorous training I came to find out that I couldn't die, which in turn the sensei made the training process much more deadly for me.

    I was there for seven years and a few months, and within that time I had learned all that the sensei could teach me. Throughout my time there, they called me by different names all based on their meaning. They called me Hideyoshi, Yuuma, Hiraku, Takuma, Isamu, Takeshi, Katsu, Shun, Ken'ichi, and Shinobu. Because I was able to learn so quickly and in such a short amount of time, they called me Shun which means fast and talented. The name that stuck with me, the name that they gave me before I left was Shinobu, meaning endurance. The sensei gifted me with a katana that I carried with me everywhere for the next few decades.

The sensei introduced me to a crew and a ship to sail back to the land that they had told me I was from. With nautical navigational skills I didn't know I had, I sailed back to North America. Only when I returned did I find out the year was 1716 and the month was September. By my calculations that meant I had awoken on that island at some time in 1708. I had landed on the coast of Virginia and I then settled there in town. I remained there for nearly four years until the locals began to take notice of my lack of aging and they rejected me for it. I moved to an isolated area in Western Virginia and became a courier there. After a while, I became acquainted with a man once known by the name of Augustine Washington and his family.

I visited him and his home once a week for seventeen years until I lost contact with the family. During those years, I very seldom saw George Washington. In 1748 I joined a surveying team were I formally met George Washington. George and I became good friends within a year as we were working in Culpeper County. While there I confided in him and shared my secrets with him; I told him about the island, Japan, that I couldn't remember my name, and that I couldn't die. He didn't find it so farfetched for he had noticed that I hadn't aged a bit since we met. George suggested that I take on the name Daniel for its meaning: "God is my judge".

While we were on the job, we uncovered an underground cavern with odd stone slabs and inscribed on them were strange writings. As puzzling as that find was, there was something far more intriguing down there; bones and no ordinary bones at that. The femur alone was four feet long which means that whoever, or whatever it belonged to was around nine feet tall. The discovery didn't get us anywhere so I just stored what we found. I still keep the findings in a warehouse today.

In 1752 George's brother died and a few days after the funeral I left to return to Japan. While I was in the samurai village, I heard about other villages inhabited by people called shinobi which are ninja. I was in search of their knowledge and skills, so I had decided to finally seek them out. When I found them I was immediately viewed as a threat. Only after a physical confrontation, losing it, waking up in a forest, and returning back to them did they accept me and train me in their ways. Just like with the samurai, the sensei didn't hold back in my training. I remained there in Japan for twenty-two years until I returned to North America with the new weapons they gifted me with.

In May of 1775 I reunited with George Washington after learning of his newly established role in government. After I made him aware of the new things I had learned, he officially appointed me as his personal assistant, when in actuality I unofficially underwent discreet jobs. George Washington is known to have been a spy master, and I can truthfully say that I contributed a great deal to everything that backs up that title. On top of that, I can proudly say that I played a role in forming both the Culper Ring and more notably the Continental Marines. During the Revolutionary War I did everything from scouting missions, retrieving vital information, some minimal wetwork, and some other clandestine work.

In December of 1783, after the war ended, I went with George back to Mount Vernon where I gave him my departure notice to go explore the west. After having spent time with the Native Americans in the west for nearly three years, I returned to Mount Vernon to drop off all that I had including some new artifact I had found. I then went and reconnected with George to share my new knowledge of the west and my self-drawn maps with him.

From April 1789 to March of 1797, I did a lot with George. My knowledge of the Native Americans allowed me to help negotiate treaties with their tribes. When George rode through towns to invoke the Militia Act of 1792, I was right there with him to help. At that same time and many others, I provided and was responsible for security for George. From time to time I did morally questionable things to help him. When Alexander Hamilton and Thomas Jefferson became aware of my actions they went to George to demand that I be expelled from the land, but George defended me so that I would stay by his side.

In March of 1797, George and I met with John Adams behind closed doors to discuss my abilities and services to George and the nation. We agreed that the same talk would be had with each presidential successor, in confidence behind closed doors. In the spring, after Adams took office, not having a place to live, I accepted George's offer to stay with him at Mount Vernon.

On the night of December 14 of 1799, George was surrounded by friends and family when he took his last breath. Anybody can find accounts of the names of people who were there in the room, but as planned and well executed, nobody can find any evidence of my existence back then. Before he died he requested that we not bury him until three days have passed, so that is what we did. The day of his funeral was probably the saddest day of my life. Close friends and family gathered around the original portico in which George once laid. At the head of the coffin was a silver ornament from which I took the surname, Silver.

I took the name Daniel as recommended by George and Silver for the ornament on the coffin. The name that I have carried with me for most of my life, Daniel Silver, is in honor of my first friend George Washington.

Chapter Nine

When I awoke, I found Sierra exactly where she was when we had dozed off. Her head still rested on my chest and her leg lied over mine. I wanted nothing more than to stay right here in this moment for as long as possible. Unfortunately, the two of us had a few things to take care of so early this morning. Paying an impromptu and uninvited visit to an infamous drug lord requires some preparation and evaluation. Part of me wants to leave without her to keep her out of harm's way; the other part of me wants to see how she handles herself in a dangerous situation. What I'm hoping for is that Sierra shows me that she can handle herself so that in the future I can be comfortable with bringing her with me on missions. Not only that, if I leave without her I'll never hear the end of it.

"Sierra", I whispered, "Sierra." She stretched herself out unfolding our legs. "We need to get ready for our trip." I gently brushed her hair away from her face as she turned her head to look at me, and I smiled uncontrollably.

Sierra leaned up and looked down at me, "I had a funny dream last night."

"Oh yeah? What was it about?"

"I dreamt about what you must have looked like back then; back in the late eighteenth century." I laughed because compared to today, the way I looked back then is very laughable. "Your face was powdered and you had hair just like George Washington does on the dollar bill." We both had a good laugh then we grew silent as we stared into each other's eyes. I couldn't help but smile at her beauty and she asked, "What are you smiling at?"

"Oh I don't know. If I had to say though, it probably has something to do with how beautiful you look just after you wake up."

Sierra brought her hand up to my cheek, "What are you trying to get with that kind of flattery? Didn't you just say we had a trip to prep for?" She lowered her head so that our lips barely touched, "Then we better get started." Sierra crawled off the bed and stretched her arms above her head. "I'll be in the shower." She strutted into the bathroom and made sure my eyes followed. She started the shower and threw her shirt in the doorway.

I loved her, but she always picked the worst times to take her sexiness to the next level. As much as I would love to join her in the shower, we have work to do and things to take care of before we can have any kind of careless fun. I rolled out of bed and stepped into my favorite pair of lounge pants.

Before we started to pack we needed to eat something. I always make sure I never go without breakfast. Not just because its my favorite meal of the day, its also my favorite. I left the sound of running water in my bathroom behind and went to the smaller of my two kitchens located on the second floor to cook up some eggs and bacon for Sierra and myself. I entered the kitchen and found breakfast already on trays held by Joey, "Ah sir, I was just on my way with yours and Miss Morning's breakfast."

I took my tray off of Joey's hands, "Thank you Joey. Leave a note on her tray and set in my room for her when she's finished in the shower. I'll quickly eat then help me start packing for San Pedro Sula."

"What? Why didn't you tell me that's where you are going? Need I remind you what happened last time you were there?"

"I knew you would respond like this, and no, you don't need to remind me Joey. Juarez knows Sierra and he might have important information on Leskov that, in case you've forgotten, we need. I'm going in as Sierra's assistant on a follow up article to the one she wrote about him. We need to leave here for the airport in about forty-five minutes to catch our flight."

I began eating as Joey was leaving the kitchen, "Send word if you need any assistance." I gave Joey a thumbs up as I continued to eat. In a minute I was finished and downed my morning shake. I placed the silverware and plate in the sink. I started to go through my mental checklist while on my way to the cave to pack while Sierra was still in the shower. I need:

- My messenger bag
- A notepad and laptop (since I'm going as a reporter's assistant)
- I should wear eye glasses to look the part. I can take the pair with a camera in them
- A knife I can hide on my person
- A disassembled handgun we can hide throughout our luggage
- Two two-way earpieces
- A belt of knives I can hide under a back brace that I'll wear
- Lastly a thumb drive to download files from Juarez's computer

That's all I could think of at the moment. I would come up with more things to pack as our departure neared. I returned to my room after retrieving all I needed from the cave. Now all I needed to do was jump in the shower and finish packing then we could head to the airport.

***

Our plane started rolling down the runway for takeoff when Sierra began asking me questions as I knew she would during the flight. "Considering how wealthy you are, why are we flying commercial?"

"Juarez will most certainly have contacts everywhere including the airport. He'll find out how we flew in. Flying in on my private jet would definitely tip him off to the fact that we are visiting for some other reason than for an interview. Remember, I'm here as your assistant for a follow-up article on the one you wrote about him a few years back."

Sierra nodded, "I see now. At least we're in first class." She turned to face me and folded her legs onto her seat, "I'm curious about something?" I placed my hand on her knee and raised my eyebrows at her as if to ask what it was she was wondering. "Why do you eat, sleep, or drink fluids if your body is self-sufficient?"

"Hmmm. That's a good question. Keep in mind that I don't know everything about my abilities yet. You know of course that my wounds heal rapidly, but what you don't know and what you can't tell anybody is that I need to be unconscious, sleeping, or in an extremely relaxed state for my body to begin its healing process. As far as eating and drinking goes, I'd have to guess that it supports the healing process. I was exploring once in some jungles when I passed out due to a lack of nutrients. I think that while I was unconscious my body, due to the lack of a better word, *fed* itself the missing necessities that I needed to continue my journey. I've learned nearly all that I know about my body through experience." I smiled at Sierra and leaned in for a kiss. "Come on, we both need as much shut eye as we can get."

She leaned to my ear and whispered, "I bet I can show you a few things about your body." I had no idea what to make of that comment. I was more confused and surprised than turned on. Sierra looked at me until she seemed satisfied with my expression, then faced forward and leaned back to rest, so I did the same.

***

We landed and waited patiently for our turn to exit the crowded plane. The moment I stepped from the plane to the tunnel, I breathed in and the scent of the tropical land filled my nostrils, rushed into my lungs, and brought a wonderful feeling of refreshment that I hadn't felt in a long time. "Doesn't it feel great?" Sierra must have been feeling the same as me.

We walked outside and were greeted by our chauffer; the man who would take us to Jamie Juarez's compound. "Hello, you must be Mr. Silver and Miss. Morning. Mr. Brixton spoke highly of you." He took our bags, "Here, we can talk more once we get on the road."

He put our bags in the trunk as I opened the passenger door for Sierra to sit, "This place is beautiful." She kissed me and smiled, "I'm glad I'm here with you."

"So am I, but unfortunately we're here for business not pleasure." She sat down and shut the door as the chauffer opened mine.

We got about a mile down the road, "I will take you as far as I can, but I cannot get you near the front gate."

"I didn't think so. How far will we have to walk?"

"His home is in a forest that runs along a beach. I will drop you off near the end of the driveway which is about a mile long. Try to stay on the path and out of the forest. There are traps all over the place in there. I'm sure I don't need to tell you that after I drop you off there is no extraction plan, there is no back up, you won't see me again. You're on your own."

"Yeah you didn't need to tell me." Sierra and I had our work cut out for us. "Did you remember to put a handgun in the trunk?" The chauffer nodded.

Sierra turned around in her seat, "Sounds like fun."

We finally reached the end of the driveway and unloaded our bags. I put on my travel pack and slung my messenger bag over my shoulder. I held a bag in each hand to keep Sierra's free. After unloading the trunk I slammed it shut and the car sped away, leaving us at the entrance of the den of the beast that is Jamie Juarez.

As we came around a bend, the corner of the compound became visible. I stopped and Sierra did the same, "Wait here on the side of the road. I'm going into the forest a bit to get a better view of the place before they know we're here."

Sierra grabbed my arm before I could go, "Remember what the contact said. Be careful of the traps."

"Please. I've spotted two dozen traps since we started walking. I'll be fine. You just stay out of sight, I'll be right back." Either the traps are just very poorly placed, or they're decoys. I climbed to the top of the hill on the bend and spotted two gunmen on the top of the walls and giant iron gates that open up to a courtyard. In the courtyard there was a fountain in the center and three more armed guards patrolling. On the other side of the courtyard were two large oak doors on the front of the building. I gathered a pile of leaves and brush to hide the gun that I took from the trunk of the car. I slid down the hill and met back up with Sierra, "I hid a gun up there just in case. There are two gunmen on the roof and three in the courtyard. Do you remember any of this from your last visit?"

She shook her head no, "There's nothing to remember. I met him at a totally different location. He must have moved after our interview." Sierra and I looked into each other's eyes as we both understood the danger we were walking into… together. "Let's go." She kissed me and we stood up.

We continued down the path, "Remember: we are not in a relationship. I work for you. You're my boss. You need to act like it. I'm going to walk behind you so it looks like you're guiding me. Our panic or danger word will be apple." Sierra walked ahead and in no time we had guns pointed at us and birds left the trees as shouts broke the silence of the forest.

Chapter Ten

When the shouting finally came to a stop four guards came out of the doors next to the front gate. Two of them rushed up to check Sierra and I while the other two stayed about ten paces in front of us with their assault rifles aimed at our faces. After the men finished searching our persons we put our arms down and one of them faced Sierra, "Quién eres?"

I don't think she knows Spanish, "He wants to know who-". Before I could finish one of the men hit me in the face with the butt of his weapon and I fell to the ground to sell it. Sierra didn't even turn to check on me. She knows I'm okay or she knows not to show emotion towards me; either way she's doing great.

Sierra defiantly looked the man in the eye, "Soy Sierra Morning y yo estoy aquí para ver el Juarez." I guess she does know Spanish. After I got back to my feet, two of the gunmen got behind us and directed by pushing with the muzzle of their weapons against our backs while the other two walked in front of us. I looked around and despite the heavily armed threat against us, this place was quite wonderful and the architecture of the compound was uniquely exquisite. Jamie Juarez must have a specific taste in architecture.

The guards lead us across the courtyard, through the front doors into the foyer, up the stairs, and into a large room on the corner of the second building. The guards left us in the center of the room and backed away. We were facing a large, well-built desk with windows in place of walls on the other side of it. Juarez is smart so the windows are probably bullet proof which means jumping through them can't be an escape route. There was a door on the wall to the right of the desk; most likely the one Juarez will enter through.

The four guards were still eyeballing us. There were pens on the desk, a few lamps, book ends on the shelf, the guns in the guard's hands, the large knives on their hips, knives on the small of my back, and of course the rest of my body; all possible weapons in the event of everything going south.

After a few minutes of waiting in silence, Juarez entered the room the way I predicted. "Hola Sierra!" He walked right up to her and hugged her, "It has been too long since your last visit." Completely ignoring me, Juarez turned and walked to sit behind his desk. When he sat he waved his hand, "Conseguir sillas para ellos." Immediately a guard set chairs behind us. "Please sit, you are guests in my home." I let Sierra sit first then I did. As soon as I bent my knees Juarez waved and shouted, "No! I do not know you. Who are you?"

This was my first impression, so I needed to sell my innocence. I avoided eye contact and answered, "I… I'm Sierra's assistant. My name is Daniel."

Juarez came around from behind his desk to me. I didn't have a read on him yet. I wasn't sure if he was going to hit me or kiss me. He put his hand under my chin and lifted my head, "Look me in the eye." I did as he asked, feigning hesitation and he gave me a quick hug, "Any friend of Sierra's is a friend of mine. Take a seat." He waved again and a guard brought him a chair to sit right in front of us, "I know it is different from last time, but after we last met I needed to move to keep myself safe. It is not that I did not trust you. I hope you understand." Juarez waved once more. "What brings you to my home?"

"Of course I understand. You need to keep yourself hidden and your whereabouts a secret; to stay off of, not only any government's radars, but your competitor's radars too." I was impressed. Sierra's heart rate was that of a resting one. She was totally calm. "And I'm simply here for a follow up interview. I want to know how a man in your line of work runs his business and how you invoke you authority. How have thongs changed for you?"

A guard set a tray next to us and poured a drink into three glasses. "Maybe I can give a demonstration when an opportunity presents itself."

We each got a glass. "Let us celebrate this reunion with drink." I lifted my glass to my nose and smelled an unmistakable drug that could only be picked up by a trained nose like mine. Juarez raised his glass, "To old friends."

I quickly drank mine and set the glass down, "Wow that's strong. Do you have anything more flavorful like an appletini?" I couldn't believe I just asked for an appletini. I reached for Sierra's glass and drank hers too. Hopefully she understood why I asked for an *apple*tini. "I'm sorry Mr. Juarez I'm just really nervous and when I get nervous I-". I slumped over and fell onto the floor. Whatever was in the drink simply paralyzed me. I would be fine in a few minutes, but for anyone else it would probably last a couple hours so I'm going to act like anyone else.

"Oh I am sorry Sierra. I was trying to be friendly; to make him feel at ease. Where did you find him? He scares like a little girl." Juarez laughed. I used the word apple, so hopefully that was enough warning to keep her from being too surprised.

"My editor assured me he could get the job done. I didn't realize he had such a weak stomach." Sierra held it together and kicked my foot most likely to show her disappointment in front of Juarez; that's my girl.

Juarez stood, "My men will take your baggage and escort you two to your room. I hope you do not mind being in the same room, but for self-assurance and security reasons I need it to be that way."

"That won't be a problem at all; he'll just have to sleep on the floor." They both laughed then I was lifted and delivered to the room with Sierra and our baggage.

"I will give you time to settle in then I will send for you when supper is ready. You are free to roam the grounds as you wish, though I should not need to warn you of the consequences if you are wandering where you do not belong. I hope you enjoy your stay."

I was laid down on the bed and Sierra said thank you as the guards left us in our room. Sierra locked the door to make sure we were alone then rushed to the bed to check on me, "Danny are you okay?" She held her head over mine and peered into my eyes when I opened them to look back at her. I opened my mouth and moaned in a failed attempt to speak, "Well as long as you're okay." She removed my glasses and pecked me on the cheek, "I'll start unpacking." I was really proud of her for handling me being poisoned as well as she did. Not fretting over my health or whether or not I would be alright.

By the time Sierra had opened our suitcases and arranged our belongings I was fully functional again. She pushed the drawer closed as I snuck up behind her and wrapped her in my arms, "I'm proud of you."

She inhaled loudly as I startled her, "Don't do that. You scared the day lights out of me." She placed her hands on my forearms, "Proud of me for what?"

I hung my head low next to hers, "For the way you handled yourself out there. You kept calm even as I was poisoned and fell to the floor. Kicking my leg was a nice touch too."

Sierra turned around to face me with her faintly blushing cheeks, "You're making a big deal out of it." She looked at me with her beautiful, glittering eyes and pushed me onto the bed. I sat up and she stood between my legs, "I love you Daniel Silver." It was like she totally forgot that there were heavily armed men outside the room that could kick the door down at any given moment and riddle us with bullets.

Right at the worst possible moment I looked over Sierra's shoulder and realized something that I should have before. It was the ceiling fan, then I looked around the room and noticed the desk, the lamp, and the telephone. I looked up at Sierra and put my finger to my lips as I stood and she stepped out of the way. I must have forgotten too that we were in a hostile environment. How could I have been so foolish?

I walked to the nearest lamp and lifted it upside down. Underneath was a small, metal piece of technology. I put the lamp down and held it in the palm of my hand in plain view for Sierra. She raised her arms with a quizzical look on her face. I gently set it down and raised a finger for her to wait. I went from the lamp to the ceiling fan, to the desk, to the phone, and then to the second lamp and held all five bugs in my hand. I went into the bathroom and lifted the window. I placed the bugs outside on the sill between bars keeping us inside then pulled the window back down.

From the other room, "What the hell was that all about?" Clearly Sierra wasn't too thrilled about the fact that I interrupted our moment.

I reentered the room, "Those were bugs to listen in on whatever happens in this room. There's a high possibility that Juarez already knows we're not who we pretended to be out there."

Sierra had her mind made up to be disgusted with my behavior, "I'm going for a walk."

"What?" I understood that she was unhappy, but now she just wasn't thinking, "We shouldn't leave each other now that Juarez knows we're imposters."

She wouldn't hear it. She put her shoes back on and walked to the door, "No! You're the imposter. He thinks I'm here as a reporter to write a story and that's what I'm going to do." She opened the door, "I'll see you at dinner," and shut it behind her. I saw her silhouette through the curtain as she walked down the hall to the right of the door.

There was nothing I could do. On the other side of that door we're not a couple anymore, we're co-workers. Forcing myself onto her would probably make things worse anyway. The best I could do with the situation at hand was to conduct some reconnaissance.

The windows were barred so the only way out was either through the door or to climb down the terrace. We entered through the front, the west side, of the building and judging by the turns we took to get to this room, I was along the south side of the building. I put my glasses and shoes back on and walked out onto the stone terrace that overlooked the central courtyard of the compound. There was another fountain here too and a few crates scattered around in the opening. I couldn't make out the writing on them, but I had a feeling they were the crates that I heard went missing during transport back in the U.S. That would explain how the guards were armed with U.S. military weaponry.

The place was well managed and kept looking pristine; too bad there were people around every corner that wouldn't think twice about killing me or Sierra. Below were vines wrapped around columns with grooves deep enough to get a grip on. There were other terraces along the wall next to mine that were within jumping distance. There were guards wandering around on the ground so going down there isn't my best option. I should try finding my way to Juarez's office for some snooping.

When being carried we took a left into the room, so I'll move clockwise around the courtyard checking each room until I find the office. When the guards walked out of sight I climbed onto the ledge and leaped to the next terrace over. I looked through the window into what seemed to just be another bedroom. I waited for the guards to walk out of sight again then jumped to the next terrace. I peeked into this room and quickly turned away after accidently exposing myself to two strangers and their extracurricular activities. An image I'd happily forget. I didn't see any more guards so I went onto the next terrace and found a desk unlike the other ones and a portrait on the wall that looked an awful lot like Juarez.

There was nobody in the room and the door was locked. The only reason Juarez would have locked the room is if he thought there was a threat which means he knows I'm Daniel Silver and that Sierra isn't here for an interview. Most of all this means I need to find Sierra and make sure she's safe. I removed my glasses and broke them to use the metal pieces to pick the lock on the door. Once I got inside I began my search with the desk.

Soon after I started I heard gun shots. Instantly my mind went to Sierra then I heard shots from a different location then another. Something was going down and I needed to hurry and get what I came for. I opened Juarez's laptop and put in the drive I brought. The decryption process had begun and the estimated time remaining displayed on the screen. I didn't have eight minutes to wait on this. I needed to find Sierra and get us the hell out of here.

Just as I was evaluating different possibilities I heard some commotion in the courtyard, "Daniel Silver! I have Miss Morning!" I looked outside the window and saw eight heavily armed guards with body armor. "I recognized you the instant you approached my compound. Leskov has issued a bounty out to all of the criminal underworld; five million for her and five more for you too." Encircled by the guards was Juarez with a gun pointed at Sierra. "Come out unarmed and call off your reinforcements and I might let her go." Reinforcements? I didn't know what he was talking about. Whoever else was here is an enemy of mine as far as I'm concerned.

Sierra looked at Juarez and I faintly heard, "You're about to get fu-" Before she could finish he hit her in the head with the butt of his gun.

The only available plan of action was attack; kill them all. I removed my back brace and pulled out the five knives I had. Nine hostiles, five knives; this shouldn't be a problem. From the terrace to the ground was two stories. With knives in hand I backed up an appropriate distance from the door and ran.

I butted the door and glass burst into every direction. I jumped onto the ledge just as everyone in the courtyard turned to see me. I threw two knives, leaped, and before I hit the ground two bodies dropped. I landed, rolled to my feet and threw two more knives that lodged themselves into two of the guard's necks. Juarez shouted, "Matarlo!" and the hired guns finally opened fire. I ran behind some stacked crates, jumped onto one, onto another, then leaped towards the nearest guard while throwing my last knife into the furthest guard's neck, three left. I hit the ground and in mid-roll retrieved a knife from one of the dead guards. I got to my feet in front of another guard and pushed his gun out of the way while thrusting the knife into his throat. I held up the body as the two remaining guards opened fire. I moved towards one guard and threw the knife into the other. Juarez wrapped his arm around Sierra's neck and began shooting at me as well. I got to the final guard, dropped the body I was holding up, dashed at him, kicked his leg out from under him and snapped his neck.

I turned and began walking towards Juarez, "Stop right there or I'll shoot." I could see the fear in his eyes and hear it in his voice. He shot thirteen times already and the Beretta he wielded seemed to have a custom mag with a capacity of fifteen. He lowered his gun to Sierra. She screamed out as Juarez pulled the trigger ripping through the flesh of her upper arm. Watching it infuriated me but one wrong move and the last bullet could hit her in a far worse place.

One bullet left. He aimed back at me. I saw his finger begin to pull the trigger and bent over to pick up a knife as he fired and missed. He pulled the trigger again and it clicked. Juarez shoved Sierra to the ground and threw away the gun. He foolishly charged at me and as he attempted to punch me I thrust the knife up into his forearm, grabbed it, turned him around, dislocating his arm, and forced him to the ground. I stuck the knife into his eleventh vertebra, twisted then whispered in his ear, "Enjoy life as a vegetable."

I rushed to Sierra and helped her to her feet, "Are you alright?"

She turned her wounded arm away from me, "What did you just do to him?" I paused unsure as to why she would even ask that. "Answer me."

"I killed him. Let me check your arm."

She looked at Juarez's limp body, "He's still breathing and he's bleeding from his back." I could see the gears turning in her head, "You paralyzed him." Sierra looked at me in disbelief, "How can you do that to him? To anyone? I don't care if he did shoot me in front of you." As she kept her wound clamped with her hand she picked up a gun from one of the dead guards, "Kill him or I will."

I took the gun she handed me and put Juarez out of his short lived misery, "There now let me check your arm." I suppose she was right about putting somebody through that. If she wasn't here I would have wrongfully left that man to live out his days in agony. I think she really would have killed him if I hadn't, but I'm making it my responsibility to make sure she never takes another life and becomes a killer like me.

"It hurts… a lot, but I'll be alright." She looked at the bodies around us, "That was incredible. I wouldn't have guessed what you just did was even possible and you did it all under a minute." I heard her but there was no room for ego in these situations.

I examined her arm and removed my belt, "The bullet went through, but I need to reduce blood flow to your arm so you don't bleed out." I wrapped my belt around her arm and tied. I then tore off my sleeve, "I need to tie something around the wound too."

Sierra kissed my cheek, "You're so hot right now." She made me smile.

"This is going to hurt." I pulled my torn sleeve tightly on her wound and a groan emitted from her throat.

As I finished tying I heard a pair of boots approach from behind me, "Step away from her now." I turned around and faced a soldier. He looked like Force Recon, but why would they be here. They're the guys that get sent to rescue the Seals. I'm the guy who rescues Force Recon.

"I respect you for being Force Recon, but if you don't put that gun down I will break your arm." He looked around at the bodies lying all over, but stood his ground. I respected his resolve but I gave him a fair chance.

Before I made a move I caught movement in the corner of my eye. I looked around the courtyard, on the ground and up on the terraces. There were soldiers all around. All with their sights trained on me.

"Wait Danny, stop!" Sierra moved me aside and looked at the soldier, "Steven? If you're here that means…" She trailed off in thought.

Steven and I exclaimed in unison, "Wait you know him."

"Stand down soldier!" Steven lowered his weapon and stepped back. When Sierra noticed the man in a USMC uniform walking towards us she warned me, "Oh no Danny. Don't say anything; let me do all the talking."

After seeing the man approaching us, I understood why they were here. He reached us and as I had no intention of heeding Sierra's warning I spoke, "Well if it isn't four star General Michael Morning of the United States Marine Corp."

Sierra looked at me confused, "You know my father?" She looked at Steven, "But you don't know my brother?"

"Brother? I didn't know you had a brother." I turned my attention back to Sierra's father. "And I do." The General and I eyeballed each other, "Although he's never had the pleasure of meeting me."

With his hands held behind his back, "It's good to see you Sierra, but I need to speak with Mr. Silver in private."

"What? Whatever the two of you have to say you can say it in front of me."

General Morning waved to Steven, "Escort you sister to my truck."

I leaned down to Sierra's ear, "It's okay, they can patch up your arm. I'll meet back up with you when we're done." Sierra looked uneasy at the thought of leaving her father and I alone, but kissed me in what felt like an intentional act of disobedience in front of her obviously disapproving father.

Steven approached Sierra, "Come on sis, let 'em talk alone." She looked at her father then me before she looked at her brother and began waking away.

When they were out of ear shot the General sucker punched me breaking my nose, "I watched your interview when I found out you were seeing my daughter and quite frankly I don't give a damn who the hell you are. I know I can't control who my daughter is interested in, but if you think for a second that I won't hesitate to personally lock you up in a hole that doesn't exist for pulling something like this again, you are gravely mistaken."

I cracked my nose back into place then it was my turn, "I'll let you have that one, but next time I will break your hand. And I don't blame you for not knowing who I really am since you don't have proper clearance. If you're talking about the hole in Southern Madagascar then you'll be happy to know I helped design it. And also I think you should know that you know nothing about me. What you should know is that though I may look younger than you I have lived many more lifetimes than you will and in turn I am much smarter and wiser than you. Lastly, general or not, I can have you dishonorably discharged then I could throw you in a pit that only I know about." I patted General Morning on the shoulder, "Thanks for stopping by. Sierra and I will be leaving now."

I went back inside and retrieved the flash drive with all of Juarez's files on it then rejoined Sierra outside next to an armored truck, "Ready to go?"

"You have no idea." She turned to her brother, "Do you mind giving us a ride to the airport?" His face said no, but he nodded so I helped Sierra into the truck and sat in the back seat.

***

Stephen dropped us off at the sidewalk in front of the airport, "I'm glad I got to meet you Steven; I just wish it was under better circumstances." We shook hands then he and Sierra said their goodbyes. I put my arm around her and we went to board a flight back to New York.

***

We landed in and walked out the front of JFK international airport. "That was fun Danny, but can we make our next trip one that doesn't result in me getting shot?"

"I truly am sorry about that." I lifted Sierra's arm and rolled up her sleeve to examine the patch work on her wound. Only little blood had soaked through and given how long it's been since we left I'd say it was done bleeding, "Luckily the bullet just missed your bone." I lifted her hand and kissed the back of it. "It should recover quite nicely." A taxi stopped at the curb in front of us. Sierra climbed in first and leaned on me after I sat down beside her.

***

When we were just a few miles from my house I woke her, "Hey. Are you awake?" She opened her eyes as the sunshine illuminated her face and her eyes began to sparkle leaving me no choice but to smile. She looked up at me and reciprocated my smile, "You had fallen asleep right after we left the air-". My sentence was cut short as I spotted an SUV coming at us from the corner of my eye leaving a split second of time for me to wrap my arms around Sierra.

The SUV rammed the side of the front end of the taxi on our way through the intersection spinning us around and leaving Sierra lying on the floor. She was conscious and bleeding from a small cut on her forehead, "Can you move?" She nodded sporadically, "I'll get their attention and you run to my house." I helped her up and I climbed out of my door.

There were three men with masks and assault rifles walking towards me. I ran at the nearest one and they each pulled their triggers unleashing a hail of gunfire. Only a couple bullets hit me when I got to the first one and formed a one knuckle fist to punch him in the throat dropping him to the ground. I began running to the next gunman when my body could no longer take anymore bullets and I fell to the ground.

Sierra and I just can't catch a break can we?

***

I woke up and an ambulance was on the scene with a firetruck. A pair of paramedics lifted the dead gunman I hit onto a stretcher. When I staggered back to my feet everyone couldn't help but stare at me; the man who appeared to be dead. Cameras and phones were in the hands of everyone looking at me with some shouting my name.

"Are you okay sir?" One of the paramedics asked. The gunman must have still had a pulse if they put him on a stretcher. I picked up the mercenaries weapon from the ground and fired into his head which initiated a series of gasps from the crowd, "I'm feeling better. Thanks for asking." A lack of police presence must mean the other gunmen got away.

I ran a couple blocks away from the scene and hailed a cab to get back to my house where Sierra should be waiting for me.

Chapter Eleven

When I got to the front door Joey was waiting for me outside. When he saw my blood-stained clothes and before he could even ask, "We were attacked on the way here and I fought them off so Sierra could get away." I speedily walked inside to make sure she got back safely, "Where's Sierra?" I turned around to see Joey's puzzled face.

"I haven't seen her since the two of you left for Honduras. Did she not return with you?"

I grabbed my phone to call Sierra. "I told her to come straight here after we were hit." Ring…ring… "Look around the house and try to find her." Ring…

The other end of the line picked up, "Ah, Mr. Silver. I was wondering when you would call." What's going on? "By now you should know my name is Boris Leskov." It is. It's the same Russian accent. "My men found Miss Sierra Morning trying to make her way back to your home."

I put my hand over the phone, "Joey! Downstairs now."

"I do admire your home." In the library. "It's not quite as large as my home though." Going down the stairs with Joey right behind me. "Do you remember what I said in the café?"

I covered the phone again, "Trace it Joey." I raised the phone back up to my ear. "How could I forget?"

"Yes, how could you. I threatened to take away something you deeply care for and now I have her." Tracing in progress. "Keep in mind: this is only the beginning. I will make things much more insufferable for you. When you want it to end, and you will want it to end, come find me. Ne do sleduyushchego raza."

"'Until next time'." I heard a sinister chuckle then Leskov ended the call. "Tell me you got him Joey."

"He made the call from an old spa house in the Russian part of the Bronx. Would you like me to go with you?"

"No. Call Howey and tell him what's going on. If I don't contact you in an hour, get Howey and come get us." I'm going to save Sierra and I'm going to eliminate anyone who gets in my way. "I'm going to get Sierra, and then I'm going after Leskov. Do whatever you can to find out more about him."

Though I've fallen in love and have been married many times, each time is different. When I fall in love, it's always stronger than the last time. Whenever I lose someone important to me, it's no easier than the last. I just get stronger so I can carry the increased weight; you never get over that kind of loss. I beat myself up whenever I lose someone for getting close again which just makes the loss much harder to bear. I've found myself in love once again. I can say this time is different, but I've said that before. I'm tired of reliving the same thing over and over. I'm going to make sure this time isn't like the others.

***

I parked a few blocks away from the sauna to approach without my presence being made known. The hour was 2300 and there's an ominous emptiness about the streets. Street lamps flickered and garbage went with the wind. I felt like I was in a horror movie, but this part of the city was always rundown like this. I stepped out onto the sidewalk and felt the chill in the air pierce my clothing.

I walked down the sidewalk, spotting the homeless as I passed each alley. Leskov's henchmen could be lying in the shadows, waiting to attack. I decided to walk around back and climb to a nearby rooftop for a better vantage point of the area. I walked down the next alley to climb the fire escape. Up ahead a man was smoking a cigarette, leaning on the wall facing me. As I continued walking, he tossed his smoke, and approached. We walked passed each other and I checked over my shoulder. He's gone.

I got to the bottom of the fire escape and I heard yelling coming from the lot at the end of the alley. I walked towards the noise and saw a man beating a woman against a car. I jogged up to the man and shoved him onto the ground. I knelt down on his chest and grabbed him by the collar. Before I could start beating some sense into him someone started hitting on my back. I turned around to see the very woman that he was beating on, hitting on me with her purse. "Let go of my boyfriend!" I threw my hands up and stepped backwards away from them. "Go! Leave us alone!" The woman tried to help him up, but he shoved her away. I thought I'd seen it all, but hey, if she wants to live like that, I can't stop her.

I walked back into the alley I came from to climb the fire escape only to find I can't reach it. I turned to a nearby homeless man, "Hey." He looked around then pointed to himself. "Yeah you. You want twenty bucks?" The man nodded, ready to hear my offer. "Give me a boost up to the ladder." The man walked over and wrapped his arms around my legs. "Hey now! Hold on." I gently pushed the man away. I interlocked my fingers and showed him what I wanted him to do. "Got it now?" He nodded then interlocked his fingers and bent over. I placed my hand on his shoulder and stepped into his hands. He hoisted me up and I grabbed onto the ladder. Once I was up the homeless man put out his hands. "I know. I didn't forget." I grabbed twenty dollars out of my pocket and dropped it to the man. He put his palms together as to thank me. "You're welcome."

I briskly climbed the stairs of the fire escape to the roof. With no buildings to obstruct its path the wind beat harshly against my exposed skin. I scanned the nearby rooftops and spotted light emitting from the skylight of the sauna three buildings away. I jumped from the roof I was on towards the adjacent building barely making it far enough to grab onto the ledge. I pulled myself up and ran across the rooftop and jumped across the much smaller gap to the next building.

Now I'm just one building away from Sierra.

I stood on the edge of my roof and peered down to the sidewalk in front of the sauna. Two shadows on the sidewalk outlined the presence of guards just inside the front door. In the corner of my eye I spotted a guard in the back taking a smoke break.

I needed to come up with a way to get inside without any of Leskov's men reporting me to the others. I don't want anything to happen to Sierra. The back way is the safest, so I'll go that way. Instead of a fire escape to get down, I have a dumpster. Dumpster diving is definitely not one of my favorite past times. I'd be at a safe height if I was diving into a swimming pool. I stepped onto the edge of the roof with my toes peeking over. It's a three story drop, but I had to jump. To keep from wasting time I stopped thinking and stepped out onto nothing.

In the brief moment before I hit the trash I began rethinking my personal policy to dress impressively. A loud crunch echoed in the alley when I landed, and I don't think it was the trash. As I began to climb out, I saw the guard flick away his cigarette and walk into the alley. He must have heard the same crunch I did. Back into the dumpster I go, closing the door on top of me.

"Who's back here? You can't be here. Leave." The guard spoke with a very thick Russian accent. His footsteps came closer to my hiding spot. He stopped. Where was he? Suddenly a loud banging echoed through the dumpster. Thanks for letting me know where you are moron. In a burst I pushed myself up, throwing the dumpster door open. The guard barely had time to even look at me when I grabbed his head and slammed it onto the edge of the dumpster. The guard slumped to the ground with his face leaning on the dumpster.

I was now officially back in the business of hurting people. And admittedly, I kind of liked it.

With no time to waste I hustled to the back door. I reached the door, but the only way through is with a key card. That's a clear sign this place is much more than just a sauna. The guard must have a key on him.

I went back to search the guard's limp body and got back to the door with card in hand. As I reached out to swipe the card, something on it caught my eye. It has the same island looking design on it that Sierra found on one of the pins back at the crime scene in the apartment building. I wish Howey or Joey would hurry up and figure out what it meant.

I swiped the card and the door propped open slightly allowing the steam inside to come billowing out. I stepped inside to find that this is definitely the women's locker room. A woman screamed and wrapped herself in a towel. As I moved on to find the door someone grabbed my arm from behind. I turned around and was caught off guard, "Whoa!" A very old and aged woman stood before me with a grin on her face. I blocked my view of her body with my arm to only see her face. "Do you understand English?" The horribly aged woman didn't respond. "Good. You're scaring me and I have a girlfriend, so if you could just move over there that would be great." I managed to break the scary old hag's paralyzing gaze and stumble out, but I had four friends waiting for me outside the locker room. I could have taken them out, but my best play was to let them take me to where Sierra was being kept, "Oh hey fellas what's up?"

Chapter Twelve

Leskov's men dragged me into the sauna where I found Sierra lying on the floor. As soon as the men let me go, I rushed over to Sierra and looked her over. "Are you all right? Are you hurt?"

"I'm fine, just a few scrapes and bruises. I'll be fine." Sierra smiled a fake smile in a failed attempt to make me feel better, "Why did you let them bring you here?"

"To find and rescue you of course." Once I saw that Sierra required no immediate attention, it was back to the issue at hand, "What's the purpose of this?"

"Leskov instructed us to bring you both here, alive. That is all." One of four armed men entered the room and set a bottle on the bench. "Here is a bottle of bleach for you. I am sure you will be very tempted to drink it to end this quickly, or you can suffer. Either way, you will die here."

"What's to keep me from killing the four of you and us from just walking out of here?" They each drew their weapons and trained their sights on us. I stepped in front of Sierra blocking their view of her. They backed up through the door and slammed it shut behind them. It sounded like they jammed the door shut but I ran over and attempted to open it anyway just to find that it was indeed secured from the other side. There was no getting out. At least not the same way we came in.

"We're trapped aren't we?" Sierra didn't move from where I had found her. "Why would they lock us in here?" She got up and walked to me.

She stared right through my eyes. "They used you to lure me here. They probably turned the temperature in this room way up, to the maximum most likely. Leskov wants me to watch you die." As I turned away Sierra grabbed my arm.

I looked into her eyes and saw fear. There was something else too but, I couldn't make it out. Past all the anger, confusion, frustration, and even guilt, there was something else. In less than a week I am to blame for her being kidnapped, beaten, kidnapped again, and possibly, her death. I can see that she knows I feel this way.

I can see now what it is that is in her eyes. What I saw was the unmistakable glint of hope.

I grabbed the arm Sierra was holding on to me with and pulled her close. I could feel the difference in heat as our bodies met. I brushed loose strands of hair behind her ear. I followed a bead of sweat run down the bridge of her nose until our eyes locked once more. We gazed into each other for what felt like a lifetime. I held her tighter, leaving no space between us. I began to slowly and gently draw Sierra's lips towards mine when the loud bang of the heating system abruptly brought us back to reality.

Our eyes broke contact and we began to wander the room in embarrassment. As I involuntarily backed away and began to wipe my sweaty palms on my pants, I became confused as to why I was behaving this way. Either it was the heat getting to my head, or the fact that I haven't been in a serious relationship in fifty years. It was okay though; this is neither the time, nor the place.

After I quickly regained awareness of the situation I put my hand on Sierra's shoulder, "Don't worry. We're going to make it out of this…together." I walked away to search the room. "Neither of us are going to die. Not today. Joey can track my phone and I told him to come find me if I was gone too long. He should be here soon." I walked to the bench and picked up the bleach.

"You aren't going to drink that are you?"

"It won't kill me, but I'm not an idiot. That man was right: not after long when the heat begins to disorientate us we will be tempted to drink this." I raised my head and pointed to the nearest window.

"The windows are too high up for us to escape, even if I were to lift you up." I cocked my arm back, and launched the bottle of bleach through the window. The glass shattered and the explosion of the bottle hitting the ground was heard even from within our smoldering prison. "Now neither of us will be tempted to drink it and some of the heat will be able to escape."

Sierra walked over and sat on the bench in the center of the room. "Well now what? All we can do is sit, sweat, and wait until Joey finds us." Sierra removed her shirt and wiped the sweat from her face, "How do you do it?" She could see that I didn't understand the question, "I mean how do you live? How have you lived like you have? Constantly facing danger and finding yourself in impossible situations. Being alone all your life with no one to burden the weight that you carry with you all the time and keeping so many secrets to yourself unable to share them with anyone."

I took my shirt off and swept the broken glass away from under the now open window. "That's a valid inquiry and I'll answer it truthfully. I've learned to avoid being pessimistic and recognize the goodness that does exist in the world. If I become a skeptic and give into possible fears, then I lose who I am." I folded my suit vest and oxford shirt to lay it on the bench then removed my under shirt to sit on the floor underneath the window. "But yeah, we can only wait. The most we can do is take most of our clothes off and sit under this window."

Sierra did as I suggested and sat down next to me, "How much longer do you think until Joey breaks down that door?"

"I'm going to say somewhere between twenty and twenty-five minutes." I looked at Sierra and put my clammy hand on her leg, where her pants were damp, and then she turned and looked at me. "I'll be the first to lose consciousness, but when I do you can't lose hope. We'll both be fine, don't sweat it." We both chuckled with the last bit of enthusiasm that either of us could find within ourselves then sat in silence.

***

About fifteen minutes of silence had gone by and I knew I was dangerously close to blacking out. In a struggle I turned to Sierra to see that she was still conscious, trying to moisten her mouth and lips. With my last bit of strength I slowly placed my hand on Sierra's. As I did my body became limp and slumped to the floor. It began to take all I had just to continue breathing. My vision became blurred and quickly worsened. Right before my visibility was reduced to nothing I saw Sierra kneel over me and grab my face. With hearing being my last operating sense I heard Sierra's dry, hoarse voice, "Daniel!"

***

I sometimes wonder what it would be like to finally die. Sometimes that's what I think about when I black out. I tell people I lose consciousness because they would never understand what really happens. There aren't any words to describe what happens to me. I'm pretty much stuck in a place between life and death. My brain is still somewhat functional. I can still think and access memories, however, all five of my senses are inactive, my body becomes a vegetable, if anything touches my body I cannot feel it; I can't even feel my heart beat, probably because I don't have one. The only thing I'm capable of doing is thinking, thinking about my current plight, how I will react when I awaken, and usually what I'm going to do the next day, when whatever mess I'm into is over and done with.

Chapter Thirteen

  I don't know how much time had gone by when I finally woke up. Before I opened my eyes flashes of blue and red shined through my eyelids, my ears were filled with the noises of sirens and voices all around, bouncing off of nearby buildings, all becoming a nuisance so soon after regaining consciousness. I opened my eyes and looked up to see Joey standing by my side. Joey wasn't wearing his glasses, or his butler tuxedo. His posture was no longer proper or professional like that of a butler's. Joey had put on his black under shirt and brown leather jacket with his olive cargo pants. He was also carrying his messenger bag that he used as a go-bag, most likely containing: water, some food, a gun, ammunition, and a few burner phones. This isn't Joey the butler, this is Joey my partner. His better half if you ask me.

"It's about time you woke up Danny. Sierra said we got you just a few minutes after you blacked out and given that, you've been out for about fifteen minutes. There were a few hostiles that Howey and I took out, probably just hired muscle since there was nothing about them that connects them to Russia or strange looking pins." Sierra! I leaned up and hopped off the gurney.

I was still weak and fell to one knee as soon as I touched the ground. Joey grabbed my arm and helped me back up. "Take it easy. You just woke up; you'll need to wait a bit before you regain enough strength to walk on your own." I spun my head around scanning the area to find Sierra, but couldn't. "If you're looking for Sierra she's sitting in the back of an ambulance. Howey is by her side on the phone with Agency Director Phillips."

I looked up at Joey for an explanation as to why the Agency was being involved in this. "Phillips called Howey. Locals heard gun shots and that's why local PD is here in the first place." Without looking Joey pulled his bottled water out from his bag for me and helped me back onto the gurney, "Here, hydrate yourself. I don't want to have to keep reading your mind just to have a conversation."

I took the bottle, unscrewed the cap, and downed the whole thing in a matter of seconds. "Thaa…" I smacked my lips and tried speaking again, "Nice man purse Joe." I laughed and Joey smiled.

"This one is yours." I leaned over to get a good look at the bag. It's been so long I didn't recognize it at first. "I dusted yours off and brought it for you. Mine is with Sierra."

I pushed myself off the gurney onto my feet and looked at Joey, "Take me to her." I followed Joey around to the backside of an ambulance. Howey's back came into view first while he was still on the phone with Director Phillips. As I came around to the back I saw Sierra sitting in the ambulance drinking from a bottle of water. When she saw me she sat the bottle down, stood up and walked over to hug me. I hugged her back, "You didn't think I was going to die did you?" She pulled away and gave me a disapproving look. "I'm glad to see you're alright. What happened after I passed out?"

Sierra licked her lips before she spoke, "I tried to shake you awake and when you didn't..." Sierra placed her hand on my chest, "I had to keep reminding myself that you couldn't die and that help was on the way."

I took Sierra's hand and held it. "We're both okay now, but I did some thinking while I was out cold... or hot, on the gurney." Sierra smiled and slightly tilted her head wondering what I would say next. "The best way, the only way to keep you safe is for you to keep your distance from me." Sierra looked at me in disbelief. "Leskov only wants you because you're with me."

Sierra pulled her hand away, "Are you saying that we have to stop seeing each other?"

"Literally yes, but I'm not breaking up with you." I pulled Sierra in for a hug to reassure her, "We just need Leskov to think we're not together anymore." I put my hands on her shoulders and leaned back to look her in her eyes, "You know I love you. I wouldn't actually break up with you. We just need him to think we have."

"Oh okay. I feel silly now." Sierra kissed me, "I love you too."

"Alright, now that we're on the same page you should head home. I'll get The Agency to post agents outside your building." I pointed to an officer in the distance, "That officer will take you home." I gave Sierra a goodbye kiss, "I'll see you later." As she walked off I felt a weight lift off my shoulders. I shouldn't have to worry about Sierra's safety anymore.

"Goodbye." Howey's phone call with Director Phillips finally ended allowing him to join us behind the ambulance. "First off I think she would be safer with you and you're wrong to send her on her own. Secondly, that was Phillips. Don't worry Danny, he called me." Howey stopped to size up Joey and his new appearance. "I haven't seen this side of you for what, twenty years. I like it, it suits you."

"That's enough about us. What did Phillips want?"

"You're right. Down to business. Phillips has been made aware of the threats made against you and Sierra by Boris Leskov himself." Howey saw the confusion on mine and Joey's faces and finished. "Leskov is the one who made the threat that if you weren't turned over to him he would attack the U.S.

and after those bombings, we now know he's fully capable of carrying out attacks of such magnitude. Somehow Leskov knew to contact Phillips to get to you and when he heard about you being at the center of the shootout here, he called me. Needless to say, Phillips wants to talk to you in person."

"You told him no though, right? That I'm done with The Agency?"

"I tried Danny, but uh… he's on his way to your house now. And when I mentioned The Agency to Phillips he said that the 'the agency' now has a new, more official title."

"Phillips really has some nerve butting his way into something that has nothing to do with him." It took me a few seconds to process what to do next. Sitting down to talk with Phillips might actually help me add a few more pieces to the puzzle. "It might be a good idea to sit with Phillips. We should head back to my house to meet him there."

"Actually Danny, I was thinkin' about sitting this one out. If I'm there I'll be forced to take sides and I don't want Phillips to know that my loyalties lie with you. Most likely that will cause him to lose his trust in me. If I lose that, I lose the resources that I've been using to help you."

"Smart. Alright, so Joey and I will sit with Phillips and one of us will get back to you on what's discussed." Howey and I shook hands and we went our separate ways.

Now we just need a ride to get back. I looked around and approached the nearest police officer. "Officer, can you give us a ride to my house?" The officer turned around and we made eye contact. I instantly recognized him as the same officer I cuffed to the parking meter when Sierra and I were fleeing the murder scene.

The officer put out his hand. "The name's Robert Price." I shook Robert's hand. "Don't worry Mr. Silver. I found out who you are and after I found out you were inside that sauna, I knew that you were involved with something I didn't understand. I don't want to arrest you and I won't tell anyone what happened, but I can't speak for the other officers you assaulted, so I would stay clear of them."

He seemed to mean what he said. Though if it was me I wouldn't let it go until I got payback. "Thanks, I appreciate your forgiveness and the warning. My friend and I could actually use your help." The officer looked intently at me waiting for me to repeat my request. "Could you take us to my house? We need to meet someone there."

"Sure. No problem." Price revealed his keys and smiled. "One of you is going to have to ride in the back of the cruiser though."

"That's not going to be a problem is it Joey?" I turned to smile at him, but he was already in the passenger seat.

Joey called out the window, "What are you waiting on Danny? Get in the back."

I climbed into the cramped space behind the cage and in just a few minutes we were on the road. "So Officer Price, I want you to tell us your story, but first I want to tell you what I think." Price looked at me in his mirror and smiled.

"Judging from your crew cut and your demeanor I'd say you served in Afghanistan. The border of your globe and anchor tattoo peaking from underneath your collar suggests the Marine Corps. You're smart and you know it. Smart enough to evaluate all the variables instead of jumping to conclusions and acting on them. That's why you forgave me so easily. You felt you didn't need a high school diploma to show how smart you were. You're still young so you probably dropped out and joined the Corps as soon as you were of age. You joined Special Forces during your second tour. Something happened while you were over there, something that made you leave at the end of your second tour, something that made you soft. You could have put up a decent fight before I cuffed you to the parking meter the other day, but you didn't. You probably won't hurt anyone unless it's absolutely necessary. Which is different from who you were before whatever happened to you in combat."

Price's face didn't reveal anything. There wasn't even a micro expression to pick up on. "Considering your flawless poker face this whole time I'd say you have experience hiding what you know. You were probably captured and tortured for information and never gave it up. The only thing I need you to tell me is how you escaped."

Robert looked at me in the mirror again. "Well you definitely know how to exceed expectations. You got one thing wrong...I did get my diploma, I just wasn't present for my high school graduation." We turned onto my driveway. "As for how I got out," Robert paused before he continued. "I was patient. I waited for an opening; a way out. I memorized my captives' routines and shifts. When they made a mistake I took advantage of it and fought my way out." Robert must have been able to see that I was impressed. "What I did was nothing special. I was Special Forces; I was trained to never break and to be able to handle anything alone."

Robert parked the cruiser under the pavilion outside my front door. "I get the feeling you were testing me to see if I was capable of talking about what happened." The three of us stepped out of the car. Robert made sure I was looking at him before he finished. "I'm not a soldier who can't live with what happened to him. I'm not some soldier who has trouble talking about what they faced in combat or gets broken up every time they do talk about it. I don't try to hide or run away from what happened to me. I accept what I went through and I'm stronger for it. I wouldn't change it if I could. It's an experience that I lived through to tell."

I placed my hand on Robert's shoulder. "I wasn't testing you. I was just curious. You might be as strong as you think of yourself to be, but for some reason that only you know; you felt the need to assert your strength and make it known to my partner and myself. You felt the need to separate yourself from other soldiers, as if you think you're better." He didn't seem to like what he just heard. Robert stood still as I met Joey waiting at the front door. I turned to leave him with one last thing, "I'm a soldier too Robert, a better one than you." Robert was stunned that I would say such a thing.

Joey opened the door. "Let's go Danny. You left him with enough to think about."

Chapter Fourteen

Joey and I walked in to find the round table that normally sat prominent in the center of the foyer, now lying over on the floor. We looked at each other and drew our guns from our bags and put in our two-way ear pieces. Joey moved to the lounge, room left of the foyer and I went to the dining room to the right. With my weapon raised I quickly moved into the dining room. No sign of a disturbance. I whispered into my ear piece to Joey, "Dining clear."

Joey's voice came back across the airwaves, "Come take a look in the lounge." I doubled back across foyer toward the lounge. I was halfway across the room when a man in a suit came around the corner at the top of the stairs. I put the man in my sights and placed two rounds in his chest before he could raise his weapon. He crumbled to the floor and rolled down the stairs. I checked the man for a pulse, but there was none. I moved on into the lounge and saw Joey kneeling over another lifeless man in a suit. "This guy's gun is still holstered and was hit once in the back and again in forehead. He didn't see the first one coming, then rolled over to see his attacker."

"So he was already in the room when he was attacked without warning." If the two men did come together then who killed this one? "We might have stumbled into the party a little late. I think it's safe to say things started before we arrived. If Phillips and his men are here then we need to be careful not to fire on them."

"I'm gonna shoot anyone who points a gun at me. Phillips or not." Joey moved into the doorway of the lounge to the hallway and I followed close behind. He stuck his head around the corner and quickly brought it back, "Another down the hall."

Most teams have to throw hand signals around to communicate silently. Joey and I know each other well enough to just look at one another and know what the other is thinking. He moved across the hall into the ballroom. Joey looked at me and continued on. I moved down the hall to see a trespasser's back turned to me. Suddenly a crash from inside the ballroom echoed and broke the silence throughout the house.

Everyone in the house knows we're here now. The man down the hall drew his weapon and stepped further down the hall nearing the entrance at the other end of the ballroom. I jogged down the hall to stop him from spotting Joey. He turned slightly and spotted me in the corner of his eye. He raised his gun and put his other hand to his ear.

In Russian he said, "He's here". After he spoke and before he could fire I pushed his gun away and shoved my gun under his chin.

"What are you doing here?" The man smiled in defiance. I don't have time for this. I hovered the muzzle of my gun over the shoulder of his arm wielding the gun. Something that I haven't felt in a very long time came over me. A smile slowly crept across my face and without hesitation I pulled the trigger. The man cried out in pain and dropped his firearm. I shoved the man against the wall and forced his head to the side.

I pushed the button on his ear piece to speak to the other person or persons on the other side, "Put your guns down now and gather in the foyer. Failure to comply will result in your death." I took his ear piece and pistol whipped him in the head. He slumped to the ground and remained motionless. I kept my two-way with Joey and put my new piece in my other ear.

I moved into the ballroom to see Joey standing over another body. "He turned around as I reached for his neck." I looked around at the mess that resulted from the ensuing fight. "There might have been a struggle."

"My guy alerted the other intruders to our presence here." We started moving as we heard gunshots coming from the second floor. Joey and I looked at each other and we moved out of the ballroom back towards the foyer. As we returned to the front of the house we heard two more gunshots and a body fell down the stairs. Joey and I looked up to see Director Phillips standing at the top of the stairs. Without waiting another second Joey raised his gun at him.

"Hey now! You can lower your weapon Mr... You know what; I don't think I ever got your last name." Phillips holstered his weapon and began walking down the stairs with his hands raised. "It's just me." I placed my hand on Joey's gun for him to lower it. "The man I came with was killed when we were attacked in the lounge. I fled upstairs to hold my ground." Phillips reached the bottom of the stairs and held his hand out. Neither Joey nor I shook it.

I took a step closer to Phillips, creating a feeling of personal space invasion. "I don't know how you got in here, but if you break in again I will tie you to a tree in the forest and leave you there for the wildlife to get to you."

"Let's not get carried away now. We're all friends here."

While Phillips and I were having a stare down, the sound of four individual windows bursting into thousands of glass shards broke our attention. We whipped our heads around to see four canisters spewing clouds of smoke out of them. "Follow me!" I turned and ran towards the study. Phillips followed behind me and Joey behind him. The front doors being kicked open was the next sound to enter my ears then the sound of bullets zinging past my head.

Once we were all in the study Phillips didn't waste a moment, "Either of you care to tell me what the hell is going on?" Joey turned around, closed the door and bolted it shut.

"Shut up for a second." I walked around to the other side of my desk and tapped a few keys on my laptop. A loud banging of cranks and gears echoed throughout the house. Steel curtains began to fall in every window and every door to the outside. A panel in the wall opened up next to the door in the study revealing a keypad and two small video monitors. Next, a humming started out quietly then became louder until darkness fell on the house and everything went silent. A few short moments later a light illuminated the study and another on the other side of the door in the hall.

"You have a lot of explaining to do Silver."

"Instead of demanding something you'll never get you should thank me for bringing you in here." I walked over to the bookshelf blocking the passage to the cave. I looked over to Phillips then to Joey. If I pulled the lever revealing the cave for Phillips to see, I would never hear the end of it. I would probably end up getting tried for treason and get locked up for a very long time. If I chose not to go into hiding of course. Joey shook his head in disapproval of me opening the door. Then again if Phillips did get into the cave Joey would probably kill him to keep him quiet.

Nobody would miss him.

At the same moment I grabbed the book more gunshots rang throughout the house. There shouldn't be any gunshots unless another party got into the house before the curtains fell. "Joey check the monitor." What good would a home security system be without security cameras equipped with night vision covering every square inch of the property?

After a few moments of cycling through the cameras, "You won't believe this one Danny." Joey waved for me to come over and Phillips followed. "Check this out." As I watched the screen I saw a figure slowly prowling through the halls. The camera had a view of a corner where two rooms met. Two other figures were moving toward the same corner. One of the figures had their gun raised and reached the corner first. The other stepped further into the darkness and pushed their self against the wall to remain hidden. When the first figure passed the corner the loner pistol whipped him in the head, shot down the second hostile, and took his earpiece. Before he stepped out of range he looked into the camera. "It's Robert Price and he's heading this way."

I walked around and sat behind my desk. I pressed the button on the earpiece I found. "Robert, this is Danny. Walk down the hall to the door on your right with the light."

"Wait. Did you say Robert Price?" Phillips seemed to know the name. "I was leading his op when he got captured. He was missing for eight months when he finally reestablished contact with me. He took photos of what we were looking for and when the extraction team reached the complex he was held in, the team reported to have found a blood bath. The team documented the incident with photos of the wake of death that Robert Price left behind. After that he quit and I never heard his name since."

More gunshots began to echo throughout the house. "Danny, it's Robert. I'm pinned down and can't get to the door."

"Alright just hold on." I got up and went to the door and put in the pin number to open it.

"Danny! What are you doing? You can't go out there."

"Sure I can Joey. Robert's under fire and can't get to us without help." The latches inside the door came undone and I grabbed the handle. "Just hang tight in here and keep an eye on Phillips." I pulled the door open and stepped into the hall with my gun raised.

I stayed close to the wall and moved along to find Robert. "I'm in the hall and I'm coming to you."

"I'm on the opposite side of the hall from the door." As he said that I spotted a figure down the hall. I fired twice and the figure dropped. More gunshots fired and I counted four more shooters, not counting Robert. I was coming up to the first room on my left and saw Robert knelt behind a shelf.

"I'm on your six." Robert turned and identified me. I signaled Robert to move down the hall while I covered him. As he started moving a shooter entered the room from the far side and another rounded the corner further down the hall. Robert, keeping low, quickly moved past me as I put down the shooter down the hall. I kept behind Robert and lost sight of the second shooter. Quietly I whispered, "Get to the door and wait." I set a flashlight on a stand and turned it on facing down the hall. I slowly backed up and waited for the target to enter my sights. Two shooters came around the corner. They fired at the light as Robert and I fired at them. There should be one more of them. I knocked on the door and Joey quickly opened up. The last shooter came around the corner and fired at us as we moved into the room. Joey opened fire and the shooting stopped. We got inside the study and Phillips shut the door behind us.

"I don't think there's any more of them. We're safe now." Phillips and Robert were looking at me with wide eyes. "What is it?"

Joey smiled and answered, "You got hit."

I looked down and saw blood running from a hole in my chest. I began to get woozy and smiled, "See you guys in a bit." I fell forward as Robert caught me and I blacked out.

Chapter Fifteen

When I finally awoke I found myself lying in the bed of the small infirmary in the subterranean area underneath of my house. I conducted a quick scan of the room and didn't see anyone. I rubbed over the spot where I had just been shot and only felt the remaining scar. Yup, I get scars. After I finish recovering from a wound it takes a few days for the scar to go away. I leaned up and stood up off the bed then noticed the bullet that had once been lodged in my chest sitting in a tray, though it didn't need to be removed. I don't know what effect it has on my body when foreign objects are left inside and the wound seals, but it's happened before. Joey must have removed the slug after getting me down here.

I walked out of the infirmary and onto the main platform of the cave to see Joey sitting in front of the computer monitors. He must have felt me nearing him because before I reached him, "I started looking over all the outdoor camera footage from the raid and learned some interesting things. Good thing you had two sets of cameras wired to separate networks because they disabled one set of them." Joey swiveled around in my chair, "How are you feeling?"

After I was finished looking at the frames Joey froze the footage, "Eh you know, just a little itching around the scar." I gestured back to the screens, "What have you found?"

Joey swiveled back to the monitors and restarted the videos with a different camera angle on each screen, "You notice anything?"

Not at first, but as I continued to watch I noticed something significant. "We know they were all Russian because we could hear them shouting to each other and in the earpiece I picked up." I pointed at the screens to show Joey exactly what I was looking at, "Here, here, here, and here. They're operating according to U.S. military raid protocol and using hand signals taught exclusively to the Marine Corps. I helped develop that protocol and taught those exact hand signals to Marines for a short time."

"That's what I noticed too, but it gets stranger." Joey tapped some keys and switched to the interior cameras from before the raid. "This is from when just Phillips and his one man were in here. There isn't any audio either." Joey started the video and I watched.

Phillips was in the lounge alone and made a phone call. He was on the phone for about two minutes when his man walked into the room behind him. Phillips quickly hung up then they began a shouting match. Phillips's man turned around and took a few steps away when Phillips drew his weapon and fired into the back of the unsuspecting man. Phillips rolled the man over then shot him once more in the forehead.

Joey paused the video with Phillips looming over the lifeless man. "He died just like we thought. Just not by whom we would have guessed." Joey swiveled back to face me again. "I'm really gonna shoot him now."

"We need to find out who was on the other side of that phone call and what they were talking about. Where are Robert and Phillips anyway?"

"I sent them out of the study once you fell over." Joey hit some more keys. The cameras switched over to the live feed and showed Robert in his police uniform apparently sleeping in the lounge with Phillips nowhere in sight.

"Check the footage from after Phillips killed his man to when we found him in the foyer. I don't like the idea of what he could have been doing upstairs. I'm gonna go talk to Robert then see if I can get some shut eye myself."

"Alright. I'll get you when I have something."

***

Before I sat down I looked around at the few of many corpses lying around my house. I needed to get the mess cleaned up and luckily I still had a guy's number from back when I was still in the business of killing. "Hello? Who is this?"

"Hey Georgie it's your old pal Rahm." Rahm was my alias back then. It was the name I chose when I started gaining a fierce reputation as somebody you don't want to cross.

"Rahm? I never thought I'd hear your voice again. I thought you were out of the business. Does your call mean your back?"

"I am happy to say I am not back. I just had a few uninvited guests that I need help with."

"Sure no problem. I'm just gonna need a little extra time to get ready. It would seem appropriate for people of our age to take it easy and not get our hands dirty anymore, but hey if you need my help Rahm, you got it."

"Take your time Georgie. They're in no hurry." We chuckled and hung up.

I sat down across from the couch Robert was snoring on and set my cup of coffee on the table in between. I took a few drinks hoping I wouldn't need to wake him. With him still sound asleep I hovered my mug full of coffee over top his arm and tilted it just enough for the coffee to run down the side and drip onto his arm. When the steaming hot coffee touched his arm he jolted awake, whipped the gun he was lying on into my face, leaving just a split second for me to lean out of the way before he pulled the trigger.

I looked behind me at the one of the many bullet holes in the wall and looked back at Robert. "Oh good you're awake. I need you to tell me why you came back after you dropped me and Joey off."

Robert used one of the throw pillows to wipe away the coffee on his arm then set it on the table with the gun lying on top. He looked up at me and spoke, "I'm going to act like you didn't do that."

"I think it's a little late for that considering you tried to blow off my head. Now answer my question."

Robert leaned back against the couch. "Why does it matter why I came back?" I simply stared at him until he saw that I wasn't playing games. "I was heading off the property until I saw multiple movements in the dark along the hedge line along the driveway, at which time I turned around. The gunshots started before I reached the front door and I entered through a broken window just before the iron curtains fell in the windows. Now you tell me why it matters."

I sipped some more coffee before speaking, "I'm just figuring out everything that went down tonight and why. Do you know where Phillips went?"

"No. He was sitting right where you are when I dozed off. What do you need him for?"

"Alright, first off, you stepped into what seems to have now turned into a war when you decided to come back here. Whether you like it or not you're a part of it now. Secondly, you are now on call for whenever I need help. You have skill, some of it you left in Afghanistan and I want to get it back for you. The first thing I need you to do is call this number." I slid a piece of paper across the table to Robert's side. "You don't need to know his name. Just tell him how you know me and everything that happened here tonight." I tried to make it seem like he had no other option than to accept, but he could easily refuse and just walk away.

Robert blankly stared at the sliver of paper then looked up at me. "I have no idea what it is you're dealing with, but that's going to need to change. As far as my skill goes you'll see it when a situation calls for it. Now I have a question of my own for you: what did you mean by 'I'm a better soldier than you'?"

I set my cup of coffee down, "It's simple, I want you to prove me wrong. I want you to show me that you can be a better soldier than me."

Robert nodded and stood up as if ready to leave. "I'll call your man as soon as I get home."

"I have an empty room upstairs. You seem pretty beat." I gestured around the corner, "You can help yourself to whatever you find in the kitchen." Robert didn't understand why I was being so generous. "You accepted the task, which makes you a part of this team now. You're welcome here now."

Joey came into the room as Robert walked down the hall towards the kitchen. "Did you find anything?"

"Nothing until Phillips left. He ran down the driveway and jumped the fence where a town car was waiting to pick him up. He got into the passenger side and they sped off. The system's running the plate and using traffic cameras to track the cars route now." Joey peaked around the corner down the hall. "He part of the team now?"

I nodded and patted my friend on his shoulder. "I'm gonna hit the hay. Talk to me when the sun comes up."

When I got out of the shower I called up Howey. After Sierra and I went our separate ways I asked him to keep an eye on her to make sure she remained safe. The phone rang four times before Howey picked up. "What's up Danny? Calling for an update?"

"Yeah. You're not busy are you?" I finished in the bathroom and began to prep my bed.

"Not at all. Just finished up some paperwork. I'll call my man on the office phone and put you both on speaker for you."

I heard Howey dial his man and the phone began to ring. Five rings before he answered. Howey spoke first, "Mike, you there? What's the status on Ms. Morning?"

There was some moaning and crackling in the speaker before we heard a response. "Boss? We were hit. My partners dead. Don't know status-". There was some deep heaving between the pause. "- Miss. Morning."

"Where are you Mike? Are you outside her apartment?" There was some rustling, on Howey's end I think. No response yet.

"Mike! Stay with me. What's your status?"

There was a loud, deep inhale and with Mike's last exhale, "Ye-". The e stretched on until Mike's life left his body. A phenomenon I would never experience.

"Still there Danny? I'll meet you at Sierra's place."

"Call me when you get there. I'll grab Joey and we'll see you there."

Not again. This is the third time now. I guess Howey was right when he said us not seeing each other wouldn't change anything. There's got to be a way I can put an end to this for good. Maybe eliminate Boris, but that still leaves his empire. I'll just have to bring that down too.

I found Joey still sitting in front of the monitors in the cave. "Joey! We gotta go, come on!" I didn't notice at first that Joey was on the phone. He quickly stood and put the phone down.

"Good you're here. Just got off the phone with local P.D; they spotted the car Phillips escaped in in the lower East Side outside an old motel. What do you have?"

"We can deal with Phillips later. Sierra's protective detail was taken out and now she's in the wind. We need to get over to her place now."

Joey jumped up out my chair and followed me down a hall in the back of the cave. It was completely dark at the end of the hall. A few more steps and motion sensor activated lights flickered to power and two parked cars became visible. One was an inconspicuous town car designed for recon and was equipped with all the surveillance you can think of. The inside of the car was lined with a special material so no signals could get into or out of the car without being wired to it.

The other I had specially made to meet my specifications. It's able to go from zero-to-sixty in three and-a-half seconds and capable of reaching three-hundred mph in times of emergencies like this. Joey and I quickly got into the car and sped off through a long tunnel with a hydraulic door that opened at the bottom of an old building that I owned. Motion sensors activated the door when I reached the half-way point in the tunnel. We exited the tunnel and pulled out onto the road five minutes away from Sierra's apartment.

***

We parked as close to the accident as the crime scene tape would allow. Howey met us there, "You busted out the fast one this time." Joey and I climbed out and walked over to Howey. "Follow me, I already took jurisdiction." We began walking and Howey continued, "Phillips has fallen off the grid and nobody's been able to reach him." Howey flashed his Department of Homeland Security I.D. to the officer on duty and we passed under the crime scene tape.

It's extremely rare that the Agency ever claims jurisdiction in an investigation. Agency personnel don't have shields or identification badges to flash when walking onto a scene. Having I.D. would confirm that the Agency actually exists. So instead phone calls are made and superiors are notified. It's been eight years since the Agency last took jurisdiction from a local department. The situation wasn't handled properly and some nosey people started poking around where they didn't belong. When this happens an agent trained specifically for said situations is sent to persuade (I use that word loosely) the curious individual to forget about everything they think they know and to destroy all research on the subject. Once there was an individual that did not heed the warning so, a different agent with a different specialty was sent to make it very clear that the matter was to be forgotten. Some form of torture may have been involved. I never apprised myself of all the details.

The accident outside the apartment was brutal. A large vehicle, probably an SUV, rammed the side of the agents' car. Driver probably died instantly and the other is the one Howey had on the speaker phone. "Some of the higher ups are considerin' a replacement for Phillips before the weeks end." We stepped through the front door of the apartment and started up the stairs. "I looked around Sierra's apartment already and didn't find much." We reached Sierra's front door. "The only thing worth looking at is in her bedroom." As we walked in Howey gestured in the direction of Sierra's room. "I made sure nobody else looked around in case there was any sensitive information or materials lying around." Being a journalist Sierra left papers and files lying all over the place.

Sierra always does an impeccable job of keeping her work and personal life separate. The living room of her apartment is littered with papers in such a manner that to the ordinary person it would appear to be a disorganized mess, but to Sierra it was the system that worked best for her; she never lost a single file or paper. Her bedroom on the other hand was spotless, completely void of work. If journalism never worked out for her she could always find a successful career in professional organizing.

I turned to Joey before I walked into the bedroom, "Take the car and see if Phillips is at that motel and you know what to do if you find him." Joey nodded and walked out.

"I take it Robert Price is part of the team now. He didn't tell me why you're looking for Phillips, so why are you and why is Joey gonna tie 'em up when he finds 'em?"

I only half heard what Howey said when I started moving towards Sierra's bedroom. "He's involved." The walk down the hall seemed to take much longer than the times before. Sierra was taken for the very reason I told her we couldn't see each other. Leskov has been getting exactly what he's wanted this whole time: for me to suffer. To feel the same pain that he must have. I got to the end of the hall and began to feel a little light headed and stumbled onto the support of the doorframe.

"Hey Danny you feelin' alright?" Howey quickly walked over to check on me. "You alright man?"

"Just need to sit." Howey walked me over to sit on the bed and Howey sat on Sierra's bedroom stool. I looked up at Howey. "There are only so many deaths and losses- so many heart breaks a person can take before it kills them."

"Whoa Danny don't go there. We'll find her, *you* will find her, alive."

"You don't get it Howey. Nobody will ever get it. I've watched my wives and my children die as the natural order of life would have it when one comes of old age." I held my stare, "And I don't think I can take it anymore. Did you know I've thought about killing myself, actually killing myself, for good? I think I know how to do it too." Speechless, Howey just laid his head in his hands. "I'm heading towards a dark place Howey, a place that I never want to go back to. The last time I was where I am now I spiraled out of control and it was bad; it was bad for the world. I did things that I wish I could forget."

Howey looked back at me. "This isn't over Danny. Don't you dare give up. We will put an end to this and not to sound cliché, but this story has a happy ending. So stand up and brush this off until we get this over with. Everything will get better."

I stood up and patted my friend on the shoulder, "I appreciate the pep talk, but there is no ending for me." I turned around and faced the resting place Sierra had been taken from.

"On a more positive note, the lab finished all the tests they could perform on you blood. They have no explanation for how you can't die, or why you remain permanently healthy other than an overpowered immune system." Howey opened his coat and handed me a vile of blood. "I figured you would want this back. It's your blood that does the magic. The lab rats noticed some abnormalities when studying it so, they ran some tests. One test included mixing your blood with an equal volume of the bubonic plague." I looked up from the vile with a surprised look. "In four hours, all traces of the plague was gone and your blood returned to its original state. The test was repeated with Marburg, Rabies, HIV, Dengue, and Ebola and the results were the same. They then concocted a mixture of different level four pathogens and in less than twelve hours your blood somehow got rid of all of the foreign samples." I held the vile of my blood at eye level as if to watch the blood cells operate.

"The only thing they were able to find an explanation for is how you don't age." I sat down at the foot of the bed again to finally hear part of the explanation for how I'm still alive. "I'll explain it all just in case you don't know. Instead of having one X and one Y chromosome like a normal male you have an X and two Y chromosomes. Though it is uncommon, it does happen naturally in newborn males and it's called Jacob's Syndrome. It usually results in brain defects such as delayed development of motor skills and speech skills, hypotonia, and motor tics. I don't know how you used to be, but you seem fine now."

Howey continued, "That's only one part though; the second part to the puzzle is the sirtuin one gene, also known as SIRT 1. Everyone has this gene, but it only becomes active after a person suffers from prolonged starvation. Once this gene becomes active it slows the aging process. This means at some point while you were thirty-eight you underwent a long period of starvation. The nerds at the lab don't know why, or how, but somehow your SIRT 1 genes clustered around your extra Y chromosomes. This being the case, the effects of the genes seem to have increased exponentially, hell, infinitely. That's why you don't age. And again, they have no idea how you can't die or why you remain so healthy."

Howey stared at me trying to get a reading on my face, "What do you think? Happy? Sad? Indifferent? Give me somethin' man."

"I don't know yet. I have too much on my mind right now. I can figure out what I think about it later."

"Okay well as long has you have blood in your body you will never age or fall ill." I tucked the vile of blood into my coat pocket. "Do you realize what this means? In your blood is the key to a universal antidote to every known and unknown ailment." Howey poked my breast pocket. "The world could really use what's inside of you."

I looked at Howey astonished, "Are you serious? My blood would be and can *never* be weaponized or duplicated. Soldiers can and will be *built* if anyone gets their hands on my blood. No one can ever get their hands on my blood," I paused and thought, "or is it my blood on their hands." Howey smiled because we both knew I was back to normal now.

"You're right Danny, I'm sorry. On another note this could mean you don't ever have to live alone anymore."

I tilted my head and looked at Howey quizzically. "You're not suggesting what I think you are you?"

"I'm not suggesting anything." Howey stood and was clearly hiding what he was really thinking, "How about we get back to finding Sierra."

"I would never subject Sierra or anyone else to the life that I lead; she would end up resenting me in the end, just causing more heart break for the both of us."

"You know me, I'm old fashioned. I believe there's a person out there for everybody, even you Danny."

"I believe that too Howey, but I'm alone; always have been, always will be. That's just how it is."

"I don't think you should have to live your life alone. Especially now that your identity is out there, you can't blend in anymore. Everyone will see you as an outsider now. Your future will be more difficult than your past ever has been. You need somebody alongside you to continue."

"I've made it this far."

"I'm sorry you feel that way, too bad I won't be around long enough to say I told you so."

I began looking around, "Yeah yeah, let's get to work." Just to be thorough I checked the closet and bathroom for any clues only to find nothing helpful. Her closet was full of clothes hung and organized by body part then by color. In the bathroom Sierra had set her clothes folded on the edge of the sink for the next morning as she always does.

I walked out of the bathroom and over to the bed side where I saw the impression of Sierra's head still in the pillow along with Leskov's signature in the form of another pin lying on it. Sierra never leaves without first making her bed and when she goes to bed she leaves her slippers neatly set next to it, so when I found her bed unmade and slippers upside down it became clear she was taken directly from her bed.

On the nightstand next to her bed something caught my eye. What appeared to be a journal or a diary had a pen placed between two pages. I picked it up and looked over at Howey; he shook his head no, but I opened it anyway. It was dated today and what I read was nothing I could have ever expected:

"Howard finally got back in touch with me regarding Danny's blood. As it turns out his blood is the key to his regenerative abilities. In theory his blood could give others the gift of long life. Hopefully this could mean I can stay alongside him for however long he lives. The only catch is convincing him. He

would never agree to an infusion of his blood. He would play the selfless hero card and say something to the effect of 'I won't let you experience all the darkness and torment that I have'. I'll just have to figure out a way to persuade him."

I turned to Howey and held up the journal, "Explain this, why did you tell her about my blood?!"

Howey sat back down and held his head low, "I'm sorry I kept it from you Danny, but you need each other. Shortly after you introduced us she asked me if your ability was transferable; before you even gave me your blood sample. She wanted to tell you herself. I didn't mean for it to seem like I was keeping this from you." I sat down to process the new information I had just received. "She's a grown woman Danny who has taken many risks in her life that have all paid off. You should know by now that she never makes a choice without carefully thinking it through." Howey walked over to take the diary and set it back on the nightstand just like I had found it. "You can protect her from Leskov and anything else in the world except herself. You can't protect her from herself."

The ring of my phone interrupted our conversation. Before I answered I looked into Howey's serious eyes, "Talk to me Joey."

"I've got Phillips tied up waiting for you."

"Has he said anything yet?"

"I didn't want to start the party without you."

"Alright good, I'm leaving Sierra's place now."

I stood up and looked Howey in the eye, "I won't let her do this and I'm going to tell her that myself when we find her." I walked towards the exit and turned around in the doorway, "I'm going to get some answers out of Phillips now."

"Don't do anything too reckless."

"Don't worry, I'll drop him off outside The Agency HQ, alive. I hope you get that promotion too."

"Oh and speaking of which it's not the agency anymore, bosses are calling it Acro."

Hmm I've only heard acro used in compound words and it means height or the top. Acro seemed like a befitting name for a secret independent agency that knows everything. "If it was up to me I would have chosen apex, but I like it." I turned around and ran to go get my answers.

Chapter Sixteen

I pulled up to the old, run down motel Joey must have found Phillips hiding out in. I climbed out of the taxi I took and paid the driver. I walked up to the room Joey texted me he was in. I knocked on the door and when it opened I was welcomed by the view of the inside of a pistol's barrel. The door opened more and Joey lowered his weapon, "Good, you're here." Joey stepped out of my line of sight so I could see Phillips tied to a chair. I walked inside and Joey locked the door shut behind me. Joey spaced apart the blinds to peak outside, "Doesn't look like you were followed."

"I didn't think I was. And I've got to tell you Joey, I'm never again going to let the Cabinet choose the director of Acro again. From now on I'm choosing the director personally." I approached Phillips and knelt down to be at eye level with him. "By now you should have figured out why we have you here. You are going to tell me everything I want to know. I do not think you will do it willingly, but I will give you the benefit of the doubt. We will start with a simple question: who were you talking to when in my home before Joey and I arrived?" Phillips raised his chin and spit in my face. I wiped my face with my sleeve and continued, "You know what I hate most in this world? When smart people make stupid decisions and you just made a very stupid decision."

I leaned up and turned around to Joey, "There's a gas station right around the corner. Can you run over there and buy a couple rags and a few bottles of lemon juice for me?" Joey nodded and opened the door to leave. "And grab whatever else you think we can get creative with." Joey closed the door behind him and I turned back to Phillips.

I sat down in the second chair at the small table facing Phillips with his head hung low. "Being the former director of the agency I am sure you are well aware of all the heinous things that happened over at Gitmo and Abu Grab. You have seen the photos, right? You have probably even been there, no? While I'm not a fan of the things that went down there, when necessary I can make the things that happened there look like child's play." Phillips raised his head and we made eye contact. "That's right, I have tortured many, many people and I have learned what methods are most effective at getting the answers. How to deal the maximum amount of pain without making you pass out. I also try new things each time just to see what works." I propped my legs up on the table, "One last chance, who was on the other end of that call?"

Phillips held eye contact and smiled, "I was made Director in part for my remarkable ability to keep the biggest and darkest secrets to myself."

I chuckled, "If whoever you are working for knew I had you they would be shaking in their boots and they would be covering their tracks because they probably know enough about me to know that I have a 'remarkable' ability to get the answers I want." I took out my pocket knife, "As technology has evolved and new methods of torture have been devised, serums and gadgets have been formulated and invented to induce immense pain without leaving a physical mark. As for me I prefer doing things the old fashioned way." I walked over to Phillips. "Let's gets started."

I grabbed his chin and forced his head back. Before I started I felt something creeping on me. I turned around but nothing was there. No. It was coming from within me.

With no resistance from Phillips I began making small incisions all over his face. Four cuts on the forehead, three on each cheek, two on the chin, and one on each eyebrow. Lastly I put the knife in his nostril and pulled it outward through his nose initiating a faint grunt from Phillips.

When stepping back and seeing my work, I felt something I hadn't in a long time. Something I've spent so many years hiding from. But why would I hide from something that felt so… good?

There was a knock on the door interrupting my train of thought and I let Joey back in. "You started without me? I thought you would return the favor and wait for me." He had a bag with the rags and vinegar and another bag of goodies that I would go through when needed. "They didn't have lemon juice so I grabbed some white vinegar instead." I happily thanked Joey and turned back to Phillips.

"So Phillips-"

Joey interrupted, "His first name is Edward. He hates being called Edward."

I smiled, "Well Edward I am going to start with a method that has worked for me in the past." I unwrapped the package of rags from their plastic. "You know what water boarding is right? I'm sure you've done it to people even." I peeled the seals off the bottles of vinegar. "I've been water boarded, but you know what's a lot worse? Being water boarded with vinegar." I turned to Joey, "Or would it be called vinegar boarded." Joey shrugged and I continued, "For starters it burns the hell out of your lungs." I went to the bathroom and soaked one of the rags in vinegar. "As a bonus, I've created small incisions all over your face. I would use lemon juice, but I'd bet vinegar hurts just as much.

I was losing myself and I knew it. If I didn't stop myself here I would get lost in the darkest parts of my mind once again. Though a part of me knew this there was nothing that could compare to the rush I was feeling right now. Oh, I was feeling good.

I signaled Joey to stand behind Edward. I poured some vinegar over his head to start and a grunt rumbled from his throat. "I haven't tried it but I could always cut off your eye lids. I'm sure that would hurt quite a bit." I looked up at Joey, "Don't you think Joey?" He nodded and I continued, "See Joey thinks so." Edward's eyes widened for a split second. "Oh Edward you just showed fear." I handed the rag to Joey and I picked up the bottle of vinegar. "Who were you on the phone with?" No answer.

I nodded to Joey, he put the rag over Edward's face and pulled his head back. I poured vinegar over his face causing him to writhe in his chair as the vinegar filled his lungs and seeped into the cuts on his face. As the bottle emptied Joey allowed Edward to lean forward as far as his restraints would allow and struggle to cough up the vinegar. I sat down and looked up at Joey, "Can you run back to the store and grab something to eat and a bucket? All this torture is making me hungry."

The darkness was swelling inside of me. I could feel it. I was having so much fun. I think after this I'll go find some people nobody will miss and rough 'em up a bit.

Joey and opened the door to leave when Robert was mid-knock. "Hey, Howey called and told me about Sie-." Robert must have caught a glimpse of what Joey and I had been up to because he moved further into the room past Joey, "What the hell Danny?"

"Relax Robert, Edward here knows the answers to my questions, but he's sadly chosen not to share them, yet. What are you doing here?"

Joey walked out and Robert sat on the bed. "As I was saying, Howey told me what happened and traced your phone to this location for me. I figured you could use some help, but it looks like you have everything under control here." Robert gestured toward Edward. "Is this where you found him?" I nodded. "Has he talked yet?"

I shook my head no. "You didn't happen to bring something I can break his legs with, did you?" A chuckle erupted from Edward's throat. "Somethin' funny Edward?"

"You're wasting your time."

"Am I? Maybe I'll rip out your nails and break your fingers next, then we'll see if I'm still wasting my time." I looked back at Robert, "I've had my nails ripped out a few times, and it sucks."

"You're a wanted ma-." Edward was stopped mid-sentence by a series of coughs. "Leskov will get a hold of you and he will make you suffer." Edward leaned forward and made eye contact, "He already has your love." If I hadn't lost it already, hearing what he said made something inside me tick. I jolted up and slammed my knife through his hand forcing out a cry of pain. I began yelling and hitting him relentlessly and my last thought was "this is it, I've lost myself again" before my rage took over and my mind went blank.

***

I woke up on the sidewalk outside the room and Robert was looking down at me with a bloody nose. "What happened?"

"I want to know the same thing. You punched him in his solar plexus then in his kidneys then proceeded to hit him with the knuckle of your middle finger at pressure points and everywhere else that hurts most. You had Phillips gasping and squirming."

"I grabbed your arms from behind to pull you off but you struggled to get free." Robert pointed to his nose, "You head-butted me, we fought, I knocked you out." He unfolded his arms and spread them, "Here we are."

I got up and we stood on the sidewalk, "What's gotten into you Danny? What you're doing is inhumane and I saw the look in your eyes when you were in there. The same look that I saw in the eyes of the ones who tortured me; you were enjoying it. You've got to stop this."

He was right, I needed to stop but, "He knows where Sierra is and who took her! If I can't get him to talk-." I didn't even want to think about what it would mean if Phillips didn't talk, "He has to talk."

"I'll get him to talk, but right now you're not the same person I met. Not when you handcuffed me to the parking meter or after you were pulled out of the sauna. You're the guy who's supposed to do the right things for the right reasons. Danny look at me." I looked up at Robert. "What if Sierra was here?

What would she think of you torturing a man out of his wits?" I could feel myself loosening up. Robert opened the door slightly, "Danny, look at what you've been doing."

Robert pushed the door open all the way. I looked at the dehumanized man tied to the chair and I suddenly couldn't stomach what I was seeing. What *I* had done. I turned away from Robert and put my hand on the wall for support as my last meal arose in my throat and spewed onto the sidewalk. I had never reacted this way before and I didn't understand why. I really have tortured several people in my life, but never once did I vomit afterwards.

I spit the remaining bile out of my mouth and turned around to face Robert, "I knew there was a reason why I brought you onto the team." I patted Robert on his shoulder, "Thank you."

"No problem. Just make sure that doesn't happen again. I'll get your answers." Robert went into the room. When I heard the tumbler in the lock turn I realized how close I was to being the monster I fear of becoming so greatly. And somehow Robert managed to pull me back from the brink.

I sat on the bench under the motel room's window just as Joey was returning with food. "Oh good you're back, I really need something to eat." He sat down next to me and began unloading the bag. I looked at what Joey handed me, then looked at him, then back at the food, then back at him, "You didn't." I unwrapped the cheesesteak he so generously got for me and began eating.

"Sure enough, the deli is still open this late." Joey leaned forward and looked past me, "You make that mess over there?"

Unable to speak with a full mouth of delicious cheesesteak, I nodded in confirmation. As we ate a yell from inside the room broke the peaceful silence. I finished my mouth full, "Robert pulled me out and said he would get answers. It sounds like he's making progress."

The door opened and a jingle accompanied it, "It's Phillip's phone, someone's trying to get a hold of him, no caller id."

I took the phone from Robert and he went back into the room. I looked at Joey then answered the phone. "Hello Mr. Silver." It was Leskov again. "I understand you have Edward Phillips and are most likely trying to get information from him. I'll save you the trouble and text you the location of Sierra and meet you there. If you do not show up I will kill her." The call ended and Phillip's phone received a text message.

I jumped up and peaked inside the room, "Joey and I are going to follow a lead. Stay and get answers." In the few seconds I was looking inside the room I saw a bend in Phillip's femur and his foot was twisted around. Robert wiped his hands with a clean rag and nodded. "I'll text you the address. Go there when you're finished here." I turned around and ran to the car, "Let's go Joey." We got into the car and sped off to where I could hopefully find Sierra and kill Leskov to end all of this once and for all.

Chapter Seventeen

Right before we pulled onto the property I turned the headlights off and parked near the abandoned warehouse. I double checked the address Leskov sent to Phillip's phone and this was the place.

"Why do you think he wanted to meet here?" Joey was just as ready to catch this monster as I was. "It could be a trap."

"That's why you're going to stay here in case anything goes wrong and I need your help." I stepped out of the car, scanned the area around me then headed towards where I was supposed to meet Leskov. I walked around the corner of the warehouse and a faint light became visible. I signaled Joey before I moved toward the light and out of his line of sight. I walked into the opening in the building that the light was shining brightly on.

"It's good to see you again Mr. Silver. I wasn't sure if you would actually answer my summons." The light was blinding me, so I couldn't see where the voice was coming from.

"Where are you coward?! Come face me!" Suddenly and without an answer, something solid and heavy smashed into my right arm. I staggered and whipped around to see nobody there. I attempted to bend my arm at the elbow, but the blow broke my arm.

"How was that, or would you like something more up close and personal?" Again I felt the weapon this time sweeping my leg out from under me. Before I could react I saw a shadowy figure standing over me and I felt the pointy end of what seemed to be rebar at my throat. "Is this enough face time for you?"

I listened to Leskov's voice, his tone, and thought about why he arranged for this to happen, "We both know why this is personal for me, but why is this personal for you? What is it that you think I took from you?" Leskov stepped back from me and back into the shadows. "What happened to you in Moscow? There's no point in making someone suffer if the victim doesn't know what they're suffering for. I'm sure you know this though."

With no response I closed my eyes and took a deep breath and readied myself for his next attack. I heard a faint step at my eight o'clock and as I dashed forward he shouted, "You killed my mother!" I turned around as I heard the sound of the rebar being swung through the space where I once stood.

"What? I've only killed two women and unless she was an assassin, I did not kill your mother." I kept my wits about me and my guard up while Leskov lingered in the shadows. With only one arm I'll have to make an effort to defend myself.

Leskov stepped out of the shadows and in front of the light allowing me to only see his silhouette. "Moscow, 1971, you killed her. What do you have to say for yourself?"

"How about I say I wasn't even in Russia at any time of that year?" I kept my guard up as Leskov stood before me.

"You are lying!" Leskov charged at me once more and I side stepped to sweep his leg out from under him.

"You're too angry to fight. Why don't we just talk?" I stepped back and put some distance between us. Leskov stood back up and I was able to see his face as the light shined onto it. He was in pain, immense emotional pain. Hate and pain that he had been holding inside for years, all directed towards me. His years as a vigilante were probably a failed attempt at relieving that hate and pain, but now he was unleashing it on me. "Tell me about her. Refresh my memory."

"I just want to make you feel pain!" He charged again with an overhead strike. I grabbed the rebar with my good arm and put my foot on his chest slamming him onto the ground.

I threw the rebar away and held Leskov down. "I've learned to ignore physical pain, so beating me won't work. Tell me: who was your mother and when were you born?"

He didn't try to free himself, he just laid there. "She was a beautiful woman with red hair. She died in 'seventy-one, five years after I was born. My father told me you did it, so I prepared and trained myself to get revenge."

"What was her name?"

"Natasha, her name was Natasha."

This didn't make any sense. I was married to a Natasha who I had later heard died in 'seventy-one. With the information that I've already acquired this could only mean one thing, "I'm... I'm your father?" I lifted my foot off of Boris's chest and staggered backwards.

"What did you just say?" Boris stood up and grabbed me by the collar, "What did you say?!"

I could imagine the blank stare on my face, "I was married to a Natasha and heard she died of natural causes in 'seventy-one. I never knew she was pregnant when I left, with you... my son."

Boris tightened his grip, "What are you saying!?"

"I'm your father. You're my son, Boris."

Boris shoved me and backed away, "No! Noooo!" Boris' eyes filled with tears. "My whole life

I wanted to make you suffer, but..." Boris wiped his face and looked at me, "If you're my father and you didn't kill my mother, then who is Dimitri Krinchov and who really killed my mother?"

Did I just hear him right? "Did you just say 'who *is*'?" Dimitri should be dead.

Before he could answer, a gunshot rang throughout the warehouse and I dropped to the ground as I felt a cold wet feeling in the back of my skull. Before I lost consciousness I heard talking and saw someone that wasn't Boris walk into the light. "What the hell Joseph? I had this."

"It didn't look like it. Besides, your father wants him back at the bunker."

Joey?

Chapter Eighteen

When I opened my eyes I was lying in the back seat of a car in motion. I laid still and looked up front to see one driver and no passenger. The driver looked back at me, "Ah you're awake now." Turns out it was Robert. "I arrived at the warehouse you gave me the address to and found you alone on the floor in a puddle of blood. It looked like you were shot in the back of the head, but the wound had sealed by the time I got there." We made a right turn, "We're on our way to your house now." I sat up straight in my seat and rubbed the back of my head where the bullet had entered my skull. Robert looked in the rear view mirror, "Before I ask what happened back there, I'd rather know what happened to the bullet that got lodged in your head."

"Just don't think too hard about it. I still don't understand it either. My best bet is that it dissolves and is then expelled from my body somehow. If you're done marveling over the unimportant information, I think you'd like to know what happened back there."

Robert readjusted his mirror, "Right, so what did happen?"

I examined my blood stained clothes and took my shirt off, "The short version: Sierra wasn't there, Leskov ambushed me, Joey shot me in the head, and I'm fairly certain Leskov is my son."

We pulled up to the front door, "Come again? Joey shot you and Leskov is your son?"

We stepped out of the car, "Now that we're on the same page, follow me." I led Robert through my bullet riddled home and down to the cave underneath.

Robert looked around at the expanse I walked him into, "Nice. Who else knows about this?"

We walked to and I sat down in front of the computer monitors, "Just Joey and Howey." I pressed the button to turn them all on, "Tell me what you got out of Phillips."

"Oh you're going to love this." Robert sat down, "He gave me more than what we wanted. He gave me the names of more than twenty corrupt politicians that are in Leskov's pocket." He pulled out a slip of paper from his breast pocket and unfolded it revealing a list of politicians. "We have names, but no evidence."

Robert was right, we didn't have anything to prosecute them with. "We'll get something on them later. How'd you manage to get him to talk?"

"The quickest way to get someone to talk is to threaten their family." I was impressed and he saw that, "I just showed him some pictures of his wife and kids I found online."

"I should have thought of that, good job."

"You would have thought of that if you didn't lose yourself in your rage. You have flawless control of your emotions, I can see that, but you stopped minding them and let your anger take control." Robert flipped over the sheet of paper with the names on it, "These are the coordinates Phillips gave me. He said Leskov's fortress is on an island in the Bermuda Triangle."

I typed in the coordinates and re-tasked Acro's satellite, purchased by me, over top of the triangle to give us an idea of what we're up against. "The points of the triangle are Miami, Florida, San Juan, Puerto Rico, and Bermuda Island itself. The powerful riptide that passes through the triangle is to thank for wreckage from ships and planes rarely ever being found." The satellite finished repositioning and displayed the same shape as the one found on the pins worn by Leskov's men. Most likely just a string to pull me along in his sick plan. "Though the triangle is known for vanishing ships and planes, many people travel within it every day and come out just fine and we're going to do the same."

"Follow me." I led Robert into the room I had turned into my personal armory. "Gear up then we'll head out." We selected weapons and changed into tactical gear.

"This is impressive. Assault rifles, handguns, rocket launchers, flak jackets, bullet proof vests, grenades; you've got it all."

We left the cave with our weapons and walked through my shredded home once more, "What's that room down the hall with the keypad?" Robert was asking about my isolation room.

This isn't the first place I've lived in that I had one though the one I have now is far more extravagant and intricate then the ones I used in the past. It's a room I had specially made for studying and research. I told Sierra in the interview that I learned everything as it was discovered which is totally absurd. My isolation room is the key to my quick learning. "It's nothing."

We walked outside and got into my every day car. "I know a guy that owes me. He's going to fly us over the island and we'll parachute out."

"And once we hit the ground?"

"We'll figure it out."

***

We rolled up to an old shack with a runway that was beginning to look overgrown. An old Serbian man came out of the shack, "You can't be here! Leave or I'll shoot!"

I opened up the car door and stepped out, "Borko! It's been far too long."

He put his weapon down, "Rahm?" He strained his eyes to make out my face through the headlights shining on him, "No! No, no, no. You cannot be here. You need to leave." Borko went back into the shack and shut the door on my foot. "You are nothing but trouble Rahm." He lit a cigar and sat down, clearly uneasy about seeing me and I can't say I blame him. "The last time I was your pilot you pushed me out of the plane and it crashed. I had to build a new on!"

I looked around at the man's poorly maintained home, "You can build a plane, but you can't keep this shack clean. I don't know how you can live like this."

Borko puffed his cigar, "What do you want Rahm?"

"My friend and I need a pilot to take us to an island in the Bermuda Triangle."

"No!"

"You owe me Borko. If I hadn't pushed you out you would have gone down with that plane. I honestly don't see why you're angry about it, you had a parachute."

"You had the parachute. I had to hold onto you for dear life."

"You're alive, are you not? You fly us there or I take your plane and you never see it again." He snarled then put out his cigar and slung his parachute onto his back. "I'm glad you've come around to see this my way."

**

The island came into view and I opened the door to jump. "Thanks again Borko!" He was ready to be done with me and waved me off. I knelt in the doorway and Robert patted my shoulder to signal that he was ready. We jumped and began to freefall in the dark of night. Freefalling is one of my favorite past times and is something I would never get tired of. We reached an appropriate height and pulled our chords to open our chutes.

Borko's plane continued over the island and in the distance I saw anti-air artillery fire and the plane burst into a ball of flames then crashed down to the ground. We weren't friends, but a life lost is just that.

We reached the ground, or at least Robert did, I landed in a tree. I drew my knife and he walked underneath of me, "You need help down?"

I started cutting ropes to get free, "No just keep an eye out. There's no doubt that if they spotted the plane then we were also spotted after pulling our chutes." I continued cutting, "If they find us you hide and I'll let them take me to Sierra." He nodded and I freed myself.

We started moving in the direction of the artillery fire and soon after heard shouting in the distance. "Well that didn't take very long now did it?" I took a brief moment to think, "Give me your weapon. I have an idea." Robert handed it over, "Now stay hidden. After they take me, do some recon and wait for us to get outside." He nodded and ran in the opposite direction of the shouting.

I held both mine and Robert's assault rifle in each hand and headed towards the shouting. I saw someone in the distance and shouted, "You lookin' for me?!" I opened fire with both weapons intentionally missing most of my shots. In a matter of seconds I was surrounded and quickly riddled with bullets. It was all part of the plan. Sort of.

Chapter Nineteen

When I opened my eyes I found myself in a well-lit, concrete room with a large window on one wall, a door on another and a curtain separating my side of the room from the other. I couldn't see through the window, so it must only be able to be seen through from the observation room on the other side. The air was surprisingly warm and clean given the setting. I tried to stand then realized I was locked into a steel chair by my wrists and my ankles. When I looked down at my feet I noticed the drain in the floor. I began to understand what was going on and why I was here.

I was brought here to be tortured.

Just as that thought entered my mind someone opened the door and a man backed into the room pulling a cart with a bent wheel and utensils rattling on it. The man had a noticeable limp and he continuously scratched himself all over, "I know, shut up! He'll think we're weird." And he appeared to suffer from auditory hallucinations. He was the only one in the room besides me.

The strange man parked his cart a couple yards in front of me and began repositioning the utensils. "It's a great honor to meet you Mr. Daniel Silver. I've been waiting a long time for this."

"What have you been waiting for?"

"For this, this moment right here; the moment you fear for yourself and realize you will suffer unimaginable pain. And I get to be the one that helps you." The man faced me and waved a scalpel in my face. "I am making him afraid! No be quiet!"

Just great. I let myself get captured only to be stuck in this quack who thinks he can hurt me. "Help me? What do you think you are going to help me with?" I looked at my restraints once more, but analyzed them this time. There were key holes in each shackle, if I could somehow get a scalpel between my teeth I could pick the lock and get out of here.

"Why don't you know Mr. Silver? You are a very sick man." The man stuck the scalpel in my shoulder and made a straight cut down my bicep. "I can see he's not hurting. Stop interrupting me!"

"If you think I am sick then I guess that means you know I cannot die and I should let you know that I have learned to completely ignore any and all physical pain. You are wasting your time." That's right I can shut off all physical pain. It's a bit more complicated than just shutting off pain though. The only way I've learned to do it is to shut off my sense of touch. If I were to do it I wouldn't be able to feel the wind blowing on me or a dog licking my hand. It took a long time to master, but now it's like first nature to me. If somebody shoots me I'll turn my sense of touch off before I can even think to do it. Like breathing; you don't think about it, you just do it.

The man put his hands on his head and walked away, "No! I am not wasting my time!" He rushed at me, grabbed my head, and whispered into my ear, "I have dedicated my life's work to the art of torture. I have killed dozens by accident because I induced too much pain, but *you* cannot die." He released my head and stuck the scalpel into my thigh.

"I have been tortured by more methods than you could ever think to implement. You cannot hurt me!" Making him angry probably wasn't the smartest thing for me to do, but it was my best chance to cause him to slip up and make a mistake, which could in turn present an opportunity for my escape.

"Shut up! I know what I'm doing!" He picked up a small knife and threw it through the curtain, but there was no noise of it hitting the concrete wall or floor. "Oh, I nearly forgot. Like you said yourself Mr. Silver: you feel no *physical* pain." He walked over to the curtain and grabbed the edge, "But what about emotional?" He pulled the curtain back and revealed what, or rather who was on the other side of the room. "It seems to have slipped my mind that Miss Sierra Morning is also here. I was just so excited to experiment on you I forgot."

The knife had stuck into Sierra's arm, that's why I didn't hear it hit the floor. She was restrained just as I was and with a gag in her mouth. I whispered so quietly I couldn't even hear myself, "Sierra?" Sierra and I stared at each other intently and as I looked into her tear-filled eyes I could see the terror and fear induced state she was in. I looked at her and began to feel that same heart wrenching pain that I have felt too many times in the past. This was once again my fault and again I would need to get us out and back to safety. I looked back at the man who held Sierra's life in his hands, "Why is she here?!"

He looked over his shoulder and responded to the voice in his head, "I know I'm supposed to remain in control. I'll let him have this one question." He looked back at me, "If it was up to me she would already be dead, but the boss said that she was the only way to get through to you, so I'm letting her li-" The stranger paused and looked back and forth at Sierra and I. He ran to Sierra and looked her in the eyes. Instinctively I jumped in my chair, but I was still restrained.

He ran back to me and looked me in my eyes, "You two care for one another?" This guy's also a little slow at noticing things. "I can see it in your eyes. Mr. Silver, you fear for her life and Miss Morning, you fear for yourself while at the same time you anticipate his rescue of you. Looks like the boss was right, she is the only way to get to you Mr. Silver. Don't worry though, that doesn't mean I can't still help you."

The door to the room opened once again and I was forced to come to terms with what had happened back at the warehouse. "Good to see you again Daniel. I truly am sorry about the bullet in the back of the head thing." I'm sure Joey could see the rage in my eyes. "Don't give me that look. You can't be surprised things turned out like this. Did you really think that I, a hardened soldier, could actually become a butler?"

"Why? What are you doing this for? Who are you doing this for?"

The strange man spoke up, "Don't answer. He doesn't get to ask questions."

"Get out Mike." So the crazy guy has a name.

"But-"

Joey raised his weapon to Mike's head, "Didn't I tell not to start with them yet? Now I said get out." The threat was enough to make Mike rush out of the room. "If it's any consolation it was never personal. Well at least not at first. I wanted to be your butler at first, but then I was approached by Dimitri Krinchov and he made me an offer I couldn't refuse. He offered me a seat in his empire in exchange for intel on you and that was enough for me. The longer I was with you the more I despised you for trading in your life of meaning and purpose that made a difference in the world for one of luxury and slothfulness. You have been brought here to provide us with answers regarding Anton Richtov's organization." Joey lost me with that and he could tell I didn't know what he was getting at. "Anton is dead, but when you killed him he took the organizations secrets with him, and you know them." His reasoning doesn't make any sense. I told him and Howey when this whole fiasco began that I never found out where Richtov's armory was. It's as if the person pulling the strings is keeping the truth from him which makes Joseph just a simple pawn in a much larger plan. That person must be Dimitri Krinchov.

"As for the freak that you just met, he's well, psycho." Joey began raising each one of the tools lying on the cart one by one for me to see. "Anton found him in a Russian prison for, not just murdering people, but eviscerating the corpses and *most* of the damage was done before the victims actually died. As you can guess, there is a long list of psychological issues with that man, too long for me to even begin listing them. Ironically, his only fear is his own death. So I suggest you start talking before he, not only starts to make you suffer, but your whore of a girlfriend too."

Joey walked over to where Sierra sat and pushed her head back with the muzzle of his gun. When he did, Sierra's pupils dilated in great fear as she stared down the barrel, "Either you tell me what I want to know quickly and she gets a painless bullet to the head-" Not that he would know, but a bullet to the head is anything but painless. "or you resist and she suffers immense pain until you break." Joey removed Sierra's gag and walked back to me and put the barrel of his gun to my knee, "You have five minutes before I give Mike the okay to start torturing her."

Joey pulled the trigger and the bullet tore through my flesh and bone and came out the other side. The sight and the sound forced a silent squeal out of Sierra. I closed my eyes, raised my head, and recited in my head, "It's only pain. It's only pain." At the end of the two short seconds it took me to push the pain out, I opened my eyes and locked them with Joey's, "Bring it on." I don't ever want to forget what pain feels like, so on occasion I'll let myself feel it. I need the pain to remind myself I'm still human and what others feel when I'm applying the pain.

Joey walked back to the door to leave, "I'll return after I deal with an urgent matter. You better be talking when I get back." Joey opened the door to leave and through the doorway I saw someone else looking in, Boris. We made eye contact, then Mike walked in and closed the door behind him.

So far there are two ways to get of here: either I figure out a way to get out of these clamps, or Boris comes around to believing I'm his father and frees us. I've got to be his father right? That's the only explanation for why he's been doing this. Krinchov manipulated him into making me enemy number one when the whole time he just wants the secrets I sent Richtov to the grave with. They kept taking Sierra to soften me up and lower my guard for this very moment in hopes to get some answers, but I won't give anything up. I mean I can't, but what about Sierra? I can't let anything happen to her, not anything more.

Mike looked into the corner of the room and whispered, "I hate Joseph too. Don't worry though, his time will come, then we can take his place." Mike walked over to his cart and situated his tools, "I have five minutes to make you talk, but I'm hoping you don't." Mike looked across the room at Sierra, "I want to see what happens to you when I experiment on her."

"When I get out I'm going to kill you slowly. Maybe I slice an artery and you bleed out very slowly." Joey said Mike fears his own death, so I wonder what he'll do when I pick at it.

"That would normally strike fear in me, as that is what you're trying to do." Mike grabbed my hand and looked me in the eyes, "But considering the fact you are in a helpless position, I am not afraid." Mike grabbed two of my fingers and bent them back until they touched the back of my hand. Each time he tried something and I didn't give the response he desired, such as pain, he became more angry, "Why," between each word, "aren't," he stabbed me, "you," in each leg, "hurting!?"

Now I can't feel anything, "Are you done yet?" Sierra was sobbing now, "It doesn't hurt. Don't worry Sierra. We'll soon be out of here."

Mike shouted as he picked up a battery operated hacksaw off of the bottom shelf of the cart and turned it on, "I will make him hurt!"

I whipped my head to Sierra, "Look away!"

He got down on one knee and cut each toe off of my right foot. Yes it probably would have hurt greatly, but like any other pain I had to remain calm and shut it off. Now if my ankles weren't locked I'd have more wiggle room to make an escape attempt.

Sierra cried out as she saw what was being done to me. I looked over at her and saw streams of tears flowing from her eyes. I would like to think it was because she saw what was being done to me, but she was more likely crying in fear at the thought of what would happen to her once Mike was finished with me.

"Sierra look at my eyes." Sierra raised her head and we made eye contact, "We'll get out of this, so just hold on." I smiled as best I could and Sierra hesitated a moment before she nodded. I looked at Mike, "Oh come on. I like my right toes. Why couldn't you have cut off my left ones?

Mike screamed in frustration at the fact that he finally met someone he could not torture. He got to his feet and punched me then ran to Sierra and punched her. I yelled out in rage then thought to myself: she really is the only way to get to me. Some would call that a weakness, but she's also my greatest strength; I need her. I know that she wrote in her diary that she needs me, but I can't imagine how much different she must feel now that we're here.

The door opened again. It was Boris this time. We locked eyes as the door swung open then he drew his gun on Mike. Before he pulled the trigger I yelled, "The knees!" Boris took out Mike's knees to make him scream and then freed me. "Help Sierra out." Well aware of the strain I'd be putting on my wounded legs I stood. I took a scalpel off of the cart and knelt next to Mike on my good knee. "I told you I would make you die very slowly." I stuck the scalpel into his carotid artery, "You have ninety seconds."

I got up and helped Sierra to her feet. "What's the escape plan Boris?" Even though I couldn't feel it, my muscles were weak, so Sierra and Boris stood on either side of me to be my crutches.

"Your friend Robert Price is waiting in a helicopter I helped him get into while Howard Brixton is on his way to us." I looked at him speechless; simply unable to express my gratitude. "Don't thank me. Let's get out of here." We limped together out of the room and down the hall.

I felt the hairs on the back of my neck stand up when a gunshot echoed throughout the concrete halls of the fortress. Before I could turn around to see where it came from, a bullet seared through the back and out the chest. Time slowed as Sierra's body twisted around and she fell to ground. I fell to the floor next to her and held her limp head in my hand. "Don't let me go…" I felt her final breath blow against my face and I felt the greatest pain I had ever felt in my entire three-hundred-some years life. My vision became blurred from an uncontrollable wave of tears. The look in her eyes… the life leaving them.

I turned around and there stood Joseph at the top of a pair of steps. The man I thought I knew. The man I thought was a friend, that I could trust anything with. But all that's changed now: I wanted nothing more than to kill him. "Did you really think we would let you leave? You belong to us now." I began to run.

I didn't care if he had a gun or if my legs were about to give out. I wanted to hurt him, then kill him.

He raised his weapon and two shots rang back to back. Joseph fell onto his blown-out knees and I saw Howey standing behind him, holding the smoking gun. Howey shot his shoulders and Joseph dropped his weapon. He was now lying on the ground face up. I waved at Howey to stand next to me for support as I looked down at Joseph's head hanging over the step, "Go to hell traitor." I used Howey as support and stomped on Joseph's head breaking his neck over the step.

Howey helped me rush over to Sierra's body held in Boris's arms, "There's an infirmary down the hall."

We got to the infirmary as quickly as we could and laid Sierra's body on the bed. I could hardly bring myself to terms with the fact that she was dead. I've been around death all my life, but this time it was unbearable. I've always told myself that being angry over the past does no good for one's future and that was the hardest thing to keep in mind, for I blamed Boris for this. After all, he did say my pain would be "insufferable" and this was that pain.

I felt like I could drop dead at any moment from simply looking at Sierra.

Howey hooked up Sierra to the I.V. and the heart rate monitor, "What are you doing?"

He looked at me then at Boris, "Watch the door. We need the room." Boris nodded and closed the door to give us the room.

"We're not outta options here Danny. We actually have only one option." I squinted my eyes in confusion for I was too distraught to think clearly. "We both know what she wants." Now I knew what he meant. First the diary then the last thing she said to me. My vision became blurred once more as tears filled my eyes and I shook my head. "It's the only way! It's what she wants Daniel! Who are you to take that away from her?!" I sat down and put my head in my hands. "You love her Danny and she loves you. I mean you *really* love each other; the kind of love that never goes away. The kind you find only once in a lifetime, even your lifetime. And when you do this the two of you will be stronger for it." I wiped my eyes and looked up at Howey. "It's what you both want."

I stretched out my arm and tapped my forearm, "You're such a romantic." We both smiled and Howey hooked me up. "It should take no longer than ten minutes before she gets the necessary amount of blood to recover. After that we take her body and go." Howey nodded in agreement.

Boris reentered the room, "An alert has gone out. Krinchov has begun the self-destruct countdown to destroy the fortress. We have fifteen minutes."

***

Ten minutes had gone by and Sierra was still dead. Howey patched up all my wounds as best he could, but none were able to begin healing because of the blood transfusion. Howey looked at his watch and stood up from his chair, "It's time to go. Boris, you carry her and I'll help Danny out."

We left the room and Howey called Robert on speaker phone, "Get the chopper ready we're headed out."

"What's going on down there? Dozens of people have been evacuating for the past ten minutes."

"The place is gonna blow in five. Make some room on the floor in there." I looked at Sierra's lifeless face in my son's arms. "We're a man down."

Robert met us when we made it outside and at first froze when he saw Sierra's body then helped us onto the helicopter. Everyone that was once in the fortress was too busy running to a safe distance to pay any attention to us. After we all finished boarding the chopper, we immediately took off and headed for home. Robert looked down at Sierra and placed his hand on my shoulder. He didn't say anything, but I heard his sympathy.

If I wasn't too late and she wakes up from this she will no longer be the same person she was before. This isn't what I wanted for Sierra, I don't want her to have to live life the way I have. But Howey was right; it's not my choice to make. Then again, she may not have to live like I have. I was alone all of my life; never able to get truly close to anyone. Yes, I've had friends like Joey and Howey, but a part of me could never truly connect because I knew that someday I would inevitably watch them die. Just like all my friends before.

When she wakes up everything will be different, not just for her, but for me too. I can finally have an unbound, untethered relationship knowing that it never has to end. I'll make sure she never has to face all the hardships or go through all the pain that I did. Ours will be a story to be told for all eternity.

Chapter Twenty

I was awoken by a nudge on my shoulder, "The suns coming up."

Robert landed the chopper in my back yard the night before. Howey helped me run Sierra into the infirmary, then went home to his worrisome wife while Robert sat with Boris upstairs. After I changed her out of her blood soaked clothes and into something clean and more comfortable, I laid her on the bed awaiting her recovery. I sat next to Sierra anticipating her speedy awakening.

I had slept all night in the chair next to her bed in the infirmary which left a nasty kink in my neck. I wiggled my toes to feel that they had returned.

She still hasn't shown any signs of life; not a pulse, not a heartbeat, or a rise of the chest. I've never done this before so I had no idea what to expect from the situation. "Boris is upstairs wanting to speak with you. Do you want me to let him down here?"

I took a drink from the glass of water next to me, "Do you trust him Robert?"

"I don't know yet. Sure he helped us escape, but what's he going to do once he realizes that what he's done is a betrayal to the man that just yesterday he thought was his father?"

"He let me get my toes cut off, stabbed in each leg, and shot in the knee. He took enough time to think about what to do and the repercussions those actions would bring. I trust him for now, but we do need to proceed with caution." I leaned over Sierra's body and kissed her on the forehead, "I'm going to talk with Boris then take him on an errand with me. Stay here and watch over her while I'm away. Call me for no other reasons than if someone other than Howey walks through the front door, or Sierra starts showing signs of life."

"Sure, whatever you need to put an end to all of this."

I pulled the collar of her shirt down to see the exit wound from the bullet that killed her. The hole had begun sealing. I lowered my head and involuntarily smiled as a wonderful feeling of warmth and relief came over me. I turned around, "Thanks for all your help on this Robert." I grabbed the flash drive and left the cave entrusting the safety of the woman I love with my new friend.

I got upstairs and found Boris waiting for me, "What do you know about Dimitri Krinchov and why did he raise me to torment you, probably knowing all along that you're my real father?"

"Come with me." I walked past Boris to the front door. "What I thought I knew was that I cut off his arm and he bled out after I killed Anton Richtov." Boris followed me outside and we got in the car, "And of course he knew I'm your father. He found your mother after I fled and somehow gained her trust enough for her to allow him to raise you as his own all the while feeding you lies that I killed her when he most likely did it himself."

"You said you cut his arm off. He's had two fully functional arms ever since I can remember. And who is Anton Richtov?"

What happened after I left? "It makes sense that Krinchov would hide Richtov's existence from you and I'm certain I cut his arm off. The only way he could have possibly gotten it back is if he somehow he got my blood and held his arm on until it reconnected, but I haven't the slightest idea how he could have done that." None of it makes sense. Krinchov didn't know I couldn't die so he couldn't have known my blood would help him.

"If Krinchov has no vendetta against you, then someone else must have used him and in turn used me to get to you." That was the only explanation that made sense so far and it wasn't much of one at all. "Where are we going?"

"Right, I almost forgot. We're going to Vancouver."

***

After flying my private jet over the U.S., Canada border, we landed in Vancouver and now we sat in a car out front of a small pawn shop. "What are we doing here?"

"An old contact of mine works here and he's going to help me with something."

We got out of the car and walked into the seemingly profitless shop. The bell over the door rang and a voice called out, "I'll be right out." I turned around the sign on the door so that "closed" was displayed to deter any interruptive customers. We approached the counter and I rang the call bell a few times, "Hold on, hold on, I'm right here."

A short stumpy man walked around the corner from the back and froze still when he saw who it was ringing his bell, "What's the matter Anthony? No hello for an old friend?"

"What the hell are you doing here Rahm, or should I call you Daniel Silver now? And you're with him no less!" He pointed at Boris, "You realize he put a bounty out on you and your girl for twenty mil right? Honestly, I laughed when I heard cuz' I thought to myself 'anybody who's stupid enough to go after Rahm is gonna get killed'." He waved at the two of us, "So you two buddies now?"

"Something like that. Did you say twenty? I thought the bounty was ten."

"Well it was. Last night I got another message saying it got boosted up to twenty. If I had to guess I'd say your alliance has made somebody very unhappy."

"Well I'm glad to hear you're looking out for me although this is not a social visit. I have a flash drive with an encryption on it that I can't break."

"What happened to learning everything as it's discovered? Shouldn't you know how to decrypt a file?"

"Maybe I'll learn how to when I get back to my house."

I waved the drive for him to see, "Of course, of course, right this way." Boris and I followed Anthony into the back, "I'm the best in the business so naturally you came to me for help."

"I don't deal with anything less than the best." We were led into a very hot room with multiple computer monitors and systems.

"The very idea of you even making a social visit is funny to me." Anthony sat down in the back of the room in front of what seemed an extremely advanced computer. Probably custom made and more advanced than the computers I bought for Acro. "Does the mighty Rahm even know how to socialize about something other than business?"

He put out his hand and I placed the drive in it. He plugged it into the side of his computer and the drives interface came up on the screen. "Hmm. This is high quality security. Whoever this info belonged to really wants to keep it private." Anthony swiveled around in his chair, "This should take me no longer than about two days, but before I get started I need to know this won't come back on me."

"Nobody is looking for this information or even knows it's been duplicated. You'll be fine assuming you get this done because if I return in forty-eight and it's not finished, you will be."

Boris walked with me back outside, "What's on the drive?"

"I got it from Jamie Juarez. As you may have had some business with him in the past you know he was a money manager for the criminal elite. I'm hoping to find money trails leading anywhere from corrupt politicians to warlords in Mogadishu on that drive."

"*Was* a money manager? What did you do to him?"

"Nothing he won't soon forget."

***

We returned back to my house as the sun was setting over the horizon, "Get some rest and find something presentable to wear. Where we're going tomorrow you're going to need it."

I went back to see how Sierra was doing, "How was your trip with Boris?"

As promised, Robert was still in the infirmary watching over her, "My previous evaluation remains unchanged; we still need to remain cautious." I combed my fingers through her hair and noticed something different about her, "When did she start breathing?"

"Just a few hours ago, but other than that nothing's changed."

Once again an involuntary smile found its way onto my face, "Thanks a lot for doing this for me. If you don't mind I would like you to do this again tomorrow."

"Sure, but what are you doing tomorrow?"

I sat down next to Sierra and held her hand in mine, "I'm taking Boris with me to have a little sit-down with the President."

***

The next morning, I woke up with a kink in my neck again. Sierra's pulse was that of a healthy person sleeping. I went upstairs for a shower then to my closet to pick out the three piece suit I wanted. I got all of my clothes tailor-made by designers that I know personally. I get my shirts, vests, suits, pants, coats, and shoes all customized to my specifications. My wardrobe ranges from all different kinds of colors and materials, I prefer dark blue wool suits, but it depends on the time of year. I was going to the White

House, so naturally I needed to dress my best. Once I suited up, I met up with Boris downstairs and we left for D.C.

***

The chauffer that was driving us around turned onto Sixteenth Street, "I thought you said we were going to the White House."

"We are. We just can't go through the front doors." Our car stopped in front of the St. Regis hotel, "We have to take a more hidden approach." We were let out of the car and we entered the hotel. "Just follow me, act like you know what we're doing, and keep a look out for any prying eyes." Next we headed over to the reception desk, "Hello I was wondering if I could get someone to fix my leaky sink faucet on the ninth floor." The hotel only had eight floors.

The woman's expression changed as I spoke, "If you could please follow I will show you your help." The receptionist came out from behind the desk and led us onto the elevator. After the doors closed she took a key out of her pocket and inserted it into a key hole on the wall, turned it, then pushed it in. The elevator began its decent and the lights on the buttons indicated what floor we were on until we continued past the lower lobby level. The doors opened up to a dimly lit concrete tunnel beneath the hotel where a small golf cart sat waiting to provide transportation, "Drive south approximately-".

"Yes I know. I designed it." Boris and I stepped out of the elevator and I turned around, "Thank you for showing us the way. I'll make sure you get a promotion." The doors shut and the lift hummed as it began its ascension. I looked at Boris, "Take a seat and let's go."

We got on the cart and started down the tunnel, "So you designed this tunnel to connect the White House to the hotel? How long ago was that?"

The gate at the end of the tunnel came into view, "This passage was finished back before that hotel was even a hotel." I parked the cart off to the side leaving enough room for Boris to get out.

We approached the left side of the gate where the booth housed the guard, "State your name and business." This man clearly had one of the most mundane jobs. He didn't lift his eyes from whatever it was he was doing on his phone.

"I am Daniel Silver and this is my colleague. We are here to speak with the President."

The man remained captivated by his phone, "Oh yeah? I'm a magician and I can pull celebrities out of my top hat." He laughed at his own horrible attempt at a joke.

"If you don't look up from your damn phone I'll call your boss Jacobs and have you fired then blacklisted." That got his attention.

He stumbled to his feet and dropped his phone, "Whoa it really is you. I am so sorry Mr. Silver, but you have no clearance here."

I couldn't blame him for not knowing that my status exceeded all levels of clearance, "I don't blame you for thinking so, so what you need to do is get in contact with whoever it is you can that can get my colleague and I through this gate. And if you make us turn around I will have you fired and blacklisted."

He picked up the landline and dialed a number, "Sir there are two men down here that are requesting access to speak with the President." A brief moment passed giving time for the person on the other end of the line to ask who we were. "Daniel Silver and his associate." Another moment passed and the guard hung up the phone, "Director Jacobs will be down in a moment."

About ninety seconds had gone by when a door squeaked open down the hall on the other side of the gate, "Daniel Silver is that you?" He waved at the guard, "Let these fine gentlemen in." The gate began sliding along the rails on the floor, "How long has it been Daniel? Twelve, thirteen years?" I conducted an interview with Thomas Jacobs to determine whether or not he was good for the Director of the Secret Service.

We walked through the gate onto White House property, "Fourteen." Once we got across I turned around, "Thomas, I would like you to meet my associate Anthony. Anthony, Thomas." They shook hands then we continued on through the door Jacobs entered by.

We walked up a flight of stairs and he stopped at the door at the top, "The guard said you're here to see the President. Can I ask what about?"

"Yes you can, but it doesn't mean I'll give you an answer you're looking for." Jacobs released a puff of air finding what I said to be humorous. He pushed open the door and then we were in the White House.

"You should know that a warrant for your arrest is being considered." This is the first I've heard of this. The choice is most likely up to the President and a few cabinet members and I can't say I blame them for wanting me in hopes that it would put a halt to the threats from Dimitri Krinchov and whoever he's probably working for.

Jacobs stopped mid-way down the hall and two Secret Service agents approached Boris and I, "Sorry Daniel, but you know protocol." I was glad to see they weren't giving anybody special treatment for security's sake.

The agents began patting us down and one was cutting it a bit close, "Hey now. I'm flattered but I'm seeing someone."

The agent moved away from that area, "I gotta tell you Daniel, I couldn't believe it when I saw your interview. I was sitting with my wife and I told her 'that's the guy who interviewed me for the director's seat'." The agents finished and signaled Jacobs the all clear. "I had to watch it again to be sure. Right this way gentleman." We continued down the hall and turned down a few more until we stood outside the one of the doors to the Oval Office. In some respects, it felt good to be back. Sort of nostalgic. We waited until Jacobs was given the go-ahead over his earpiece.

Jacobs pushed open the door and followed us inside. He was turned around and looking out of the front window, "Ah Mr. President it has been far too long." Jacobs seemed astonished by my lack of manners and respect. "Thank you Thomas for showing us the way and you did a superb job of following the protocols I put in place, but my associate and I need to speak with the President in private, so if you and the other agents could please excuse us it would be greatly appreciated."

"What? No. I can't do th-". The President waved his hand for the Secret Service to leave us alone. Immediately each agent left through the door they were guarding. All had left except for one man that stood next to the President's desk.

He sat down behind his desk and appeared to be perturbed, "Before we begin I need you to verify that you are the man described in the presidential journals." As one might guess, the presidential journals are where all presidents write down anything and everything they feel might be useful to their predecessors.

"Unless you want to be the first president, no wait, second president, to have a man shot in the head within the Oval Office you're just going to have to trust that I am who I say I am. And honestly, how could I have gotten here the way I did if I was anybody else?

The President seemed minimally satisfied with my answer, "Why are you here Silver? Why show up here now after declining my invitations in the past? Why finally make contact with a president after so many years?"

I sat down in front of the desk and Boris stood behind me, "Despite the nostalgia of being back, I loathe being here. Some number of years ago, before you were born, I became unhappy and I'm still unhappy with this countries turn out, but extenuating circumstances are what have brought us here together."

I think I said something wrong, "How dare you come here saying these things to me. You have no right to bring judgments down on this country or my presidency."

"I have been around since before the conception of this nation. My dear friend George Washington had a vision for this country and knowing him as well as I did, he would be rolling in his grave if he could see where it is now. When I saw down the road this country was on I knew there was nothing more I could do to keep his vision a reality, so I created Acro to protect it. And as for your presidency I don't blame you for the state the country is in; you were voted into an impossible situation." The President seemed lost for words, "Don't get me wrong; I have a great deal of respect for you and I believe this is the greatest country in the world and I'll do everything in my power to make sure it stays that way." I've never been able to really answer the question as to why I've done what I've done or do what I do. The best answer I've been able to give myself so far is that I do it to honor my friend's legacy and to continue what he started. I kind of enjoy the spy life too.

"Now if we're done with the small talk I'd like to discuss why I'm really here, but before I can, that man needs to leave." I pointed to the suspicious man still standing next to the President's desk. He didn't leave with the rest of the agents and he didn't wear an earpiece so he wasn't here for security. The simple fact that I've never seen his face makes him a possible threat. I make sure to know all the faces that come in and out of the White House on a daily basis.

The President looked up at the suspicious man to his right, "No he stays." He waved his pen, "What about your man? Why can he stay and mine can't?"

He had a fair point and he deserved the truth, "This is my apparent son although to be quite honest I'm not entirely convinced just yet. I'm not even sure if he's completely trust worthy. Mr. President, I would like you to meet Boris Leskov."

The President looked utterly astonished. He jumped to his feet, "What the hell Silver? How dare you bring him here!"

He was angry, but would understand soon enough, "Sit down Mr. President. I would say you have absolutely no right getting flustered over me bringing a terrorist into the Oval Office." He must have understood what I meant when his gaze fell to the floor and he sat down. The man reached behind his back, but before he could pull anything I aimed a gun at him, "I relieved one of the agents of their service weapon. I knew as soon as I entered this room he was a spy and judging by the micro expressions you were unable to tame when I revealed my associates name, I would say you work for Dimitri Krinchov." The President didn't recognize the name and I didn't think he would. Krinchov is one of a handful of criminal masterminds that only Acro knows about. "Dimitri Krinchov is the man behind the organization that wants me, and Mr. Leskov used to be a part of." It started with a giggle, then the spy began laughing loudly which made no sense to me.

I still had my sights on the spy, but he was in a position to attack the President at any moment. I waved to Boris and he went to relieve the spy of his weapon, "Would you mind telling me what you find so funny?"

Boris handcuffed the spy, "You took an agents weapon, I took handcuffs." Boris shoved him onto the nearest couch, "I agree, he works for Krinchov, but I have never seen this man before. Whoever he is, I must have been kept separated from him on purpose. Whatever the reason may be, I cannot think of it."

"Mr. President, I hope you understand that this is an extreme security breach of absurd proportions. Why you allowed this to happen is of no concern to me; just know it is unacceptable." He turned his chair to the side as if he couldn't bear to face the situation at hand. "Is a routine security sweep still done of the office at dusk and dawn?" I could see from the side of his face as he nodded that he wondered how I knew that, "If you are wondering; I put that protocol in place. The real reason I came here is to suggest that Howard Brixton be made Director of Acro and to *tell* you that I will personally decide who becomes director for the foreseeable future. Your grave error in choosing the last director has brought me to this decision." I stood to my feet and adjusted my suit, "We will be taking the spy with us to find out how bad the security breach is and you will never speak of this to anyone ever. I don't care if it's in a frail attempt for forgiveness or an admission of guilt while lying on your death bed."

The President nodded guiltily. I walked around his desk and looked down on him as he looked up at me, "This is not your problem anymore. I will see to it that this madness is brought to an end then I will come back here and tell you myself that it is done and over with."

I seemed to have reassured him of the plight when he stood to shake my hand, "Thank you Mr. Silver."

I chuckled, "If you have read the presidential journals, then you know I have handled things such as this many times in the past. Speaking of which, it will be your entries that will tell the tale of my return to the President." I walked back to mine and Boris's captive, "Could you call Jacobs in here so we can have an unimpeded escort out of here?"

Jacobs came in after being called and stopped in the doorway with a flabbergasted look on his face, "It's alright Jacobs. They just need an uninterrupted escort out with their prisoner." Jacobs nodded, still unsure of what could have possibly happened since he left us in here.

I approached Jacobs, "Here is the weapon one of your agents is looking for and I'm keeping the one this spy had on him." He accepted the gun still confused, "Let's go, I have work to do." Jacobs nodded again and he escorted us out so I could get back to New York with my captive and check on Sierra's recovery progress.

***

Our transport helicopter landed in my back yard and I shook Jacobs' hand in thanks before we got off. Boris followed me with the spy on his shoulder through the back door of my house and down into the cave, "Robert!" I saw him step out of the infirmary from the next platform over, "We come bearing a gift."

Boris and I crossed the catwalk, "Uh, what did you two do?"

"There was a spy in the White House. When I mentioned Dimitri Krinchov he laughed. I want to know why and why he was there. If you don't mind, can take him into that little room over there and find out what he knows." I pointed to a small hole in the wall on the far side of the cave, "There's a closet in there with everything you might need."

Robert took the captive off of Boris' shoulder, "Sierra's vitals are normal and she turned onto her side, but hasn't awakened yet."

"Alright, so Robert you get started on him and Boris you can come with me upstairs." I looked at Boris as his head swiveled around looking at all that was in the cave, "I forgot you haven't been down here." I went into the infirmary and checked on Sierra. She was just as Robert said.

Boris and I walked upstairs, "I guess that's how you got away from us when we raided your home."

"Got away? We killed them all." Boris looked around at the lack of dead bodies lying on the floor, "I called somebody to clean up the mess." We walked down the hall to the kitchen, "You can get something for you and Robert to eat, then help him."

I turned around and headed down the hall, "What are you going to do?"

"I'm going to study everything that happened in Russia since I left to see if there's anything I missed." I didn't have to see Boris's face to know he didn't think what I just said was even possible.

***

I arrived at the door Robert had asked me about earlier. I punched in the seven digit passcode onto the keypad and the latches in the door frame came undone. I pushed the door open into what the ignorant would think is just an empty void of a room.

I stepped into the darkness and let the door close behind as I removed my shoes. The room was so dark I couldn't see my hand in front of my face. I placed my hand on the wall next to me and the floor became dimly lit so that I could see where I was stepping. The room had a circular floor and off to the side sat a desk with a chair behind it. This is the room I use to rapidly learn anything I wish. I've always had a room that I've devoted to learning though they've never been as nearly elaborate as this one.

I walked around the desk, opened the bottom left drawer, and pressed a button underneath of it. It became visible that the room was a sphere when the floor became clear and tiny lights all over the wall, floor, and ceiling began illuminating the room. I built the room personally by hand to simulate the appearance of space. All the lights matched up with the locations of all known stars, constellations, and planets in real-time.

"Give me everything on Russia since 1969." Suddenly files, articles, and government documents appeared transparent on the floor. I looked at the floor and once I was satisfied with the layout of all the info I lifted a glass out of the drawer that I opened. The inside of the drawer stays warm at all times to keep the tea I leave in there fresh.

Time dilation is a very tricky subject that is part of the theory of relativity. Simply put, when one experiences time dilation, they experience anywhere from an hour to a week of time in a matter of minutes. This way I can learn things that it would take centuries to learn, and even I don't have that kind of time to spend on just learning. Back in the interview when I said I learned everything as it was discovered, I lied. I mean how could I possibly learn everything as it's discovered? That doesn't even make sense, nor is it even possible. I was shown by the samurai when I was training with them an ancient tea leaf (yes it sounds like a poor and generic origin story, but it happened) that can induce time dilation when ingested.

    I built the room to be sound proof and inaccessible to anyone other than me. I learned the hard way that if something outside of a controlled environment interferes with someone experiencing time dilation, it can distort the mind and cause brain damage. Luckily for me my body can repair itself. If I want to end the time dilation, I simply go to sleep. Since I'm in a controlled environment I actually can't tell if the tea is taking affect; I just have to trust that it's working. I tilted my head back and emptied the glass of tea. I put the glass back and sat down on the floor then began learning all I could in hopes of finding out something I didn't know before.

Chapter Twenty-One

The simplest way to cancel the effects of the tea leaf is to sleep. After I awoke from my nap, I speed-walked back into the cave. I sped past Boris, "That was quick. What did you find out?"

I barged into the room and grabbed the spy by the throat, "Are you working for Anton Richtov?" I tightened my grip, "Answer me!" His face began to turn purple.

Robert grabbed my arm, "We need him alive. He can't talk if he's dead." I released my hold on his neck, "All he's said so far is that Dimitri Krinchov works for somebody far more powerful."

"I know. They're working for Anton Richtov."

"You said you killed him. Why do you think he's still alive? And running things no less?"

Boris entered the room to listen, "In my research I noticed dozens of incidents and payments that fall in line perfectly with how Richtov worked back when I had infiltrated his empire. I don't' know how I never noticed before. And Dimitri was never very smart to begin with." The spy began laughing hysterically. "What are you laughing at?"

When the laughter came to an end he answered, "You never 'infiltrated'." A smile remained on his face, "He knew who you were the moment you walked into his bar. He let you stick around."

"What do you mean he knew?"

He began laughing again making it difficult to understand what he said next, "He's like you Daniel Silver. He cannot die either!" I didn't understand. I mean I did, but how was it possible? I had so many questions. How could somebody like me exist and I not know about them? What happened to him to make him this way? Are we connected somehow?

"This guy is clearly mad Danny. We can't trust what he says."

"Mad men speak the most truth Robert." My phone began to play Howey's ringtone, "Continue interrogating him and Boris you come up with anything that may or may not help." They both nodded and I exited the room, "What's up Howey?"

"Did you pay a visit to a certain somebody and happen to use my name?"

"Why do you ask? Did a certain somebody come through for you?"

"Considering you're talking to the newly appointed director of Acro, I would say yes. How's Sierra doing?"

I went to check on her, "She's alive, but hasn't awoken yet."

"Glad to hear it. How's your investigation coming along?"

"Boris and I captured a spy in the White House and he says Anton Richtov is not only still alive, but that he is also like me in that he can't die." There was brief pause, "I gotta tell you man; it kinda sucks knowing that there's another guy out there like me. I always viewed being one of a kind as a negative, but now that I'm not, I wish I was." I sat down next to Sierra.

"You still are one of kind. He might not be able to die either, but that doesn't make him anything like you. People like him kill for the fun of it. You kill people like him. Speaking of which, do you have any ideas on how to do that?"

"Just a couple. Thanks for the pep talk Howey."

"No problem man. Thanks for talkin' to the President for me." We said goodbye and I leaned back watching Sierra as she laid on her side facing me.

She began mumbling inaudible words. I leaned forward in an attempt to hear her. She began wiggling and her mumbling turned into heavy breathing. I put my hand on her shoulder, "Sierra. Sierra, its Danny wake up." Her eyes opened wide, she jolted up, and her head slammed into mine. I ignored the pain and focused on her. She was breathing heavily, "It's okay Sierra, it's okay. You're safe now." She looked around, at her hands, then at me. She stared at me as if she was trying to remember.

I saw only one thing in her trembling eyes: sheer terror, "I know it's frightening but you're awake now." She experienced the same thing I do; being trapped in your own mind waiting to come back to reality.

Tears streamed from her eyes and she wrapped her arms around me hugging tightly. She held onto me as if for dear life, "There was nothing there. I was trapped within my own mind, left with my own thoughts."

"I know. The first times the worst, but I've got you now." She was shivering and had started a cold sweat.

She wiped her eyes and looked up at me, "Thank you." She kissed me amorously then asked, "What got you to do it?"

"What do you mean *got me to*?"

"Howey talks to me just as he does you. I know you want to protect me. I know you don't want me to go through everything you have. I know you didn't want to bring me into your life." She let go of my hand and looked down and felt the scar on her chest, "Does this mean… I'm like you?"

I smiled, "To an extent. I've never done this before so I'm not too sure. I don't think you can die." The corners of her lips stretched from ear to ear. "I don't think you have all the perks I do though either. Like the scar on your chest; I don't think that'll go away. You won't recover as quickly as me considering you've been unconscious for nearly forty-eight hours."

"Forty-eight hours?! What's happened in that time?" She looked around again, "And where are we?"

"We're in the infirmary that's in the cave that's underneath my house." Her eyes got wide, "The cave is the surprise that I told you about back in the coffee house before all this started. And for what's happened…" I trailed off as I realized the truth of what I was about to say, "We aren't the only two that can't die." She smiled, most likely because I said "we", then she looked confused as she thought about the second part. "As it turns out, a very dangerous man that I thought I killed a long time ago cannot die. Boris, who is now on our side, was being manipulated by Dimitri Krinchov who turns out to be working for Anton Richtov who cannot die." I pushed Sierra's hair behind her ear, "But enough of that. You just came back to life. How are you feeling?"

She thought for a moment, "I feel wonderful; better than I ever have. I feel like I can do anything." She looked at hand and followed her veins up her forearm, "You're blood is flowing through my veins."

"I'm happy to hear it." I lowered my head before I continued and Sierra lifted it, "You can't die now. You will live much longer than any average person. I understand that this is what you wanted; to be with me forever. And don't get me wrong, I want that too, but the whole world will seem different to you now and the things you will experience in the future will affect you differently than they normally would have." My life hasn't been easy. It's been one hardship after another and in a way I've put on a front to the public and to my friends and to Sierra before, but not anymore.

"Danny don't worry. Look we'll be together until one of us dies somehow. We will face whatever happens to us and the world together. Because we're different from anybody else. We're match-made. We're better together than any other two people. Not only is this amazing for me, but you're not by yourself anymore and I'm ecstatic that I can be the one to accompany you on your adventures. Whatever front you've put up for all your life, you don't have to keep up with me." Like she read my mind. Sierra smiled and added, "We'll be the team that goes down in the history books of the future."

I kissed her, "I'm glad that it's you with me. And now that you are I think it's time you see things for the way they are and must be."

I took Sierra's hand and helped her out of the bed. She looked down and stepped into the slippers I sat next to the bed, "How did I get into these clothes?" I looked off into the corner of my eye as if to hide something, "I see now. You get a girl unconscious then take her to your cave." I threw my hands up in surrender.

We smiled together, "Come on, I'm going to show you something." Sierra staggered as she attempted to walk on her jelly legs.

I held my arm around her as we walked out of the infirmary, "Wow, this is definitely something." I helped her walk across the catwalk and I took her into the room where Robert and Boris were with the spy. Luckily all they had done so far was break his fingers so Sierra wasn't exposed to too much gore.

All three of them looked at us when we walked in, "We heard the noise from in here." It dawned on Robert that Sierra hasn't met him yet, "Names Robert. It's good to see you on your feet again."

"Thank you." Sierra's eyes went from the prisoner to Boris. She stared at him for a couple seconds then walked herself over to him and landed a punch on his jaw.

The momentum from the punch nearly pulled her onto the floor before I caught her, "Okay, now you've got that out of your system."

"I want to hit him again." Boris massaged his jaw and Sierra turned her attention to our captive, "Who's he?"

"A spy that works for Richtov. He's the one that told us about him. Has he given anything else up?" Robert shook his head no.

"All you need to know about him is that he lives to create chaos. He will stop at nothing to make you suffer and eventually kill yourself."

"Robert can you help her?" Robert helped Sierra stand and I grabbed the back of the steel chair the spy was locked to. I dragged the chair out of the room, "We won't get anything else out of him." I set him on the edge of the platform. The others stood behind me, "This is the stuff I wanted to keep you from Sierra, but now that isn't possible." I placed my foot on the chair, "Richtov will be joining you shortly." I gave one push and the chair tilted over the edge with the man still in it. A couple seconds went by before a crash was heard.

Sierra slowly walked herself over to me and I stopped her before she got too close to the edge, "How many people have died down there?"

"That makes two." I walked her away from the deadly drop off, "You two can go do whatever you want. Sierra and I are going to Vancouver to find out what Tony got off the drive."

Chapter Twenty-Two

Our chauffer was taking Sierra and I to the pawn shop to meet Tony, "I can't get over how different; how much better I feel. I feel so much more capable of anything. My body feels rejuvenated and invincible." She placed her hand on mine, "Thank you again." I gripped her hand in mine. Now that she could live long like me somehow I was afraid for her. "When did you come all the way out here to drop off the drive?"

"The morning after we returned to my house I brought Boris with me." The car came to an abrupt stop as we turned onto a gridlocked street.

"Can we trust him? After all he is the one that started all of this." Traffic still hadn't moved.

"I started all of this by not making sure Richtov was dead and he's the one that manipulated Boris into what he is now." I looked around at the cars outside, "We're not getting anywhere like this. What do you say to walking the rest of the way? The shop is only a couple blocks away."

"I'd love to walk, but we can't even get our doors open." She said it knowing either one of us could easily open our doors.

I smiled at Sierra then pointed to the sun roof with my eyes, "I've climbed through the roof of a car many times. I actually did on my way to meet with you for coffee just last week."

Sierra undid her seatbelt and used me as support to stand through the roof then looked down, "Try not to get your overly-nice clothes dirty." She limberly climbed out and jumped across cars to reach the sidewalk.

It was my turn to car hop. When I got to the sidewalk drivers shouted obscenities and I waved and shouted back, "Love you too!"

Sierra was smiling with big eyes, "Why are you so… gitty?"

"I don't know." She grabbed my arms and let go in an impulse to release energy, "I guess it's just exciting to do things that most people find taboo. And again I just feel good." I put my arm around Sierra and we started walking down the street, "Is Anton Richtov really so bad?"

I thought carefully before I answered, "The best way for me to put it is that he is the closest thing to Satan walking on earth." I saw out of the corner of my eye Sierra look up at me surprised, "And what makes him truly dangerous is his patience and his sanity. If he was about maximum destruction he would be in a league of his own above Hitler and all the other baddies you can think of."

"If you've devoted your life to stopping people like him then what does that make you; a hero?"

I noticed a man tailing us from across the street, "To stop evil people you can't play by the rules of a hero. You have to dirty your hands and fight with stakes that they understand. Hero's don't take lives; they do everything in their power to save them. I won't hesitate to take a life if it means saving two more." Sierra remained silent, "I'm not saying I'm right in my choices to kill, but when there's nobody else to make the hard choices, I do. And a lot of times that means being judge, jury, and executioner." We were one block away from Tony's shop, "I carry all the weight of everything I've done around with me and because I know what that's like I'm going to do everything in my power to make sure you don't have to carry that weight."

"What, so you're going to make sure that I don't kill anybody… forever?"

We neared the door of the shop, "Hopefully it won't be hard." We stopped at the front door, "Keep your eyes on me." Sierra looked like she was expecting me to say something profound, "Somebody's been following us. Observe your surroundings and pay attention to everything.

Consider this training." We went inside then I flipped the sign to "closed" and locked the door.

Tony was already at the counter, "I've been waiting for you Rahm. I've got your drive sitting in the back. I see you brought the pretty little lady with you too."

We approached the counter, "Just take me to the drive."

Tony went into the back and as we followed Sierra whispered, "Why did he call you Rahm?"

"Back when I was involved in the criminal underworld I went by that name. Criminals hired me to knock off their competition. When my reputation reached every corner of the world I started to only get offered contracts to take out good people that hindered criminal organizations so, that's when I got out. I can count on my hands the number of people that know me by the name Rahm. They're all very old and everybody else that knew that name is dead." We got to the back of the heated room where the drive was, "One of which died helping me rescue you from the island." She seemed saddened by the fact.

"Here's your drive." Tony handed me what we came for. I heard the breaking of glass and judging by the lack of their reactions they didn't seem to hear it, "You're going to be blown away by what you find on there." I grabbed the drive and put it in my pocket then rushed back out front and saw a couple SUV's parked on the sidewalk and about a dozen armed men funneling in through the front door, "What's going on?"

"Is there a back way out of here?"

He nodded and led us through another hall further back, "I thought I heard something, but I told myself it was my imagination." I was surprised to find Sierra heard them break in; I barely even heard it myself.

We got to the end of the hall and Tony pushed the door open to the outside. Before he could get back inside, a flurry of gunfire came at us filling him with bullets. I shoved Sierra back and pulled him in with the door. When I saw her was unhurt I knelt next to Tony, "Is there another way out?"

He hardly lifted a finger to point at a door we had run past and coughed on his own blood, "Storage." He exhaled his final breath and I closed his eyelids.

I jumped to my feet, "Come on!" I grabbed Sierra's hand and pulled her with me through the door and down the stairs. Bullets pinged off of the wall and door as we ran down the steps. We got to the bottom only to find a short hall and a couple small storage rooms, "Dammit Tony! This is a dead end." I looked around and took in the environment, "Go to the room at the end of the hall and stay there until its safe."

Sierra ran and I searched some nearby crates for anything useful, but found nothing. "Danny in here!" I ran to where she called from and saw her standing over an open crate full of weapons.

I picked up an assault rifle at the same moment Sierra grabbed me and kissed me intensely. I pulled her off of me, "Really? Here? There are hostiles coming down here to try and kill us. Now is not the time."

I went back into the hall and crouched behind a crate. I looked back at Sierra giving me a pouty face and was evidently unhappy, "Why do you always do that?"

The enemies kicked the door down and were on their way, "Do what?" I knew exactly what she meant.

"Whenever I get on you like that you stop me and make an excuse. We haven't even had sex yet because you keep stopping us. Why?"

Bullets started coming and Sierra stood in the room with her arms crossed, "In my defense you really do pick the worst times." I peeked up and dropped a body. "As for not having sex yet-" I fired some more and dropped another body, "-I'm old fashioned. Not like when you were born old fashioned." A grenade rolled next to me and I threw it back, "I mean eighteenth century old fashioned." The grenade exploded and blew debris over my head without phasing Sierra, "Not only do I only sleep with women I'm married to I only get into and stay in a relationship if I think it has the potential of turning into marriage." A hostile came around my crate. I turned him around and used him as a bullet shield.

Sierra knelt down next to me while still safe inside the doorway, "Hold on. Are you saying you want to get married?"

My gun was empty so I threw it down the hall, "Can I get another gun please?"

She ran back to the crate and came back with another weapon, "So do you?"

I shot some more, "Yes!"

Sierra became ecstatic, "Are you proposing to me right now?!"

I looked at her with wide eyes, "No!" Her excitement turned to hurt disappointment, "If I propose to you here, while we're under a hailstorm of gunfire, what would that say about the future of our relationship?" She thought about it, "I'm going to wait until we are no longer being hunted."

"You could have just told me you wanted to wait until we got married."

"I didn't want to scare you with the idea of marriage if you weren't ready for it." Bullets continued to hit the wall behind me.

She looked at me like I said something stupid, "Have you forgotten that you gave me your blood? We're bound, not by just our feelings for each other anymore, but by our blood. You're stuck with me. Heck, I'm stuck with you." I couldn't help but smile with relief at the fact that we were on the same page now. "We won't be, we can't be, satisfied by anybody else, but each other." I fired a few more shots and Sierra grabbed more ammo and a couple grenades, "Because I'm the only one that won't leave you and you won't leave me."

She pulled the pin on a grenade and raised her arm to throw it, but before she could I grabbed it from her hand and threw it myself. Sierra clenched her wrist and cried out. She had been shot.

I tore the sleeve off of the dead body next to me and grabbed her arm, "Wounds will come with this life; it's inevitable. And I told you I wouldn't let you kill anybody else." She looked up at me with tear filled eyes. I tightened the knot and she reflexively slapped me. She held her hand over her mouth to try and hide her laughter, "Oh you think that's funny?" I peeked over the crate and lobbed another grenade, "I took out about ten of them so far which leaves us with five or six. Sit next to the chest and slide me weapons when I need them." Sierra nodded and the gunfire stopped. I whispered to her, "Sit over there and keep your heart rate low; the wound will clot faster." She moved further into the room and closed her eyes to focus on her breathing.

"I don't want to hurt you or your lady friend Rahm." That voice sounded familiar, "If you show your face I promise they won't shoot."

I looked at Sierra focusing and stood up to face our assailants, "Oh it's just you Marvin. I thought we were in some sort of danger." The old man stood ahead of me with most of his weight on his cane, "Aren't you a little old to still be doing stuff like this?" He must have been here for the bounty.

"You only taught me how to thrive in this life, but never how to get out of it." Back when I had assumed the role of Rahm I took Marvin under my wing and mentored him in the world of criminals. It's something I wish I could take back now that he's a notorious international criminal.

There were five armed men standing around Marvin, "As always you blame everybody but yourself for your own ignorance." I walked around from behind the crate I used as cover from the gunfire, "Why are you here? You should know better than anybody else that I can't be beaten." Marvin shifted himself on his cane and the armed men raised their weapons.

"Isn't it your cockiness and false sense of security in the public eye that has brought forth your recent misfortunes?" I guess he was right to an extent. "Call out Miss Morning and come with me; no more blood needs to be spilled here."

"I agree, but if you do not leave us then I will be the one leaving you here."

He turned the nob on the top of his cane, "One line comes to mind as we stand here: 'the student has become the master'?"

"Not if the master was me."

Marvin whipped his cane and the sheath launched at me revealing the sword hidden within it. I narrowly dodged the cane that was immediately followed by a swing from Marvin's sword. I managed to lean out of the way just enough so that only my vest was sliced through. When his attacks stopped I paused to gather my thoughts, "How? You're so old."

"You were the one who taught me that the aging process was just a hindrance on the mind meant to be overcome."

"Of course I would say something like that; I don't age." I stood ready to fight, "You can't catch me off guard again so you better make your next move count." He raised his sword and cut the air as he lunged at me and brought his blade down from above. I turned sideways as the blade came down in front of my face and forcefully kicked Marvin in the chest launching him backwards and knocking the sword out of his hands. I caught the sword and before the threats could raise their weapons I swiftly cut down all five of them.

I wiped the blood off of the sword and sheathed it into the cane, "It truly is ironic that you tried cutting me down with the very weapon I gifted you with. I think I'll rescind my gift and add it to my collection of keepsakes." I looked down and felt where my vest was torn, "I really don't want to kill you, but if you're still here when I turn back around to leave, I will."

I turned around and went back into the room to retrieve Sierra. I found her sitting on the crate with eyes still shut. I knelt in front of her and noticed her breathing was shallow, "Sierra." She opened her eyes and looked around as if she had forgotten where she was, "You alright?"

"Uh yeah I think I just dozed off." I unwrapped her wrist to check her wound, "What?

How?" The bleeding had stopped and only a shallow, open wound remained.

"I don't think you fell asleep. You just shut out your environment when you slowed your heart rate like I said allowing it to start healing so quickly." I helped Sierra off of the crate, "It's time to get back."

We walked back into the hall and Marvin was gone, "I'm not sure I'll ever get used to how you can do all of this on your own."

"It took a life time of training to learn how to fight like I do." We walked over the bodies and up the stairs.

"Not just that, but the killing too. You've never had someone to carry that burden with you; the weight of all those bodies piling on top of you."

"I know what you meant." We got upstairs and stepped over everything that was broken during the raid, "I don't keep you with me to have to face my struggles or share my burdens. The only reason we're not on a beach in some exotic country is because we won't be safe until we bring down Anton Richtov."

"I know I could have chosen a different, safer path for myself, but I stick around knowing that I'll inevitably have to face things with you and I *want* to help you face them." We walked across the broken glass to get outside.

I stopped us, "I love you and when we get through this we are getting off the radar and out of the public eye to live on a beach somewhere."

She stretched her neck upwards and gave me a quick kiss, "I would like that." She brushed off my shoulders and pulled my sleeve down, "You have the drive right?"

I patted my breast pocket and signaled with my eyes at our chauffer that had just pulled up to the sidewalk, "Let's go find out what's on it." I helped Sierra into the car as all passersby stared at me.

No.

Us.

Chapter Twenty-Three

My jet landed on my private runway a few miles from my house. We were met on the tarmac and from there were on our way to meet up with Robert and Boris at my house. Sierra had her head rested on my shoulder when we approached the end of my driveway, "Sierra. Look." As we pulled through my front gate onto the driveway a bright orange glow could be seen coming from my house.

Sierra straightened up and leaned forward between the two front seats, "What the..." As we got closer it became clear that my house was burning to the ground. She shouted at the driver, "What are you waiting for? Go faster!" The driver sped up and we got to the front of the house much faster thanks to Sierra.

We jumped out and my phone started ringing. Right when I looked at the screen to see Howey calling I saw someone in the smoke slowly coming out, "Here, talk to Howey and find out what he wants." Sierra took the phone and I ran through the frame of the front door to help whoever it was I was looking at.

I got to them and put their arm around my shoulder, putting most of their weight on me. We got outside and when they fell to the ground I saw that it was Robert, "Danny just got Robert out." He had something wedged into the side of his thigh and was bleeding badly, "Yeah Robert's injured send someone to help. No we haven't found Boris yet."

Now wasn't the time to worry about how this happened, but to make sure everybody was safe, "Do you know where Boris is?"

When he finished moistening his mouth he answered, "We were eating in the kitchen." He took a moment to catch his breath, "He walked out just before the explosion."

Sierra hung up with Howey, "He's on his way with an Acro medical transport from the nearest sub-station."

"Make sure Robert stays conscious while I find Boris." Sierra nodded and I turned around to face the flames. There was no way of telling where he could possibly be and there was no time to check the whole building even if Sierra helped; the place was crumbling. I closed my eyes and listened; if Boris was calling for help I would hear him.

"Danny what are you doing?" I focused on the noise from inside the house. Flames flickering, the crackling of wood, I tuned it all out. "Danny!" I tuned out Sierra and the noise of the wind that was blowing against my face. Past all the interruptions the only thing left to hear was the heavy breathing and the shouts for help coming from my son. He sounded like he was in the bathroom down the hall from the kitchen.

I ran into my crumbling house; into and through the fire and flames. I hurdled a fallen beam and ran into the hall as the flames began to sear my flesh. I continued down the hall until I reached the door that was burning and falling off of its hinges. I grabbed the door and pulled it out of the way as my hands burned to the touch of it, "Boris!" I saw a hand rise from the floor. When I grabbed it it became limp. I lifted him up onto my shoulder and left the bathroom.

The way I had come was now inaccessible. The quickest way out was through the window down at the end of the hall. I began running as fast as I could with a full grown man on my shoulder. About half way through the hall a piece of the ceiling fell from above. I was quick enough to raise my free arm to deflect it, but now I was on fire. I continued to run, stepped onto the window sill and hurled myself through the window. My trajectory was off leaving me unable to land on my feet, so while in mid role I laid Boris on the grass and got back on my feet. I waved my arm around until the fire went out unvovering the third degree burns on my arm.

I knelt next to Boris and resuscitated him. He choked as he struggled to fill his lungs with fresh air,

"Let's get you to your feet." We grabbed each other's forearms and I pulled him up. I put my arm around him and helped him walk around to the front of the building. Sierra was keeping Robert's head up as they both stared into the building waiting for us to come out, "Waiting for us?"

When Sierra whipped her head around I could see her beady eyes fearful of my safe return. She let go of Robert and ran to my aid, "Oh my god look at you!" She covered her mouth in shock, "Your arm!"

"I dislocated my shoulder too, but I'm fine. Grab another bottle of water out of the car for him." She remained staring at us, "Go Sierra!" I didn't want to yell at her, but she appeared to have gone deaf. From what I've been able to deduce, she's perfectly fine in any situation as long as I'm not hurt and if I am then she becomes hysterical. She's not ready for stuff like this just yet and I don't want her to have to be.

The Acro medical unit screeched to a stop and Howey jumped out. The unit opened up the back of the van and grabbed Robert while Howey ran over to take Boris for me. I shifted my shoulder to put it back in place and he looked me up and down before he walked away, "You're good right?" I nodded and he took Boris to the back of the van.

Sierra handed Boris the water and came back to me. She looked me over once more but more thoroughly this time. She took note of the lack of flesh and the visibility of my veins and muscles. She hovered her hand about an inch away from my arm as if debating whether or not she wanted to find out what it felt like, "Are you going to be alright?"

"Yeah I'll be fine." I wrapped my good arm around her and we walked over to the back of the van, "Can I get a swig of that?" Howey handed me the bottled water and I took a couple gulps.

Boris sat on the step in back with no apparent injuries while the unit worked on Robert's leg, "We're going to pull this out then we'll need to cauterize the wound."

"Yeah yeah I know the drill. Just get it over with." The team counted down then pulled the piece of metal out of Robert's leg which was followed by a quiet grunt. Due to the units limited resources on such short notice they used a blowtorch to seal the wound. The flesh glowed red and the bleeding slowly stopped. When enough of the pain subsided Robert said what we were all thinking, "So, what the hell?" We all looked at each other with no answers, "I was in the kitchen then the oven blew up and considering it wasn't being used I think it's fair to say this was an attack."

It was fair to say that and I think that's exactly the case, "I agree. We'll set up shop in the cave, take the night to rest up, and then tomorrow we'll comb through whatever the security cameras may have picked up."

Sierra spoke up, "And if we don't find anything? That island base is destroyed and we don't have any leads on Richtov or Krinchov."

"We still have this." I took the drive out of my pocket, "Whoever or whatever is on this will give us what we need to stop those two."

The glow and the crackling of the fire drew our attention as the warmth came over us in the cool of night. Sierra pointed into the fire, "What is that?" In the distance and through the smoke the dome of my secret study was barely visible.

"That is my secret study." Sierra cocked her head and opened her mouth as if about to say something, but I think she had too many questions and not sure what to start with, "You know how I told you that I learn everything as it's discovered?" Sierra crossed her arms waiting to hear my confession, "Well that's not exactly true."

She surprisingly didn't seem surprised, "It's about time you fessed up." She sat sideways on my lap, "I hope you know how ridiculous that sounds," she looked up and waved her arm to mock as she quoted me, "'when you've lived as long as I have you learn everything as it's discovered'. Anybody with half a brain laughed at that, I know I did. I almost called you out on it in the interview." Everyone laughed and I lowered my head to cover my face with my hand in a poor attempt to hide my embarrassment. She lifted my head and kissed me, "So what is it?"

"How bout we set up in the cave then I'll show you. I'll take out the cots and blankets I have down there. Robert, I have an old pair of crutches you can use and Howey, well, you have a wife to get home to."

Sierra and I stood up, "That's great and all, but how are we getting down there?" I took Sierra's hand and Boris followed us as I walked her onto the patio underneath the canopy.

I pulled out a brick from one of the support columns and placed my hand inside, "We're standing on a hydraulic lift." Before we started going down I remembered Robert. I ran to the back of the van and helped him out, "Almost forgot you." We stepped onto the patio as it began its descent. I waved to Howey, "Thanks for your help."

He waved back, "Anytime."

Chapter Twenty-Four

Sierra looked around at the four walls, "You never cease to amaze me babe."

"Oh I'm 'babe' now?"

"Just trying it out." She shrugged her shoulders, "I don't think I like it though."

"Come on. Could you please wait until I'm not around to discuss pet names?" We all laughed at Robert's plea as the lift neared the bottom.

"The cave doesn't extend this far, so we'll have to take a walk down this hall." The lift stopped and I opened the gate to the hall. We got off, I closed the gate, and the lift rose back up to the surface.

We got inside the cave and I retrieved the crutches for Robert from the infirmary. I took two cots and blankets from the closet and set them on the main floor, "I could only find two cots so Boris and

Sierra you can each get one. Robert you can have the infirmary and I'll figure something out."

Before I could walk away to preform my next task Sierra got all of our attention, "Are we not going to talk about what just happened out there?"

I understood her concerns though I didn't quite share them at the moment, "Yes, what just happened was a deliberate attack against us, but there's no need to worry about it right now and we're not in any immediate danger." Judging by Sierra's tenseness, what I said served no good towards her relief. I neared her and softened my voice hoping she would sense my calmness and relax herself, "Don't fret. We've been through a lot today and the best thing for us to do right now is rest." I was thinking in her best interest. I could go another couple days without a wink of sleep, "We should clear our mind and get a fresh start in the morning."

Sierra's posture showed little relief, "Is that alright?" She nodded and that's enough for me to know that she would be able to sleep through the night not worrying about what was ahead of us tomorrow, "Good. Wait here I need to go grab something then I'll be right back."

I went into my trophy room to retrieve something; I didn't like calling it that because it sounds boastful, but that's exactly what it was. I pulled out a drawer full of jewelry and searched for the right piece. I rifled through different necklaces, bracelets, and rings that I've collected over the past couple centuries and each were worth a fortune alone.

I found the most valuable of the collection and took it in my hand.

I walked back out onto the main floor after securing the ring in my pocket. Boris and Robert were preparing their cots for the night, "They'll use the cots. We can sleep in the infirmary." I wonder what she had to say to Robert to reserve the bed for us, "So what's in there?" She looked past me.

"Just a collection of stuff I've kept over the years."

"What did you get from it?"

"You'll find out." I locked onto her dazzling eyes, "Why don't I show you what's inside that dome?"

"I would love that, but how are we going to get inside? The house is burning." She looked wonderingly then registered the scheming look on my face, "Of course another hidden passage." I placed my hand in the small of her back and we began walking, "What is it this time; an elevator, escalator, knowing you it could be a teleportation device." We approached a hidden door along the cave wall and I opened it to reveal our method of transportation, "Or it could be stairs." I flipped the switch on the wall and the stairwell lit up. We climbed to the top of the stairs where it appeared that they led only to a short hall to the right that was a dead end, "Where to now?"

I placed my hand under her chin and lifted then we both looked up at the latch above us, "Ran out of space during construction so the only way to go was straight up." The space directly above us was right in front of the door to the dome where on the other side was the fire destroying my house. I grabbed the pole in the corner to push open the panel ten feet above us. I knelt down on the floor and interlocked my fingers, "I'll boost you up."

She rolled her eyes at me with a grin, "Because a ladder would be too easy."

"I've got to make it a little fun." She took notice of my still-charred arm before raising her leg, "It's fine, it won't hurt."

She stepped one foot into my hands and I lifted. When her foot reached my shoulder I let go with one hand and turned the other for a better grip. Playfully I placed my free hand on her right buttock and she gasped, "You're supposed to be helping me get up here."

I could hear her pitch rise and pictured her face blushing, "Like I said, I've got to make it a little fun."

"Well you can grab my butt later." Now my face was red. She got her arms on the edge and I extended my arm over my head for her to climb up. She stood to her feet and looked down at me, "I can't see anything up here. How are you getting up?"

"You're in a narrow hall, stand against it."

"Okay, but how are you getting up here?" I backed up to the end of the dead end hall. I sprinted forward, put my foot on the wall, pushed up, grabbed the ledge, pushed my feet off of the inside of the floor panel behind me, and rolled back onto my feet. I placed my hand on the wall and the hall dimly lit. Sierra and I looked at each other, "So for the fun of it?" Having rolled onto my injured arm I winced in pain, "I thought you could shut off pain?"

"Yes, but to do so I need to cancel my sense of touch completely." I gently kissed her on her lips, "And if I did that I wouldn't be able to feel your lips on mine." I closed the hatch on the floor, took her hand, and led her down the hall, "You're the only other person who's ever been in here. You'll be the only other person who knows what this place even is, or what it does."

We walked into the open space under the dome, "So this is where you learned most of the stuff you know?"

"Not here. In the past I've just used isolated locations, but this is the most elaborate of the places I've studied in."

I left her standing in the center of the room while I walked around my desk, "Have you ever just looked up at the stars and wondered?"

She smiled and chuckled, "What?" I actived the dome and the simulation began. Sierra began turning in circles, looking up, looking down, and everywhere else. In the light of the stars I could barely see that her smile vanished into a look of surprise and speechlessness, "This is…" She searched her mental vocabulary for one of the few words that could describe the sight before her, "Unbelievable. Breathtaking."

"Most of what I would say in this moment has already been spoken between us." She looked away from the walls and at me as I walked over to her. I looked into her glittering eyes as the stars reflected in them, "You told me that when I decided to save you that we became bound by blood. And that from the moment I made that decision we became an inseparable team."

The beads of water in the corners of her eyes sparkled in light from the dome, "Danny what are you-."

I put my finger on her lip to shush her, "And I told you that I never got into a relationship if I didn't see it going anywhere." I got down on one knee and took the ring out of my pocket. The light from the stars made the diamond ring sparkle, "I love you Sierra and I want us to spend the rest of our lifetimes together. Will you marry me?" She put her hand over her mouth and looked around in the overwhelming moment as tears flowed from her eyes.

She wiped her eyes and extended her hand. As clearly as she could in her emotional state she answered, "Yes. Yes I will."

I slid the diamond ring onto her finger and she looked at it then at me as if she didn't believe what she was looking at, "The ring itself is a diamond band. I cut it myself some time ago and saved it for a rainy day. But from here all I can see is sunshine." Some key words triggered effects on the walls so when I said 'sunshine' everything in the room became a bright orange as the sun became visible.

Sierra wiped her face once more and smiled, "I hope you know how cliché that sounded." She hugged me tenderly, "But it was still lovely."

"I've been using cliché lines since before they were cliché."

Sierra fiddled with the ring on her finger behind my back then pulled away, "It's a bit loose."

I took her left hand and raised it to my lips for a short peck, "No problem. I'll just pull some equipment out of storage and forge a thin band of silver to wrap around the inside of the diamond. It'll fit perfectly."

Sierra smiled, wrapped her hands around the side of my neck, and pulled my head down for a deep kiss, "I love you."

"I love you too." I gently brushed her hair with my finger, "Why don't we head back and call it a night?"

We got back into the cave to find Robert and Boris already lying down. I walked with Sierra into the infirmary and closed the curtain. I opened one of the cabinets and took out some clothes, "I kept a spare set of clothes down here when you were unconscious. While you change I'll go add that silver band onto the ring."

"You don't have to worry about that now."

"It'll take less than thirty minutes." She slid the loose ring off her finger and stared at it while it sat in the palm of her hand, "I'll bring it back to you then we can rest up for the night."

After melting a silver ring into a malleable metal, flattening it out to be as thin as a hair, and wrapping it around the inside of the diamond ring I returned to Sierra with it. She was sitting in the chair waiting for me and her hair was now in a ponytail that made me wonder what she looked like in high school. I knelt down in front of her, took her hand and slid the snug and improved ring onto her finger, "It fits like a glove." She fidgeted with it to test how secure it was, "I don't think I'd be able to take it off if I wanted to."

We both laid down on the bed meant for one and snuggled next to one another leaving little space between us. Sierra sniffed a couple times, "Uh when's the last time you showered?"

So much had been going on the past couple days none of us have had the opportunity to bathe, "I could ask you the same thing." She slapped my wounded arm unwittingly. She saw me wince and laughed, "I'm so sorry."

"You don't need to apologize." I smiled at Sierra then laid my head back letting it sink into the comfort of the pillow and closed my eyes, "Goodnight."

I could feel her gaze on the side of my face. She gently lifted my wet-to-the-touch and fleshy arm and rested it on her waist then kissed me on the cheek, "Goodnight."

Chapter Twenty-Five

"Wake up you two love birds." I opened my eyes only to see Sierra's arm lying awkwardly over them. I turned my head and saw her next to me face down. I had conditioned myself to wake up at six a.m. every day, but when I did this morning she was still sound asleep, so I chose to enjoy her company and stay in bed. I attributed her extended slumber to the fact that it was her first sleep since she changed. I guess her body was still getting accustomed to the changes. Granted, we didn't get to bed until five earlier in the morning.

I cautiously moved my head out from under her arm and laid it back down on the pillow to give me the freedom to lean up, "When did you get up?"

"Boris woke me at eight. We checked the cameras that are still intact and saw that the fires were out. We cleared the passage through to your study to get in and out. As you can guess it's still pretty hot up there. We went to the nearest hotel to wash up then grabbed a bite to eat. We brought you two some carry-out."

"We also checked the footage from the past twenty-four hours and didn't see anything out of the ordinary." Robert woddled a few paces closer, "My best guess is that during the assault the other night somebody planted a device in the kitchen. I haven't shared this with Boris because he was still fighting against us at that time. I'm not saying I think he knew about it, but I didn't want to tell him what I'm thinking in case he did." The idea was thought provoking, but I wasn't going to worry about it until I had the chance to ask Boris about it directly.

I looked up at the digital clock mounted on the wall that read 1300, "Is it really one in the afternoon?" Robert nodded and his face said he was as surprised as I was that we slept so late into the day.

"We also met up with Howey. He gave me the spare set of clothes he said you kept at his house." He set the clothes on the counter next to him.

I had forgotten that I kept a change of clothes at Howey's place for just-in-case situations like this one, "Thanks. Did you happen to check out what was on the flash drive?"

"As a matter of fact we did. Only minimal things stood out to Boris but it's too much to explain to you right now. Why don't you two eat and get cleaned up then we'll get to work."

I was impressed with his initiative and his natural authoritative tone so I couldn't resist, "Aye aye captain."

Sierra rolled over and mumbled, "Is it morning already?" And with that Robert did a half salute and exited the room. She squinted at the clock on the wall and jolted up, "Is it really one o' clock?"

"Yeah. I'm unhappy about it just as much as you are." I hated sleeping in. If I woke up after ten a.m. I was unhappy, but given the fact I woke up next to my fiancée I couldn't help but be happy.

Judging by Sierra's tone and alertness she didn't feel the same way at all, "No, you don't get it. I've lost so much of the day; to sleep no less. I absolutely loathe sleeping in." She jumped out of the bed, "Do you have any more clothes in here for me?" Before I could answer she found them in the first cabinet she opened.

For each second that passed I understood more and more how much she really hated waking up late. She began undressing and it occurred to me that it didn't matter that it was just me or if on stage in front of thousands; she was going to make the best of the remaining day.

"Don't look at me like that. We're engaged now and I'm not going to waste another minute of dayli-." She had one leg in her pants then froze and thought about what she had just said. She raised her left hand and stared down at the rock wrapped around her finger. She looked at me and smiled from ear to ear, "We're engaged." Sierra stopped and took a deep breath.

I walked over to her and placed my hands on her hips, "Yes we are. We're also standing in my personal infirmary in my secret cave underneath the crumbled remains of my house."

She nodded in agreement with the peculiar situation, "Speaking of which I'm sorry about your home burning down."

"Oh, don't be sorry. This wasn't my home." I didn't expect her too and when I saw her face crinkle cutely like it does I knew she didn't understand, "With all the moving around all my life and the many different places I've been to, I've never been able to call a single place home."

A look of sadness fell upon Sierra's face, "Well that just won't do. When this is all done and over with we'll have to find us a home."

I smiled and picked up her shirt off the bed, "There's no need for that because wherever I am, as long as you're there with me, I'll be home." Sierra laughed out loud and I threw her shirt at her, "Oh you think that's funny huh?"

"No no no. Well yes, but only because it sounded so cheesy." I hid my smile as I turned my back to grab my clothes that Robert dropped off. I was about to walk out without another word just to tease her when she stopped me by the arm, "Danny wait." She turned me towards her and I cleared my face, "Yes I thought it was funny, but what you said was sincere and from the heart and for that I find what you said to be very beautiful." I looked at her and laughed so that she understood that my feelings weren't hurt. She playfully hit my arm for making her believe I was upset, "Hey look at your arm." Starting at my shoulder she rubbed her hand down my arm. Amazed she looked up at me, "It looks just like it did before."

"I told you I would be fine." I took her hand and turned it palm up, "Just like the wound that was once here on your wrist." I briefly caressed her wrist then remembered we only had a few hours of sunlight left, "You don't need to be in a rush every morning anymore. You're not running out of time." She knew she liked the reminders that she could rapidly recover from wounds and that she wouldn't be aging anytime soon, "How about you keep the shirt you slept in on so we have clean clothes to change into once we wash up?" She poked her head through the neck hole and pushed her arms into the sleeves, "We'll take our food with us to eat on the way."

"That sounds good and all but I still have a career of my own." In light of recent events I've seemed to have forgotten the fact that she has her own life, "If you don't mind I need to check my e-mail for any potential story updates." I parted the curtain and walked her over to the monitors. I rolled the chair behind her to sit and I put in my password to gain access to the computer, "Thank you."

She typed a few keys to get online and then signed into her work e-mail. The most recent event was a shooting that left a man critically injured and was time stamped two hours ago. Sierra sighed in disappointment. She moved the cursor to the top of the page and clicked refresh in hopes of there somehow being an event occurring between the time she logged on and now. After a few seconds a new headline appeared at the top of the list in all caps "GUNMEN IN BUROUGH OF MANHATTEN COMMUNITY COLLEGE". The subheading mentioned hostages, "Well there's my new story."

Sierra stood up and walked away from the monitors, "Uh how do I get out of here?" I headed for the stairs that led into my study expecting Sierra to follow, "Where are you going?"

"With you to the college." I added a sense of urgency to my voice.

"Why?"

I neared her so that she would understand the importance of what I had to say next, "A reporter is who you are and that's okay, but being who *we* are, having what *we* have; our job is to keep the headline "gunmen in college" instead of "massacre in college". To not report the tragedies, but to prevent the tragedies from becoming anymore newsworthy." Sierra was struck off guard by my intensity, "You look at that headline and see an opportunity for a story because you're a reporter and you can keep being that. When I see that headline I see lives that need saving, not a chance to write about the ones lost. So while you're watching what's going on from the outside I'll be inside preventing the deaths of innocent people."

I had never spoken to her that way before and her speechlessness suggested she didn't know how to take it. I looked past Sierra to Robert and Boris pretending to straighten up their already made cots as if they were too preoccupied to be listening, "One of you contact me with anything relevant to what's happening at the college." They looked over like they didn't know I was talking to them.

I turned my attention back to Sierra, "I'm sorry, but that's how I feel." I caressed her cheek apologetically with the back of my hand, "Let's go."

I speed walked to the bottom of the stairs and noticed her lagging behind, "Are you going to help me or not?"

Chapter Twenty-Six

We arrived on campus and exited our car with the infiltration kit I grabbed before we left the cave. There were crowds of worrisome, nosey bystanders, vans and cameras from several news outlets, and people simply looking for excitement in their dull lives. In the distance Sierra spotted her cameraman, the same cameraman from our interview. We waded through the dense crowd and approached him from behind, "Tom what do we have?"

Tom turned around and was clearly surprised to see Sierra, "Whoa! You actually showed up for a story." Sierra looked up at me then quickly looked away when I met her eyes, "I thought I was going to lose my job without a reporter to work with." He looked us up and down, "What happened to you two? Looks like you went through hell." Sensing there was something going on between Sierra and I he continued, "It's good to see you too Mr. Silver. The gunmen are held in the second theater with nearly a hundred hostages and nobody's sure how many baddies are in there. About twenty minutes ago one of the gunmen sent out a video to all news outlets. All he's said is that he's looking for somebody and every fifteen minutes he doesn't have them he's going to kill somebody." He almost seemed giddy when he said it, enough so I had to restrain myself from punching him, "I think he was bluffing though since no gunshots have been heard yet."

"Has there been any indication of who he is or who he wants?"

"Oh yeah he did say his name was Dimitri. Though nobody has any idea who the hell Dimitri is." Before I could devise a plan another video from the gunman started broadcasting on the TV's in the news vans.

He wore a ski mask and the hostages were visible in the background. If it really was Dimitri he was speaking without an accent to keep everyone from thinking Russia was behind this, "I've just received word that the man I'm looking for has arrived on the scene. If you're watching Mr. S, I suggest you come in unarmed or more people will die." There were murmurs all around from people asking who Mr. S was. "That would be me" I thought to myself. He pointed the camera at another gunman with his assault rifle's muzzle against a hostages head, "Every fifteen minutes." The gunman pulled his trigger and screams erupted as brain matter spewed out onto the remaining hostages. The live feed ended.

Sierra gasped and grasped my forearm. Tom looked away from the screen, "Whoa did you see that? That was sick man."

He had a smile on his face. He actually had a smile on his face. I set down my briefcase then grabbed him by the collar and slammed him against the open door in the back of his news van, "Are you really smiling? That man just died and you're smiling. How bout I drag you in there so they can shoot you next then we'll see if you're still smiling." I saw the fear in his eyes that should have already been there.

Sierra grabbed my hand and tugged, "Danny stop. This won't help anything." I looked around at the people staring at me, watching what I would do next, so I backed away and Tom adjusted his shirt. Sierra stood between us, "He doesn't matter, the people inside do." She lipped something else so nobody could hear, "They need your help." I mentally reprioritized and took out my phone to analyze the blueprints Robert e-mailed me.

Tom massaged his clavicle, "Jeez Sierra. I think you need a new boyfriend."

I raised my eyes from my phone to see Sierra lift her left hand to Tom's face and watch his eyes nearly pop out of his head when he saw the ring, "And you need a new personality." I turned my attention back to the blueprints and identified the best possible route to get inside the building.

Tom eagerly changed the subject, "So uh, who do you think this Mr. S guy is?"

"Your guess is as good as mine."

Sierra stood next to me and held her hand over my phone to block the glare on the screen, "How are you getting in?" I scrolled to the corner of the building and zoomed in on the gymnasium, "That's on the other side of the building. How are you getting to the theater?" While zoomed in I scrolled over the path I planned on taking, "So across the gym, up the stairs to the third floor, down the hall and across the bridge, back down the stairs, then down the hall to the theater." She took my phone and searched the building herself, "Why not get into the building through one of the many closer entrances?"

"Entering at the farthest point guarantees a far less possibility of them knowing I'm inside before I want them to."

Tom interrupted, "Hold on. Did you just say you're going inside?"

"No. I didn't say I that."

"Okay cuz' I was gonna say there's nothing you can do." I raised an eyebrow at him to elaborate, "What? I'm just sayin' you're a billionaire that wears suits all the time; it's not like you can save them." Tom's face contorted and somehow he figured it out. He started pointing his finger at me and opened his mouth but nothing came out.

I took one step closer to Tom. He backed up fast enough to hit the back of his head on the open door behind him, "I don't see you going in there to help them and if you tell anyone what you're thinking

I'll pay you a not so friendly visit at your home." My phone started ringing and I answered, "What do you have?"

It was Boris, "We scanned the gunman's retina and confirmed that it is Dimitri though I knew it the instant I heard his voice in the live video. What's your plan?"

"I'm going to kill him and save as many of the students as I can."

Tom got bug-eyed when he heard what I said. I opened the kit ever-so slightly so nobody could see the gun inside. I took out the black carbon tactical gloves and the three pack of throwing knives then gave the rest of the kit to Sierra. I kissed her as Boris started giving me info about the campus that might be useful, "Be careful." I assume Tom tried recording me walking away when I heard Sierra, "Put that down you moron."

I reached the doors to the gym but they were locked. I stepped back and kicked the locks off the door. I got inside and closed the door before anyone noticed me. I hurried to the other side of the empty gym and looked around into the vacant hall before I stepped out and into the stairwell. I got to the third floor and cautiously moved out into the hall. The only threat so far was on the ground floor of the second theater, the rest of the building had evacuated and was now vacant.

Right before I stepped onto the bridge connecting the two sections of the building I heard heavy breathing coming from one of the classrooms. I doubled back a few paces and slowly approached the doorway. When I noticed the shadow of somebody right around the corner they came around and lunged at me very sloppily with a knife. I grabbed his wrist and pulled the knife from his hand as I swung him around me onto the floor. He pushed himself across the floor until his back met the wall. He turned away and covered his face with his arms, "Please no Mr. Silver he made me do it!"

What did he mean? I worked my brain to decipher his words and went over everything I did or did not see since I got into the building. Dimitri and his men were only seen in the theater. I've gotten this far and haven't seen anybody until right here and right now. This kid is terrified, but of course he would be, there are men with guns on campus. The only door obstructing my path so far was the one to get in. Every door was shut and probably locked for security except for the ones I went through. Dimitri must have known which path I would take and left the doors open for me. And lastly he knows my name so why would he attack me unless he was acting under duress?

When I finished brainstorming I heard feet scuff the floor behind me. I whipped around and threw the knife into the chest of the hostile behind me. A man with a ski mask and gun crashed to the floor. I walked to the student on the floor and extended my hand, "Come on its okay now." He looked up at me and took my hand, "Go down the hall and leave through the gym." He thanked me then turned around to leave. I grabbed his arm and he looked back, "Don't tell anybody you saw me here. I'll know if you do." He nodded spastically and ran off.

Now that Dimitri is expecting me to take a specific route I need to change my plan. I had already chosen a back-up so I knew where to go. Instead of taking the stairs down directly on the other side of the bridge I continued down the hall and across the plaza to the registrar's office and used the stairs there to go down to the second floor. Since the hostages were being kept on the floor it was a safe bet that at least one gunman would be posted on the back watching over.

I looked around then moved quickly and lightly across the lobby to the door to the theater. I slowly pushed the door open making sure nobody was watching. There was an eerie silence about the theater. I passed completely through and quietly closed the door. There was one gunman walking along the back of the theater like I expected. His back was turned to me so I stayed low and moved along the wall in the opposite direction. I moved up to the back row of chairs and looked over to see all the hostages cluttered on the floor. There were four guards standing in a half circle around the hostages. I couldn't tell which one or if any of them were Dimitri. It's possible that there's more guards that I can't see too. My mission is to secure the safety of all the remaining hostages and the best way to guarantee that was to eliminate every threat. The secondary mission is to capture Dimitri.

The ideal situation would be for Acro to be on the scene, but they can't operate here, not with all the attention that this situation is getting. Luckily I'm here acting on behalf of the agency I founded. If I wasn't here Howey would probably send someone with far less notoriety than me to do exactly what I'm doing now. Though I'm willing to bet Dimitri was counting on this whole scenario.

I heard some talking coming from the hall on the floor where I couldn't see. It was definitely Dimitri speaking fluent Russian, but it was impossible to actually hear what he was saying. The guard on the opposite side of the walkway was on his way back. The first move is to always get a feel for the lay of the land and second is to take out the overwatch. I hid in the aisle and waited for the hostile to walk past. I quietly rose to my feet, put one hand on his chin, my other on the back of his head then twisted breaking his neck. I held him and slowly lowered his body to the floor to keep from alerting the others to my presence.

I prefer knives over firearms; they're silent, serve multiple purposes, require more skill to use, reusable, and I don't have to reload them. I could easily take out three of the gunmen with three throwing knives then use the assault rifle on the floor next to me to take out a fourth. That still leaves Dimitri and any other guards I haven't made yet. I can't, in good conscience, risk the lives of the students. I needed to go around back stage to get a view of the rest of the theater.

The floor plans suggested there was a walkway on either side of the theater between rows of chairs extending from the floor to an exit below the upper level. In that corridor there was a door that opened into a back room with another on the other side that could get me back stage. I stayed low moving along the back row of chairs to remain hidden. I reached the railing preventing any unfortunate souls from falling several feet to find an injury at the bottom. I peeked up to make sure none of the hostiles would see me then vaulted over the rail crouching low on impact with the floor to keep from making noise.

I looked up to make sure I wasn't spotted and saw four hostages with blood stained clothes looking back at me. I raised a finger to my lips and they each nodded then they turned their heads looking upwards at something out of my line of sight. "What are you looking at?" I heard in a thick Russian accent.

I turned around and hurried into the side room that looked like a storage space. I waited around the corner of the door in case he decided to investigate. The door opened again and the muzzle of a U.S. military issued assault rifle poked through the doorway. I didn't take note of it before but these guys must be equipped by the same shipment of weapons Sierra and I found in Juarez's compound. I'll have to get Howey to run the serial numbers through Acro's database.

The hostile stepped through the door and I swung the side of my hand into his throat knocking him backwards. To keep from making noise I grabbed his shirt and stepped back out to grab the back of his neck. Movies and TV shows like to dramatize fights when it's more realistic when the seasoned pro (me) just makes one swift move to end the fight before it even begins.

I looked down the corridor and the same four hostages were still watching with fear all over their faces. I wasn't feeling it but I smiled anyway to reassure them but it was clear that it didn't work. I pulled the body into the room with me and gently closed the door. I took the weapon and shined my phone's flashlight to memorize the eight digit serial number.

I used the light to navigate to the other side of the room without making noise. I cracked open the door and looked down the hall on the side of the theater that leads to the backstage. Where the hall opened up to the side of the stage I saw the back of a guard. I could throw something across the room to distract them but then they would know I'm here and that would cause them to act erratically almost ensuring the death of another hostage. I could silently move past him; his mask blocks his peripherals so he wouldn't see me.

I took one step when my phone started vibrating with a call from Robert. I stepped back into the room to answer, "Now's not a good time."

"Boris left. I'm willing to bet he's coming there to face Dimitri himself."

"Thanks for the heads up. You talk to Howey yet?"

"Yeah. He has agents on campus waiting for you to finish up so they can clean up the mess."

"Text me if you have anything else." I hung up then texted Sierra to keep an eye out for Boris and to keep him outside. I put my phone away and heard shouting outside.

"You have fifteen seconds Mr. S until your fifteen minutes are up and another hostage dies." I walked down the hall and the guard that was once there wasn't now. I needed to make a move before anyone else was killed. I could rush around the corner and identify all remaining hostiles eliminating the one tasked with killing the hostages first then improvise the rest of the way once I've used my three knives.

Thirteen seconds. I moved quietly down to the end of the corridor. Ten seconds.

I spun around the corner and threw my first knife into the back of the neck of the man with the hostage. The hostages covered their heads and Dimitri spun the camera around to look at me, "Who do we have here?" Seven seconds. My second knife found a resting place in the eye socket of another hostile. "What is Daniel Silver doing here?" Dimitri is showing the public who I really am.

I raised my third knife to take out the final hostile when Dimitri shot me in the shoulder with his sidearm forcing my hand to drop it. I caught it in mid-fall with my other hand and lodged it in the chest of the final gunman. Four seconds left. Dimitri continued to shoot as I dove next to one of the downed guards using his weapon to quickly fire off two rounds. One in his shoulder forcing him to drop the camera and another in his knee forcing him to fall and drop his weapon.

Times up.

I kicked the gun away from Dimitri and picked up the camera with the lens facing me, "I'm coming for you next Richtov." I tossed the camera and turned to the hostages, "You're free now, leave."

They all frantically got up and ran out as Boris pushed through them and stood over Dimitri with me. Sierra followed close behind, "I'm sorry Danny. He wouldn't stay put." She looked at my arm but didn't scream, cry, or lose her composure, "You've been shot."

Before I could tell her I'd be fine something behind me had grabbed her full attention. They had all left except for two. A girl was kneeling and weeping next to the hostage that had been executed. Sierra walked over and knelt down next to her and placed her hand on her shoulder, "Who was he?"

She looked at Sierra with tears flowing from her red eyes, "My brother."

An Acro agent came through each entrance of the theater, "Two of you walk with her and carry her brother outside. Look like you were hostages when you get out there. The rest of you get ready to carry the bodies out of here." They all moved to perform their respective duties.

Two of them stood by Sierra waiting for her to finish up, "We will get the man responsible for all of this then I will come see you personally to tell you. What's your name?"

The young woman wiped her eyes, "Sam. Samantha Barker." She thanked Sierra then helped Sam up. The agents walked her out with one holding her brother in his arms. I was struck by Sierra's sincerity and compassion. It made me love her all the more.

I turned my attention to Boris hovering over Dimitri and they started talking in Russian, "You've betrayed me, your father."

"We both know you are not my father." I was surprised Boris was also able to keep his composure. I was expecting him to lose control like he did with me back at the warehouse.

"I raised you as my own. I treated you as my very own son."

"You made me a murderer and made me believe my true father killed my mother when it was you all along."

Dimitri fell silent and Boris' eyes watered, "We'll get answers out of you Dimitri. I'll make you feel the greatest pain you've ever experienced." I kicked his arm, "I hope you haven't grown attached to your new arm cuz it'll be coming off again though probably not as cleanly as before." He turned his head away and I called Robert to find the most inconspicuous way out, "We're going out the north east side."

"This is far from over Daniel Silver. Nobody is safe. Not even the innocent people you fight so hard to protect. It's because of you that so many lives have been lost and so many more will continue to be lost." I kicked the terrorist in the face and turned away.

Sierra walked up to me with saddened, burdened eyes by the promise she had just made. I hugged her, "I'm proud of you." I wiped the only tear from her cheek that managed to squeeze its way from her eye, "It won't be easy but I'll help you through this." My words hadn't reassured her but she knew I meant them.

I called for the last agent left in the room, "Give me your zip-ties." He handed them to me and I bound Dimitri's hands behind his back. "Boris you can carry him."

"Sir?" came from behind me, "Sir?" It had been so long since somebody called me sir I wasn't used to it anymore. I turned around to one of the agents that was bent over the compact camera, "It's been recording this whole time. I've stopped the recording but this was its angle."

The world has seen that Sierra Morning is involved in this.

I analyzed how it was positioned. The camera was facing the doorway the freed hostages evacuated and Sierra and Boris entered through. Dimitri's head was probably in the shot too, "Get it to Howard Brixton and tell him I sent you." The agent nodded and walked off with the camera.

    I pushed Sierra's hair behind her ear, "Let's get going." I took her hand and we left the bloody scene behind us.

Chapter Twenty-Seven

We got back to the cave underneath the rubble of my house without being spotted or followed. Every news station in the country is playing the footage recorded in that theater. By the day's end not only will every person in the country have seen or heard about what I've done, but they'll know that Sierra Morning is involved. Soon enough there will be rumors about what I spent my life doing before the interview. How the public will react, I have no clue. One thing is for certain though: Sierra and I can't stay here once we finish with Anton Richtov.

"Dimitri is prepped and ready for you." Robert had taken Dimitri to the "interrogation" room for me while I sat with Sierra.

"I'll be right back once I get some answers okay?" She barely nodded. What Sierra had seen and experienced in the theater had shaken her pretty badly but this was the life she chose. I lifted her chin, "I'm not going anywhere. If you need anything I'm right here with you." On my way over to our captive I stopped Robert, "Keep an eye on her for me."

I took one step when he grabbed my bicep, "If you get carried away like before I'll pull you out. You can't be losing it anymore, not now that you've got her." I looked back at Sierra then at him and patted his shoulder. He was right I couldn't lose control. The last time I did and nobody was there to stop me I went on a killing spree and even killed a few innocents. I'm not by myself anymore, I've got Sierra now.

I walked into the room where Boris was standing behind the chair Dimitri was attached to. "Boris are you okay to do this?" He didn't understand the question, "Are you stable mentally?" It was an odd question, but a necessary on. He broke eye contact in uncertainty, "If I think you're losing it I'll stop you." He nodded in agreement. It takes a toll on a person when you torture somebody. It's not an easy thing to do and if it is you've gone way too far and you need somebody to pull you back. I have Robert and Boris has me. "Take the hack saw and cut his arm off." Dimitri looked at me as if to ask for mercy but only muttered a curse under his breath in Russian.

Boris took the hacksaw and a few seconds to mentally prepare himself for what he was about to do. He wasn't about to just torture some random captive with answers. He was about to torture the man who raised him; the man who taught him how to do just that.

I sat on the stool in the corner of the room and chose to close my eyes as Boris started cutting. Dimitri screamed so loudly it definitely reached the top five of most wretched, blood curdling screams I've ever heard. I thought of Sierra and what she must be hearing so I carefully kept my eyes clear of his arm as I duct taped his mouth shut. Now that his screams were kept to a minimum I was able to hear the blade of the saw grinding against the bone. I cringed and told Boris to stop before leaving the room unable to and not wanting to hear that nauseating sound. I told him to stop for me but Boris had only gotten through half the bone and that would create more unbearable pain for Dimitri.

Across the catwalk I saw Sierra standing with horror in her eyes. I got halfway to her when she turned around to leave. I called out to her but she continued on her current path up the stairs. "Robert stay with them and get answers. Text me when he starts talking."

I followed Sierra outside onto the crunching rubble and through where the walls used to be to the back yard where the sun nearly blinded me. I saw her a few yards away as she dropped to her knees and started sobbing. This was too much for her to handle and I knew it would be. I ran to her and knelt in the grass beside her and wrapped the blanket around her I had grabbed on my way out. "I'm sorry Sierra. I am so sorry."

She put most of her weight onto me nearly toppling me over. The past few days she had been handling everything quite well, but today's events are too much and now everything is hitting her all at once. And just like that the tough hardened exterior that she kept up in front of everyone came crumbling down revealing the compassionate, sympathetic part of her she worked so hard to keep hidden. "I never wanted you to go through any of this." I had warned her but I wasn't about to say 'I told you so'.

"We should go eat something." She looked at me as though I had said something ridiculous granted it did sound that way. We needed to do something normal, something to take her mind, and mine, off the day, "Come on let's go eat something."

"Can we just lay here in the grass?" An odd request but I liked it so I laid down with one arm behind my head and the other around her. She kept her weight on me and draped the blanket over both of us. She must have noticed her head was lying on my wound, "Am I hurting you?"

"Yes." She started to lift her head but I stopped her, "But don't move." There were countless, more comfortable places that we could be laying but at this moment in time, this was the perfect spot. The brisk air was slightly chilling yet the warmth of the sun was still easily felt. I could feel the heartbeat of the woman I loved in synch with mine. And we were both calm, actually relaxing in the midst of recent, and current, events.

While my eyes were closed to take in the environment I heard a pair of feet in the grass coming towards us. "Did you get anything out of him yet?"

The lack of a response forced me to open my eyes. What I saw caught me way off guard. "Come on Sierra get out of the way." Her brother Stephen grabbed and pulled her up and away from me.

The second pair of boots stopped next to me and when I turned my head to see who it was I got a swift kick in the face. While in mid-roll back up to my feet I thought that if the brother was here then the father must be too. "Nice to see you again Mr. Morning."

My sarcastic greeting was met with a quick jab that I took a short step back so that his fist missed just by a hair leaving a slight breeze on my face. "I don't want to hurt my future father-in-law." He stopped just a moment to register what I told him then his face turned red with rage. His next failed punch came with much more ferocity than the previous. "Try again and you'll hit the dirt."

Sierra screamed for her father to stop but both my warning and her plea went in one ear and out the other. With the next punch I grabbed his arm opposite mine and stepped to the outside. I snap kicked the back of his knee forcing him down onto it. While still holding onto his arm I pushed my free hand down onto his shoulder blade keeping weight on it, "Resist at all and this will get a whole lot worse for you." His fist clenched and I forced his arm back causing a pop to rupture from his shoulder.

Sierra broke free from her brother and shoved me away from her father, "Stop it!" Michael got back up to his feet and faced me but before he could do anything Sierra stood between us, "What the hell! Both of you!" She directed her attention to me, "You didn't need to dislocate his shoulder!" Then turned to her father, "And you! Don't touch him again. I know you punched him back when you met. I love him and we're getting married and if you can't handle that you need to stay away from us." She took a brief pause to take a deep breath and calm herself, "Why are you even here?"

In his gravelly voice he answered, "I warned him that if he got you into any situation like the one in South America I would be back for him."

"While I appreciate your paternal impulse to protect your daughter, I don't need your protection." Sierra quickly turned the tables on him, "That wasn't the first hairy situation I've, no, we've found ourselves in and today isn't the only one since. Where were you for those times if my safety is actually your main concern?" She stepped closer to her father the General, "That's right. You weren't there. You know who was?" She pointed behind herself at me, "He was! My fiancée, that's who." There was a tick in the man's eye, his only tell since she stepped onto her soap box.

Sierra calmed herself before continuing, "He keeps me safe Dad. And because of how much my relationship differs between the two of you, Danny can keep me safe when you can't." She took his hand and held it, "Now if you can understand what I've said I really hope you can get over whatever it is you have against him and, maybe not yet, but eventually find a way to be happy for us."

The large man pulled his daughter's forehead to his lips and stared right at me. He released Sierra and walked around her to come to me. He raised his hand to elbow height, "I think I can find the approval for the man that can protect my daughter when I'm not there to."

I didn't trust him but I thought I'd play along. I met his hand with my own and we shook, "When this is over I'll make sure nobody can hurt her."

He looked over his shoulder at my old house, "I don't know what you've gotten yourselves into and if we're being honest you seem more than capable of handling yourself, but if you're ever finding yourself in need of some extra man power just tell me it's because she's in trouble and my team will be right there to help."

"I might just take you up on that before this is over."

Sierra came over and wrapped her arm around me, "Now was that so hard?" She looked up at me and we kissed. Stephen joined and Sierra checked with him next, "I'm not going to have to worry about you now am I?"

He smiled, "He had my approval when I saw him drop all those bodies in Honduras." He read the question on my face and answered before I could ask it, "Yeah sorry about the gun in your face, but orders first." I nodded in understanding. Whenever I give out orders I expect them to be followed down to the letter.

The ring of my phone broke the awkward silence between the four of us, "What have you got Robert?" Sierra hugged her father and brother goodbye then I shook their hands sending them on their way.

Sierra hugged me tightly. "I had to pull Boris out but just before I did Dimitri started talking."

"What'd he give you?" I wrapped my arm around Sierra.

"The location and time of a black tie auction for the criminal elite. He said Richtov will be there, hosting it actually. And that he could put us in contact with somebody that can hook us up with invitations."

"See if you can get the contact's name then give it to Howey so he can run it. What's Boris' state?"

There was a pause, "It might sound strange but I think he might need his father."

It certainly did sound strange, "Alright I'll be down in a minute." I hung up and hugged Sierra with both arms, "We're making progress."

"What did Robert say?"

"I meant with your father."

She pulled away, "That reminds me." She slapped my bad shoulder, "You didn't have to dislocate his shoulder." She was smiling so I knew she was being playful but still meant it.

"He wasn't going to stop until I was unconscious." I caught her hand in mine.

"We both know you could have stopped him without dislocating one of his joints."

I pulled her hand bringing her into my grasp, "I didn't stop him you did." I lifted her into both of my arms, "You saved me Sierra. You saved my life!" This was new for me. A sense of satisfaction and accomplishment made me feel different and happy… happy. Something I haven't been in a long time. I was literally holding my happiness in my arms. So in a way she has saved me.

Chapter Twenty-Eight

While Robert was getting specifics from Dimitri, Sierra sat in the infirmary eating the pizza I had ordered for all of us and I sat with my son. I'm not a huge fan of pizza but it was delivery and a quick eat.

"What happened in there?" Boris had wiped Dimitri's blood off of him as best he could but there're some stains that just never come out.

He couldn't maintain eye contact, "I thought he was my father. He made me believe he was." He took a moment to gather his thoughts. Having to think about his words forced him to realize what they meant, "I thought you killed my mother. I spent my whole life on the path Dimitri set me on in preparation of confronting you about killing her. And avenge her murder."

"Is that what you were trying to do? 'Avenge her murder'? Because you certainly weren't trying to get information out of him. Exacting revenge on someone will never make you feel better. Take it from me, someone who knows what a path of vengeance leads to." Boris mulled over my words and finally brought his gaze to meet my eyes, "I was never much of a father figure and luckily for the both of us I don't have to raise you. The best I can do is offer a friendship. You seem to need one of those more than a father anyway."

I stood for my final words, "If you need to talk you can come to me because I guarantee I've been through something similar and I've come out on the other side looking like this." I haven't had to attempt being a father for nearly one hundred years and I wasn't very good at it then so I doubt I'd be any better at it today.

Robert came out of the room wiping his hands with a rag, "I sent the name to Howard and got a probable location for the meet. The auction will be held in Zurich Switzerland two days from now."

"What's the contact's name?"

"Jordan Welch."

"Ah Jordan. He's from Indonesia and his real name is something I've never known how to pronounce. I can get him on the phone right now to set up a meet. We'll probably end up meeting him at some coffee shop he likes in Bel Air Maryland."

"There's a Bel Air in Maryland? Not just Cali?"

"That's right. I've met with him there once before and from the way he talked about that place I doubt he's been able to wean himself off of their house brew."

Sierra came out of the infirmary swallowing the last bit of pizza she had left, "Where are we going?"

I looked at her and couldn't help but smile for no given reason, but I guess that's love, or happiness, or a combination of both. She cocked her head for not knowing why I was smiling but she reflected it. "On second thought we'll go unannounced, first thing in the morning. Robert you call Howey and ask him to keep us posted on Welch's whereabouts."

"I asked where we were going."

"Bel Air Maryland. We can leave at sundown, swing by your apartment so you can grab some clothes then we can grab a room in a hotel once we get there."

I turned back to Robert, "Do you think we can get anything else out of him?" He shook his head no, "When you call Howey arrange for a pick up too. He'll have Dimitri delivered to a black sight and get more intel out of him regarding different items." Robert took out his phone to make the call then I turned to Boris, "Why don't you eat something then get some shut eye." I'm sure he didn't want to but he nodded and went into the infirmary.

I turned to Sierra with a smile, "Ready for a road trip?"

***

We decided to leave that afternoon and spend the night in a hotel. We stopped at Sierra's apartment to fill suitcases with her clothes. I told her I wanted to visit my tailor to pick up some new suits since all my other ones were burned to a crisp and I didn't keep any in my safe houses. She said "suits are good sometimes but they're not meant to be worn all the time" and that she would pick me out a whole new wardrobe. I wasn't too keen on the idea of somebody picking out my clothes but I have to admit she did a good job. After we finished shopping she had me wearing a long sleeved Henley with the top two of the four buttons undone and light brown jeans that looked like kakis.

Now we were in our master suite of a hotel just over six miles from our meet. "What's the name of this place we're meeting Welch at?"

"Apparently it came under new ownership not too long ago and now it's called The Jaded Bean. When I was talking to Welch on our way here he said they re-did the whole place. New floors, new lighting, and a bunch of other stuff. He says he likes it more than he did before." I laid down in bed ready to call it a night, "I have to admit I'm a little eager to see what the place has turned into."

"Sounds like a nice place." Sierra stepped out of the bathroom in her night gown and I felt my face redden, "Easy now." She rubbed her eyes and came to bed, "I'm beat and feel like I could sleep for a whole day." I took her in my arm and she wiggled her way as close to me as physics would allow.

I made sure not to go into detail when reflecting on the day, "A lot happened today and I'm surprised at how well you handled it all." I gently turned her head so I could see her eyes, "I'm proud of you." We kissed then she smiled and her eyes fell shut as she struggled to keep them open. I stretched my free arm over to the lamp and switched it off.

***

I automatically woke up at six a.m. the next morning and gently pulled myself out from under Sierra's sprawled out arms and legs to wash up and get dressed. I ordered breakfast from room service and despite my plea for silence the employee had bumped the door with his cart awakening Sierra. I tipped him with a fifty and sent him on his way.

I wheeled the cart of eggs, sausage, bacon, O.J., and coffee over to the foot of the bed. Sierra propped herself up with pillows against the headboard, "That for me?"

"Good morning to you too honey." She tilted her head and gave me a fake smile. I made her a plate, put it on a tray, and set it on her lap. "Did you sleep well?"

She began cutting at her eggs, "In your arms? Of course. What time is it?"

"Shorty after seven. We meet Welch at nine and the drive will take about fifteen minutes so we have an hour and half before we need to leave." I made my plate and sat on the edge of the bed next to her. "I would like to leave early so we can visit the old armory in town. The inside is nothing like it was during the Civil War but the outside doesn't look all that different except for some renovations to keep it from falling apart."

When she finished her mouth full, "Okay mister mathematician. When I forget what two plus two is I'll be sure to ask you."

"I don't even know what to make of that." We both laughed and continued eating in each other's company.

***

After I retraced my steps with Sierra in and around the armory and shared the stories that accompanied those steps she was thrilled to have walked where I did so long ago while at the same time disheartened to hear the dark stories of that time.

On our walk down the street to The Jaded Bean, "If I had known your memories of that place were so gruesome I wouldn't have wanted you to go back."

We stopped at the end of the block for a passing car, "I know and that's exactly why I wanted to take you: so you know what I've come from. And I want you to know more." She stretched her neck to peck me on the cheek and held onto my arm as we continued walking.

We walked the rest of the distance and after opening the door to walk in behind her I was able to really see the changes made since I was last here.

I looked around and didn't see Welch anywhere. We approached the counter and saw fresh bagels along with scones in the glass case at the end of it. "Hello!" The young lady greeted us when we reached the counter across from her. Sierra returned her warm welcome and eyed the chalk board listing the variety of hot and cold drinks.

Already knowing what I wanted I placed my hand in the small of Sierra's back for her to order first, "May I have a small latte with skim milk?"

She tapped in the order on the sleek touch-screen register then looked up at me, "Anything for you sir?"

"Yes. I'll just have a large coffee, black."

She turned around and handed me a cup, "The coffee is all self-served at the end of the counter."

I leaned back to get a view of the end of the counter where the thermos's sat then paid the bill for our coffee and latte. "Would you happen to have a regular customer that comes in here by the name of Jordan?"

Her ears perked up at the sound of his name, "Oh yeah Jordan." She started working on Sierra's latte, "He's here nearly every day. He always orders a small coffee and sits at that table over there next to the shelf facing the front door. He either reads a book the whole time or takes the occasional phone call. Nice guy. Always enters and leaves through the back door too." I leaned back again to look down the hall through the back to see the door to the outside.

She placed the lid on the cup blocking the billowing steam and handed Sierra her latte. Got more info than I even asked for, "Thank you for your help."

I walked to the end of the counter and read the labels on the thermoses. Never heard of Java Raven, must be the house blend. Guess I'll try that. "Well she was friendly. And now we know all about Jordan. Even what she doesn't know she told us." I stayed silent to hear what she was thinking, "Those occasional phone calls might be for whatever business he's involved in. Most likely criminal stuff since we're here to get his help." Sierra noticed that I was impressed with her thorough observation and accurate conclusion. "What? I investigate for a living."

I filled my cup and started down the hall with Sierra behind me. If Jordan was going to meet somebody here it would be out back. We got outside and nobody was there. I checked my watch and it was two after nine. On second thought if Jordan was comfortable with sitting in plain view whenever he was here I doubt he would care to stand outside in the cold just for a meet. We walked back inside hoping he had come in the front door in the short time we were outside.

We walked back into the sitting area and the girl behind the counter pointed, "That's him." I thanked her as we approached Jordan from behind where he sat in his usual spot.

Before I entered his line of sight, "It's been a while Danny. Or Rahm. I think Rahm is cooler." When we walked in front of him he looked up at us, well more so at Sierra. Jordan stood up, "Who is this lovely lady?" He took her hand and kissed the top of it then saw the ring, "That is just the most beautiful piece of jewelry I have ever seen." Sierra smiled but I couldn't tell if she was flattered or annoyed. While still holding her hand he looked at me, "Is this your work Danny?"

Jordan Welch is a con-artist and a fence for stolen goods such as artwork and jewelry. The youngest and one of the best. I discovered him on the streets of Miami before he was even twenty, either swiping or conning elderly people out of their precious items. I caught him and gave him a choice: I lock him up or he works for me. He chose the latter so he's been an informant for me ever since. He was still young, handsome, and the primary quality of all good con-artists, he had the charm.

I took Jordan's hand off of Sierra's and turned his hand over, "Haven't you learned that you can't get anything past me Pretty Boy?"

He frowned at my barb and opened his fist revealing the ring lying in his palm, "Never hurts to try." Sierra took the ring and we looked at each other. I saw what she wanted to do and I shook my head as slightly as I could. Jordan would probably enjoy a swift slap to the face from an attractive woman.

He touched his hand to his head and looked around, "Where are my manners? Please, have a seat." I pulled the chair out across from Jordan for Sierra and pulled up a chair for me from one of the other tables. "You know I almost didn't recognize you without a suit or at least a suit vest. You've lost your sense of style Danny. Are you drinking the Java Raven? That's my favorite. All I get when I'm here."

"I am an old man so what do I know about style and as much I miss our time spent together this isn't a social visit." Jordan's swagger façade vanished and he became serious. "A little birdy tells me you can get us invitations to the auction in Zurich tomorrow."

Jordan leaned back and considered all of his options. "You know that video that's been playing all over the news? Of course you do. You two are all the news can talk about. You know how that terrorist leader was taken out in the Middle East the same day as that hostage situation? Well that took second page in the papers while you two took the cover page all over the country. Even in local papers. Considering the events that transpired in that college and all the other things I'm hearing, you really need this. And since you're here talking to me, I'm your last option." He was good when I found him in Miami but he's clearly stepped up his game since we last spoke. "So what can you offer in return for my services?" He lost his charm too as he eyeballed Sierra creepily and smiled.

I grabbed his arm and squeezed, "If you saw that video then you would be smart not to piss me off. I'm not here to negotiate so you're going to give me what I want and in return I don't drag you into the woods to put a bullet between your eyes." I pressed a finger between his eyes and his confidence left his face and I could see the submission in his eyes.

"Fine." He opened up his jacket and pulled out two envelopes, "I suspected why you wanted to meet with me so I came prepared." He handed me the invitations and we all stood, "Be careful Danny. I've done business with Richtov's men and he's a bad dude." I nodded and we shook hands. Having been showed weak he smiled impishly to Sierra. We turned around to walk out when Jordan called us back, "Hey Danny don't you want-".

I didn't turn around but just raised my hand for I knew what he was going to say, "You can keep it." We walked out onto the sidewalk and I rubbed my wrist where my watch used to sit.

***

We got back to my property in New York and saw Howey with two men pushing Krinchov into the back of a van. Our driver stopped next to Howey's car and we got out, "Boris really roughed him up." He and Sierra hugged, "It's good to see you walking around."

"Yes it is." We all three smiled, "We got our invitations to the auction."

"Right. Robert gave me the names on that drive to run through the system. It's a list of payoffs from Anton's organization to politicians with intelligence access. Dates correlate with terrorist attacks around the world. Of the names on the list two are congressmen and one a senator: Congressmen Michaelson, Cramer, and Senator Rachel Maddox. Here's the kicker: all three are stayin' in the same hotel in Zurich right now."

"That's huge. Why hasn't Acro known about them?"

"We've been keepin' an eye on them for a few months on suspicious activity. None of which would have led us to believe they were connected to anythin' like this. No way to tell if either of them knows about the other's involvement either."

Sierra spoke up, "So we get into the auction, hopefully identify those three, and take them down with Richtov. But how?"

"You and I fly in there privately, attend the auction, do some surveillance, possibly ask around for any helpful info. Most people there will recognize us or at least me. The public knows of my wealth so everyone will think I'm there as a potential bidder with you as my arm piece." Sierra glared at me giving me an opportunity to save myself, "They'll think you're just my arm piece when we know you're my fiancée and we're actually spying on them." When she looked mildly satisfied I continued, "We'll then locate and capture Richtov."

Sierra and Howey both looked at me as if they were waiting for me to correct myself, "If we weren't lied to and Ricktov really can't die like us then we need to capture him first then figure out a way to kill him."

"Alright well just let me know what you need from Acro. I'll take this guy to the black site and get what I can out of him. We'll keep looking into the three traitors to determine if they could be useful or not."

"And if they're not?" Sierra wanted to know what exactly the "not" scenario entailed.

"They've committed treason and are each responsible for countless deaths across the world. Their own deaths would be a gift from us to them compared to what they deserve." And with that Howey wished us luck and got into his car.

Sierra didn't look like she liked what Howey said but understood it, "The world that protects the blissfully ignorant is a dark one, and we're in the middle of it." I couldn't have said it better and I didn't like that she had become so involved in this world that she was gaining an understanding of it.

To supply comfort I hugged her, "We need to go pick out a tuxedo for me and a dress for you before we leave for Zurich."

"I already have something in mind and you might regret saying that after you pay for it."

Chapter Twenty-Nine

The party was scheduled to start at six pm and the auction to start one hour after that. It was all taking place at the Kameha Grand Zurich hotel and the whole place was rented out for the day and twenty-four hours prior. The invitations included a one-night's stay at the hotel free of charge so after landing in Zurich at about eleven pm local time Sierra and I had gotten into our room by midnight.

"This place is amazing." Being an investigative reporter didn't provide Sierra with any opportunities to stay in any luxurious hotels such as this. I didn't care what she said, I bought a new suit just for walking through the foyer of the hotel and I convinced her to pick out something new for the same reason. "I could live here. Well not really here in this hotel, but in a house like this."

"Maybe next week we can start building one on the beach somewhere." Sierra's face lit up and she came over to wrap her arms around me, "A long driveway away from everything with a gate at the entrance. When you step out back through the French doors you're standing on the hardwood deck and after just a few more steps you can feel the sand between your toes and hear the sound of crashing waves on the shallow shore of our very own personal beach."

"That sounds perfect except for the part where I help you build."

"Well at least watch and learn. A knowledge and understanding of architecture will be useful in the long run. We'll wake up at six am to go down to the restaurant for breakfast to become familiar with the faces of the guests and get a better lay of the land." Getting a hold of the guest list would be a waste of time since all the guests are criminal masterminds and too smart to leave their real names. And on top of that with an invitation guests didn't need to leave their names. Everything was arranged to preserve anonymity, until you shake hands and decide to exchange names.

"How about we get up at five and make sure we're down there by six. That way we can take our time in the morning. And you said our outfits would get here before the event begins right?"

Due to how quickly everything came together we didn't have time to go pick up our clothes so I called my tailor and told him what Sierra and I wanted and where to have it delivered. He said he would make a few calls and get what we needed to our rooms by noon the next day. "That's right so we'll sleep the next few hours away then get up for the big day." I set my trio of throwing knives on the nightstand next to my side of the bed. We laid down together, switched the lights off, and kissed each other "goodnight".

***

We woke up at five as planned, washed up then went down stairs to the hotel's Italian themed restaurant where most of the guests were already at. For the criminal elite the day starts early and runs late. We walked into the restaurant and eyes turned to us. To the world I'm just a rich guy who can't die while to the criminal underworld I'm a legend and only those closest to me know my connections to Acro. The room was populated yet nearly silent and quite peaceful. Sierra and I seated ourselves at one of the round tabled booths and ordered our breakfast.

"Recognize anybody yet?"

"Most of the older men and a few of the younger guys, but only from when they were up and comers. Some of these guys aren't even on Acro's radar, yet. The one's I don't know must be new to the business." A few eyes were still locked on us, "Don't avoid eye contact. Locking eyes shows you're not afraid of them. Ignoring the stares and minding your own business shows you don't care."

Right when I finished talking the notorious Joaquin brothers twins sat down, one next to me and the other next to Sierra, boxing us into the booth. The first brother Isaiah, "Good morning Mr. Rahm." and the second brother Eli finished, "and soon to be Mrs.

Rahm." The twins are the leading drug runners in the Spanish countries. They offed their mentor to take over his operations and they've been co-running it ever since, "A lot of people were doubting that you'd show up with a bounty on your head." "Not only did you show up you brought your fiancée with you." "That takes stones. Both of you." "Though there are very few people bold enough to take you on."

"More importantly it's an honor to meet you." They each extended a hand and I shook both of them. They each stood, "It's been a pleasure meeting you too Miss. Morning." They walked away and sat down at the other side of the room.

"Is it common for people to talk to you then leave before you say anything?"

"Only if they're trying to prove a point. For those two they were only asserting themselves. They boxed us in, brought up the hit on us then feigned respect towards me. I expect them to attack us later."

Sierra leaned towards me and her eyes widened, "You gathered all that that quickly?"

"The big give away is that they're into drugs. Most people in the drug business are jokes. They also killed their mentor so they're incapable of showing respect." I sniffed my coffee to make sure it was clean then took a sip, "Don't worry though. We're expecting something from them now." I looked over Sierra's shoulder at an older gentleman approaching us, "This one on the other hand proves to be enjoyable company."

I stood as he approached our table, "Antony! It's good to see you again." We hugged and he pulled a chair from one of the other tables.

Before he sat he took Sierra's hand and kissed the back of it, "It is truly a pleasure to meet you Miss. Morning." He sat down and his coffee was delivered with mine and Sierra's food. "When I heard Daniel was seeing someone I had to find out who it was to decide if she was good enough for him. Ever since I found out who you were I've been unable to figure out why such an extraordinary woman such as yourself would stay with him."

"I've been wondering the same thing." Sierra's eyes fell and she blushed. Her bashful cuteness brought a smile to my face, "How have things been going for you? Decide to settle down yet?"

He held his cup of coffee wrapped in his hands, "As a matter of fact I have. I've gotten myself out of the fencing business for the most part. Now I'm living on a beach with a wonderful woman I've met." Antony took a sip of his steaming beverage and added, "You two should try it after you're finished with whatever it is you're caught up in."

Sierra and I looked at each other and I reflected her mouth filled smile, "What do you mean for the most part? Something holding you back? Do you need help?"

"Oh no no. Nothing of the sort. I'm completely out unless I receive an invitation I can't resist. Events like this only occur once every other decade you know?" He eyed me and registered my age, "Of course you do." Antony finished off his drink then stood and I did the same, "It's been good to see you again Daniel but there are others I need to speak with." We hugged once more and he spoke quietly into my ear, "Keep that extra eye open. There are many here who would like to claim that bounty on you two." I patted his back and we released each other. He said goodbye to Sierra then left to the adjoining room.

"What did he say?"

"Look out for anybody who might be looking for a payday."

"If he knows you as well as he seemed to I'm sure what he really said had a greater meaning than that." Either spending time with me has made her more intuitive or she's been holding out.

"He pretty much told me to protect you." Sometimes I get the sense that others don't think I appreciate Sierra as I should; like they feel they need to remind me of her importance to me.

"Well that's sweet."

"What is?"

"You two think I need to be protected." Sierra had a slightly cocky look.

I looked around the room, "You have no idea." She almost looked insulted. I nodded to a man behind her, "Simeon Petrovic, Serbian arms dealer." I pointed my thumb to another, "Olek Szczepanski,

Polish hitman, small time." Another, "Mara Kurucz, Bulgarian hitwoman, likes to poison." Sierra hesitantly swallowed her food and pushed her plate, distancing herself from the potentially poiseness food.

I pulled the plate to me and stabbed a piece of egg with the fork, "You might be able to hold your own in a street fight with a random stranger but not against professionals." I fed myself and swallowed, "Don't worry though. I'll train you to beat anybody." I took a gulp of coffee, "Anybody that isn't me of course."

"So what are we going to do until the party starts?" She took my coffee and drank it.

"I'm hoping more people will introduce themselves. We'll check in with Howey then go see Robert and Boris down the street to make sure they're ready for tonight. If we have time left over we can go sight-seeing."

"Sounds like fun. What I'm most excited for is getting to wear that gown tonight." Sierra had chosen a one-shoulder satin column gown designed by Oscar de la Renta for tonight's event.

I smiled, "I'm excited for that too."

Another familiar face I was hoping to see came over to our table, "Daniel-san! Good to see you." He sat in the chair Antony left at the table and looked at my waist band, "Are those my knives?"

"I don't use anybody else's." Ryou Yamamoto, traditional and professional weapons smith from Japan. Nearing eighty years old and still mobile enough to travel to a foreign country. Bald on the top but a very well-groomed white beard. I make an effort to acquire all of my blades from him seeing as he's the best in the world, but comes in second to an old friend of mine.

"You have still yet to let me see that katana you've told me about."

Sierra looked at us, "What katana?"

"It's made of a special material I found a couple centuries ago. An unknown material that I've never seen before, or since actually. I had a hard time not setting myself on fire just trying to make it malleable. I keep it mounted back in the States with my other collectibles. The blade is extremely dense weighing about forty pounds, sharp enough to cut through most solid metals, and as black as night." Just hearing me talk about it brought a huge smile to Ryou's face. "I was actually hoping to see you today. I was wondering if you could make a katana for Sierra."

Sierra's face had a mixed expression of surprise, confusion, and excitement, "Of course, of course. I just need to ask you a few questions to learn about you so the katana is just for you. A katana is an extension of the wielder so I must make it special just for you. No one else."

"It'll be a nice change of pace being on the other side of an interview, but why do I need a katana? That's more your guy's kind of thing."

Ryou looked to me to speak for him as if he couldn't tolerate Sierra's ignorant question, "Like I said I'll need to train you to fight and protect yourself. Some of that training will require the use of a katana and other blades. And as Ryou said you'll need a katana made specially for you. And if you'd like you can start coming up with names for it." Sierra looked at me like I was talking about an imaginary friend and laughed, "But hey if you don't want to that's fine too."

"Did you name yours?"

"I did, but don't laugh." Sierra's face turned overly serious to the point it almost felt like she was already mocking me, "I named it Bisha. Short for Bishamonten. In Buddhism he is a god known for many things, but only a few of which I chose his name for. He defends the nation, in my case North America. He punishes criminals or evildoers, as I sometimes do. He is the god of warriors and known to be turned to for victory in combat. He's also known for blessing his followers where as I'm always helping people through my work." Sierra's expression hadn't changed at all, "What, nothing witty to say about my katana's lame name?"

"That sounds umm..." she was looking for a word hoping not to hurt my feelings, as if that were possible, "interesting." She didn't totally reject what I had said but she couldn't quite bring herself to get on board with naming a katana either.

Before the silence extended too long Ryou spoke up, "I think it's a wonderful name for a katana that is second to none. I have some materials I need to retrieve from a couple locals. I suggest you start thinking of names that mean something to you. And we will meet later so I can ask you questions, yes?" Sierra nodded then Ryou said goodbye.

"I'm not sure about this. Naming a katana and it being personalized for me."

I guess it was a normal thought for anybody that wasn't familiar with the Japanese culture and the katanas significance, "It's not like you have to talk to it but any good swordsman has a connection with the weapon that he wields and that's also why Ryou needs to learn about you. You will be the one he's thinking of when he's crafting your katana." Sierra looked a bit disturbed at the idea of a stranger having her on his mind, "Or would you rather he be thinking of the prostitute down the street when he's crafting the thing you'll be holding in your hands?"

"Alright I'll start looking for names and give it to Ryou when he interviews me."

"It might seem strange now but believe me; when you hold the katana, *your* katana, in your hands, you won't think so anymore." I placed the tip on the table and stood up, "You might even thank me."

Sierra got up and stood close to me, "Maybe, I don't think so, but maybe. Why don't we go sight-seeing now?"

I was just about to comply when I noticed Sierra's phone still sitting on the table. I picked it up and looked at the screen. The recording app was open and sound waves were crossing the screen. I tried to remain quiet to avoid attention and make it clear I was unhappy at the same time, "What the hell Sierra?"

"I was just-" I pressed my finger to her lip then grabbed her arm and walked her out to where no one could hear us. I waited for her to talk but she just glanced at my hand around her arm. I let go and she spoke, "I'm an investigative reporter. You don't honestly think I would come to a place like this and not take advantage of it do you?"

"Yes, actually I did. Because I thought you were smarter than this. No good can come from this. Why are you even doing this? It can't be to improve your reputation since you're already a household name and now associated with me and what happened in Manhattan."

"You don't get it. I do what I do because it's in my bones. I can't help but want to inform people and the public about things they would otherwise never know. Tell me what would be wrong about giving this recording to a news station and letting it get out there."

"Wow. I never thought we would have such conflicting views like this. Telling anybody about what's going on here would do no good. It would only cause panic and unrest. And two of the people we spoke to are friends that I don't want to expose. Acro solely handles people like this covertly for a reason: if too many people, like the public, knew about them it would cause an endless list of problems for the people trying to bring them down. If you can't help but inform the public so much how did you think you would be able to live on a beach away from everything?" Sierra broke eye contact but didn't say anything.

"Let's say the public did hear what you have. We would be hunted by everyone we expose and by everyone they hire to catch us." Her eyes fluttered when I said we, "I might be mad about this but that doesn't mean I would make you face the repercussions on your own." It was clear that Sierra was holding back a smile, "I won't let a disagreement distance us but do know that in my line of work you do come to find out more and more that for the people out there, ignorance is bliss. I hope, in time, you come to find that out too."

I handed her phone back, "Come on. We need to check in with Howey then we can go wander the city."

Chapter Thirty

After meeting with Howey and roaming the city Sierra and I got back to our room at about 1730. I had Sierra stand in the doorway while I did a sweep of the suite first to determine it was safe and nobody was waiting for us. Our garments for the party had arrived earlier and were hanging for us in the bureau. My tuxedo was hanging there next to Sierra's red satin gown with her Patinana Strass Sandals by Christian Louboutin sitting on the floor under it.

About thirty minutes after Sierra stepped into the bathroom and closed the door behind her I saw the handle on the door turn. I was highly anticipating this moment; to see Sierra in this gown. She opened the door and then I saw her. There she stood in all of her glory, the gown hugging every curve of her body. No amount of imagination could have prepared me for the sight before me. In all my years I have never seen anything, or anyone of such beauty. My mouth became dry and my face became hot.

She stood in the doorway and spun around, "Well, what do you think?" I was speechless, "Is that childish look on your face good or bad?"

I stood up from the side of the bed and walked over to her, "Shakespeare wouldn't be able to find the words to describe the way you look." Sierra blushed, "Let's just hope there isn't a bidding war over you tonight."

She couldn't stop smiling and I couldn't take my eyes off of her, "Stop staring at me. After a while it starts getting uncomfortable."

I raised my eyes to meet hers, "Sorry. It's just that you're so...stunning."

"Yeah well you can't stare at me all night. We need to get downstairs." She was right but she still had to turn me around to take my eyes off of her.

***

The event was taking place in the Kameha Dome which has a square footage of 7,546. It was a half hour after six once we exited the hotel elevator on the ground floor. Most guests were already under the Dome and what few people we passed couldn't help but stop and stare.

There were two security guards standing outside of each entrance to the ballroom. They were all equipped with a radio and a sidearm; neither of which were they attempting to conceal from wandering eyes. The guards must have memorized names and faces for this event because when we approached the one said, "Mr. Silver and Miss. Morning welcome."

They each pushed open a door and we entered with Sierra's arm wrapped around mine. The large ballroom was full of guests that were all occupied or socializing with one another until they saw the doors open. It seemed like all at once all heads turned to see who entered and once they saw, the room fell silent.

Sierra leaned towards me and whispered, "Why are they all staring at you?"

It's true that I'm the most notorious and it's also likely that I'm the most talked about guest here but, "Trust me, they're staring at you." While all eyes were on her I scanned the room.

I identified many of the criminals in the sea of faces before me. Bankers, hitmen/women, assassins, drug lords, arms dealers, spies, and so on. Four of which I wouldn't be surprised if they tried for the bounty tonight. I didn't however see anyone from the restaurant this morning.

Along the lengths of the room were pedestals with cloths draped over whatever was sitting on them; the nights merchandise.

A waiter approached us with a tray of glasses of wine. Judging by how prompt he was my first thought was that the drinks were poisoned and somebody wants us to drink them. Since I'd rather have everyone think that I'm either ignorant or fearless I took a glass for Sierra and one for myself. I took a whiff of her glass before I handed it to her. Either of us blacking out here tonight would cause major complications to our task.

One of the nearest people to us was a U.S. senator. I softly pulled Sierra to get her mind off of the few people that were still staring at her and we walked over to meet the Senator. Senator Rachel Maddox was one of the few U.S. government officials that Robert found out would be here but not the one that has knowledge about Acro. The microphone disguised as a button on my shirt would deliver audio to Howey, Robert, and Boris while the camera in my right contact lens would deliver visual.

"Good evening Senator Maddox." She appeared to be caught off guard by the fact that I chose to speak with her first over all the others here.

We shook hands, "Please, we're not in the U.S. Call me Rachel." She took a sip of her wine, "May I ask what your business is here?"

It irritates me when people ask if they can ask you a question, "Well as you know I'm a very successful business man and such success requires a hand in all markets of every type." The last thing a U.S. Senator wants is for her country to find out that she's attending an event for criminals, "And I thought this would be a good opportunity for Sierra to experience the underbelly of the criminal world first hand." The Senator tensed and the heads of nearby eavesdroppers turned their heads to us, "Don't worry though. She's only here to observe, not to report."

Her tension didn't seem to release, "Now for you: what are you doing here?"

"Same thing we're all doing here Daniel: networking. Making new acquaintances for future endeavors." She leaned into my ear opposite Sierra, "There are more people within our government that know about you and Acro than you'd think." Those words carried weight when spoken by somebody that shouldn't even know what Acro is.

Rachel stepped back, "Now if you wouldn't mind there are others that I need to speak with."

The Senator walked off and Sierra came back having not noticed she had even walked off, "I think I just received a threat from some woman and now that I think about it-" She looked around before she finished, "-why are there so many women giving me death stares?"

I looked around and heads turned away, "Could be one of two reasons: They're mad because you look better than them or because they want to be the one with me." I sipped my wine and smiled at her, "I think the latter is more likely." Sierra's mouth opened and she gently hit my arm with the back of her hand, "Or it could be both." I scanned the room for faces once more and identified more of them, "Most of these women are dangerous so you need to keep a third eye open since they've got you in their crosshairs."

"Third eye?"

"It's a term Howey and I came up with. In some lore's the third eye is the all-seeing eye. So by keeping your metaphorical third eye open, you won't miss a thing."

Sierra processed and considered what I said, "I think I can get on board with that."

The socializing portion of the party was ending and now it was time to start what we were all here for. We all gathered in front of the stage at the far end of the Dome. Sierra and I had finished our drinks and I advised her not to take another to avoid being poisoned for the rest of the night.

As we waited for somebody to walk up on stage and begin the auction I spotted some movement off to the side. I made sure Sierra and I had gotten close to the stage but there were still some heads in the way blocking my view of what was going on. Just as quickly as whatever was happening started it stopped and somebody walked up on stage.

I couldn't believe my eyes. We were told that he was alive but to see it for myself, "Good evening ladies and gentlemen. My name is Alexander Hunt and I am this evening's host. I thank you all for your patience." I guess he burned the Anton Richtov alias back when I thought I killed him, "Before we get started I would like to give a special thanks to this events designated honored guests." He gestured his open hand towards us, "Daniel Silver and his bride to be, Sierra Morning."

The room became filled with the sound of clapping as Sierra and I were recognized though I highly doubt anyone meant the welcome that the clapping implied. It was simply proper etiquette to do so. *Hunt* only announced me to make my presence known to everyone else and to make it clear that he's been keeping tabs on me.

"Without any further delay, let us begin." The curtains were pulled off of the cases to reveal the items within them. While everyone else was observing the items available for bid I was watching Hunt as he handed the mic off to somebody else and walked off the stage.

I kept my eyes on him until he walked outside. There was no way I could tail him without his knowledge, he's too smart for that. I took out my phone to call Boris who was waiting in a car outside watching and listening to everything on a computer. Howey and Robert saw the whole thing so they knew to keep an eye on Hunt via satellite.

"Boris, that was Anton Richtov who's now going by the name Alexander Hunt. He just left with a couple of body guards. Follow him and connect with Howey, he should have a visual on Hunt."

"On it." Before I go after Hunt I need to make sure I capture all items for sale on camera.

I looked around for Sierra and found her in a crowd of people grouped around one of the showcases. When I approached her from behind I could see what was on display. There was a large sign with a long description of the item for sale. Next to the sign was a large television streaming live feed of a child in an iron barred cage. The sign gave no name but described the child to be seven years old and "a hard worker".

I looked at Sierra and saw her astonished face and compassionate eyes. I put my arm around her and walked her away from the crowds and into an open area away from the screen. I looked her in the eyes and her lip began to quiver, "Hey hey hey. Yes it's cruel and inhumane but this is what happens in the world. You can mourn and feel bad or you can resolve yourself and fight to put a stop to it." She took a deep breath and wiped her eyes, "Besides, showing any emotion or sympathy here will make you appear to be a weak and easy target."

I turned and looked around the room, "There's artifacts and artwork here too. Those won't sadden you will they?" She smiled and we walked around to view what was held inside the other showcases.

There was a totem on a pedestal that I recognized from the early eighteenth century that I had held once long ago. Last I heard it was stolen from a museum. There was a missing piece of artwork once belonging to Hitler's collection. In one case there was just a sign with details pertaining to a nuclear warhead. I made sure my lens camera got a clear view of the sign so that Howey and Acro can deal with it later. We walked around and saw all the pieces of ancient currency, artifacts, jewelry, and artwork. I even identified Congressmen Michaelson and Cramer for Acro to deal with later.

The last item for sale that we came across was another child. As soon as we got close enough to tell what was in the case I turned Sierra away, "We're going to save those children right?" I walked her further away from the crowds to make sure nobody heard.

Leaving those children in their cages isn't something I want to do but they aren't the priority either, "Hunt is the priority. The kids are secondary. If we find them we will save them but right now we have no idea where they are and we can't spend the night looking for them." Anybody could look at Sierra and know that she didn't like what I just said, "Look, we'll go after Hunt and if we're lucky he'll lead us to the kids. If we lose him countless more children will end up dead or as slaves."

"When we find those boys they become the priority alright."

"We will handle it *if* we find the boys. Come on, we don't need to be wasting time here talking about what might happen."

My phone began to ring and I answered, "Hunt stopped outside and entered a warehouse. City files say it's abandoned. Good place to store illegal merchandise like slave children. Boris is a safe distance away awaiting your arrival." Sierra and I headed for the exit, "Is she going with you or are you dropping her off here?"

"We don't have time to stop. Make sure reinforcements are on standby by the time I get to that warehouse. And tell Robert to meet us out front with the van."

Sierra and I walked out the same way we entered but as soon as we did the guards stopped us and placed their hand on their weapons, "No one is permitted to leave until the auction has concluded."

"Right. Of course. I'm sorry." I turned Sierra around and we walked back inside.

"What was that? You could have easily taken them out."

We continued walking heading for the back doors, "I know but with guards it'll be smarter to do it from a less used exit further from the guests and wandering eyes. You strapped that diving knife to the inside of your thigh like I said right?"

"Yeah. Why? What are you thinking?" There was worry in her voice.

We walked out the back door and just like before the guards stopped us, "We can't let you two lea-"

Before he could finish and paying no attention to the guards, I shoved Sierra against the wall outside the door and pressed my cheek against hers, "Raise your leg with the knife."

She extended her neck and exhaled deeply as she ran her leg up along mine. I guided my hand from her hip down her leg until I felt flesh at her ankle. I then brought my hand back up until I reached the knife all the while she was breathing heavily on my ear. Before I pulled away she whispered, "We'll pick this later."

I heard one of the guardsmen un-holster his weapon, "You two need to go back inside."

I whipped around launching the knife at the combat-ready guard's neck then jumped at the other punching him in the throat. They both toppled over and we ran around to the front of the building where Robert was waiting for us in the van. He pushed the back doors open and I helped Sierra in, "You two do realize that whole scene was recorded right?"

"Are you asking for copies Robert?" Sierra laughed and I climbed into the back of the van. Robert just looked at me unamused, "What are you waiting on? Get us to the warehouse!"

He jumped into the driver's seat and we squealed off, "Hurry up and get changed if you want to go in with me."

Sierra's face lit up and she began undressing, "Aren't you changing?"

I untied my bowtie and unbuttoned the top button of my shirt, "I don't know when you'll let me wear a suit again so I think I'll make this last as long as possible." Sierra hung her gown on the overhead rack and I caught a glimpse of Robert's eyes in the rearview mirror, "Hey! Eyes front."

***

"We're pulling up now and it looks like all your backup is here."

Sierra finished dressing as we rolled to a stop, "I realize you brought me the appropriate outfit for a combat situation but next time I want to choose what I wear."

I had packed her normal combat clothing, maybe not the most comfortable stuff but definitely practical, "What do you have in mind?"

"I was thinking more along the lines of Trinity from *The Matrix*."

I chuckled at the thought of her in that outfit, "Admittedly that's something I wouldn't mind seeing but that was a fictional movie. Dressing that way isn't practical."

Before Sierra could get her next word out the back doors opened, "Dad? What are you doing here?"

"Daniel called me last night to call in his favor. He gave me what I assume are the bare minimum details."

"Oh don't you trust me General?" I hopped out of the van and helped Sierra out.

Stephen, Sierra's brother, walked over with a bullet resistant vest for her, "I don't need that."

"The hell you don't. You'll get yourself killed without it."

"You don't need to worry about that."

General Morning looked back and forth between Sierra and myself, "What the hell did you do to my daughter?" He drew his sidearm and held it pointed at my face.

Sierra raised her hand to her face and mumbled, "Not again."

"I only did what she wanted and I'd like you to remember what happened last time you got hostile with me." He didn't move, blink, or even seem to breathe; he was like a statue, "There's two children being held as slaves, maybe more, and a lead on a nuclear warhead. You can continue to try my patience or we can search for the kids and the bomb."

He blinked once but remained still. Stephen placed his hand on his father's, "Sir, we have work to do."

Michael holstered his weapon, "What's your plan?"

"Stephen you come with Boris and myself into the warehouse. General, you position your men around the Kameha Dome and either when we find the children or when the auction ends get your men in there and detain everyone. After that, coordinate with Howard Brixton whom I've already given you the contact number for. As for you I would like you to stay in the van with Robert and run reconnaissance with him."

Michael laughed, "I'm not going to sit and do nothing."

I looked at the front door of the warehouse and pointed, "You can stand guard at the door if you want but I want you and Robert to remain within earshot of each other at all times. He'll keep the van right here."

Robert opened the chest in the back of the van and handed us the weapons stored inside. I lifted an assault weapon over my head to sling it over my shoulder, and attached a holstered pistol to my hip. Boris equipped himself with a shotgun and a sidearm. Steven was already armed to the teeth with an assault rifle, a sidearm, a k-bar knife, and his pockets were stuffed with enough ammo for all of us.

"What about me? Where's my weapon?"

"Sierra you'll remain in the van with Robert to keep out of harm's way. Michael will be here to."

"I'm not staying here. I told you I'm going in there." Sierra's stubborn father wouldn't let up.

"We've already been over this. I don't need you with me. Any more than a three man team would be too much. How about you stop being a soldier and try being a father for once in your life." I calmed myself and spoke softly, "Your daughter will be safer with you by her side." He only stared at me and said nothing.

I fidgeted with my ear piece, "Howey. Can you still hear us?"

"Loud and clear." Came the voice over the radio frequency.

"Good. Robert and Howey keep in contact until the op is finished." Robert nodded in confirmation, "Alright then."

We started to move out when I realized I almost forgot something, "Oh yeah Robert, you have my special order on board?"

"I've got it right here." Robert leaned back and pulled something off the top shelf. When he leaned forward he handed me my katana.

"Ah. There she is." I took the sling off of my assault weapon to equip Bisha instead. I had made my own special harness that allows Bisha to hang at my hip on the left side clipped securely to a sling over my opposite shoulder and a belt around my hip.

"Should I be jealous Danny?"

I unsheathed the seventy-two centimeter, black-as-night blade, and twirled her around to re-familiarize myself, "You have nothing to worry about. Then again I never have to worry about Bisha arguing with me." Sierra gave me a hard shove with the muzzle of a gun she picked up.

"What good do you think you can do with a mere sword when a firefight breaks out?" I expected as much from a Marine such as Michael Morning.

I sent Bisha back home into her scabbard, "I can get more done with this than I did with five throwing knives back at Juarez's compound." I looked around at the team that surrounded me, "If we're all ready, let's move out."

Chapter Thirty-One

The three of us approached the door, "I'm going to take point, Steven you cover the rear." They both moved into position and I looked to Sierra, seeing the worry in her eyes. The General gave me a look that said, "I hope you never come out."

With our weapons ready I pushed the door open ever so slightly, "Lights on." We flicked on the flashlights mounted on our rifles and I moved through the doorway into the dark warehouse. I pushed myself up against one of the large crates near the door while I waited for Boris and Steven to quietly enter. There was only one other light besides ours and it looked to be all the way in the opposite corner of the warehouse. Judging by that it seemed the warehouse was just one big room.

I signaled Boris and Steven to get a view on the light and they peeked their heads over their cover for a view. When they did shots broke the silence and muzzle flashes expelled the darkness. I could picture it, Sierra running to the door at the sound of gunfire and her father stopping her.

Boris and Steven were both well experienced in combat so I didn't need to direct them on how to eliminate the enemy. I signaled that we split up and so we did. Steven took the left flank, Boris took the right, while I went up the middle. As I moved, firing in short bursts, I had only come across crates and pallets, nothing of noteworthy significance. The lamp that we were going for was on the opposite side of the room and it seemed like the hostiles were coming from whatever was underneath of it. Shots continued to ring out and the yells of enemies hit accompanied them.

I put my finger to my ear, "I'm pushing forward. You two move further to the outside." I moved around from my cover keeping low and my weapon raised. I quickly moved, preemptively eliminating targets as they attempted to take a shot at me. I sensed somebody behind me and as I turned around a bullet went through the head of the man standing over me. To my right was Steven. I would have thanked him but there were still threats to be dealt with and he knew that.

I reached the lamp and saw what was underneath of it. I approached the hatch doors on the floor and radioed in, "I'm clear under the lamp." Slowly two lights came from either side of me.

"That was a little too easy if you ask me. Most likely a distraction." I was with Steven on that.

Boris looked down at the doors, "I agree. What do you think's down there? A cellar?"

There was no way to tell just yet. I waved for them to keep an eye out, "Howey we've found doors leading to a sub-section of the warehouse. See if you can find any records of what might be down there. A map would be best. And Robert tell Sierra we're fine." They both confirmed with an "okay".

"Alright one on either side." Boris and Steven got into position and I counted down on my hand. Three. Two. One. I pointed my weapon down when they lifted the doors open revealing an empty stairwell, "Back in line." We began our decent in single file line led by me.

We moved down the stairs where at the bottom it opened up to a very long, seven foot wide corridor running perpendicular to the stairs. I pushed myself against the right wall and Boris came down to press against the left wall. I silently counted down from three then we both moved around our corners looking down opposite ends of the extended hall and Steven came down just as fast.

Boris and Steven could take the left while I take the right but without knowing how many halls or rooms are connected to this corridor or how extensive this sub-level is it would be unwise to split up. "Howey do you have anything yet?"

"Yeah but you're not going to like it. There's a whole network of tunnels down there that were supposedly abandoned and sealed off by the city. The maps I have are all very old and possibly outdated."

"This place looks new. If the tunnel system is old then somebody went through a lot of trouble and put in a lot of effort to make it look new." The whole corridor was well lit, had steel walls, a concrete floor, and pipes running along the wall in the corner of the ceiling, likely for water and ventilation. "Thanks Howey."

"It's too risky splitting up not knowing what we might encounter." I looked both ways, "We'll stick to one wall single file with me still in front."

"Why not cover both walls?" Steven had a valid question and if I wasn't here that would be the way to proceed.

"If you're behind me I'm more likely to get hit before you, potentially saving your life." Without any argument from them we continued.

We got about twenty yards down the hall before we came to the first room. I stopped at the doorway and Boris moved around to the opposite side while Steven moved to the other side of the hall to see past us. He nodded and I quietly turned the door knob. Boris was able to see in the room first and nodded when, from his point of view, he determined it was clear. I silently moved into the room and raised two fingers for Boris and Steven to see, indicating two hostiles.

They were sitting in chairs watching television leaving their firearms lying on the floor next to them. Boris and Steven entered the room and I handed Steven my rifle. From that, Boris put together what the next step was. He slowly lowered his weapon letting it hang at his side. On my hand I counted down from three. We each dashed at a man sitting in the chairs.

I tipped the chair backwards bringing it down with the man in it. Boris flipped his chair forward knocking the man on his face. Steven kept the door cracked just enough to peek through, keeping an eye out for any unwanted visitors. Boris held his man stomach down holding his arm behind his back and pressing his knee down on the side of his head. I had my knee digging into the man's ribs and applying pressure from my elbow down on his face.

Now that we had struck the fear of God into these men it was time to question them. While Boris already started beating his man I would start by asking a question I already knew the probable answer to, "Who do you work for?" He only begged for his life in Russian. Russian was probably the only language they understood so that's how I would continue. I punched him in his kidney, "Who?!" He only cried out in pain.

In the corner of my eye I saw Boris choke out his guy then walk over, "He said this guy is his boss." The man screamed that he was lying, "Well we'll never know since he's dead now."

"Well if he's the boss I wonder what information we can get out of him." The man squirmed and cried, "He doesn't seem very cooperative so we'll probably need to force it out of him." I grabbed two of his fingers and raised them in front of his face, "I'll just break his fingers, then his toes then some bigger bones and joints." I twisted and bent his fingers backwards.

His expression and demeanor changed, "Okay okay! I'll talk!"

"You speak English huh?" I put more pressure on his head, "Is it just you or should I expect everyone I find to play stupid?" These guys are well-trained if they're able to come off as incompetent in the face of death, "Answer my question." I applied more pressure with my knee onto his ribs cracking two.

He screamed then answered, "You know who I work for. What you want to know is where you can find the kids." He said with arrogance.

"Boris wake him up and bring him over here." I picked up my man and held his fingers interlocked behind his head. Boris slapped the man awake and walked him over for them to face each other, "First one to tell me what I want to hear lives." Boris's man glanced at my sidearm. I drew Bisha and thrust her through his heart, "He had the wrong idea." I flicked the blood onto the ground and put her back home.

"Alright I'll tell you. This side of the complex is the storage and personnel section; where you'll find the kids. You'll find more opposition on this side than you will on the opposite side; the research and development section of the complex."

"Where can I find Hunt?"

"I don't know. Honestly. He doesn't tell anybody where he is or where he's going. The only people that get to know where he is are his top guards. They always have his back."

"Anything else you want to share? Specifically what's going on in research and development?"

He swallowed, "Only the technicians, scientists, and a few authorized guards are allowed over there. I have no idea what they do there. I swear."

"I believe you." I nodded to Boris and he punched him in the throat. I let go of the suffocating man and he fell to the floor, "He cooperated. I wanted you to knock him out not kill him."

Steven tossed me my rifle, "How was I supposed to know that? You only nodded."

"From now on if they cooperate we don't kill them." Boris agreed reluctantly.

I buzzed in with Howey, "Did you get all that?"

"Yeah. I don't like the sound of a R&D section."

"Neither do I. We'll continue our current route and when we're finished on this side we'll go see what we can find over there."

"Alright just keep me posted."

"Are we clear Steven?" He nodded and swung the door open for us to move out.

Down the length of the corridor more doorways were visible, "We're going to need to speed this up. We kick in doors, shoot first, questions later. We need to find Hunt. Got it."

They nodded and we moved out of the door and down the hall at a fairly fast pace to the next door. Faster than before, Boris moved to the other side of the door, I kicked it down, rushed in, shot and killed two hostiles as they reached for their weapons, then Boris and Steven came in behind me. We swept the room and cleared it then moved on.

The shots alerted the other hostiles as expected. Before we left the room guards were already in the hall searching for the intruders. I pulled a flashbang off of Steven's gear and threw it down the hall. After the explosion all three of us moved into the hall, keeping formation, eliminating the disorientated threats in rapid succession. The next few rooms having now been vacated, we each searched one individually.

I finished checking mine and waited outside the next room. When they joined me I kicked the door open and instantly gunshots came out of what looked like a vast storage area. I had moved out of the way just in time for a bullet to only graze my arm. Boris and Steven payed no mind to my superficial wound and shot short bursts into the room when they felt it safe enough to do so.

I signaled to them that I would move in first so they fired suppression rounds until I got to a safe spot. Then I supplied the cover fire for them to get in. The shooting stopped and familiar voices called out, "We've been waiting for you Rahm." It was Isaiah Joaquin. "This is the end for you and your merry band of do-gooders." And that was Eli.

"Anyone who knows me by that name knows I can't be stopped." I signaled for Boris and Steven to move but to stay together. Steven tossed me an extra mag for my rifle that I pocketed.

"Where's Hunt and the kids?"

"The kids are in the back of this room over here. You'll have to find Hunt on your own." A grenade landed next to me forcing me to leave my shelter. I dove away to my left and shot a few rounds, taking out a hostile as I moved to safety behind a forklift. I turned my back to the grenade when it exploded, shielding myself from the flurry of debris that was once a crate. On the other side of the room I could still see Boris and Steven shooting back.

Having others with me was a distraction. Boris, my long lost son, and Steven, my fiancée's brother. If they weren't here it would be much easier to focus and I'd be able to sweep through this complex much faster. If only-

Before the thought even crossed my mind I watched a bullet rip through Steven's thigh. He slumped against the barrier he was leaning against and fell to the floor. He stood back up on his good leg and continued to shoot back at the enemy; like a true soldier. But now he's a liability.

Gun fire was exchanged for another thirty seconds or so and Steven fell back to the floor. I waved for them to leave but he shook his head no. He attempted to get back up to show he could still help but failed. I ran over to them, "Get him out of here Boris."

"I can still fight!"

"Even so, you're wounded which will only slow us down. And to be honest I'd be going a whole lot quicker alone." Both of them looked insulted, "Leave me some mags and flash bangs and get out the same way we came in." Boris didn't argue. He probably felt that Steven's wound needed to be treated too. When I threw the flash bangs Boris grabbed Steven by the back of his collar and began to drag him as Steven fired at whatever moved.

When they got through the doorway and I was sure they were out of the line of fire, I moved, "You're two men down Rahm." I rounded a large crate and slammed a hostile in the throat with the butt of my weapon, "You're all alone now."

I paused behind a barrier to reevaluate my environment when a grenade landed next to me. I quickly grabbed it and threw it back. Just a second later it blew up and an arm fell from above, landing next to my foot.

I've spotted two forklifts and one was back where I came from. There are plenty of crates and barriers to find safety behind. If I move quickly and use the obstacles to my advantage I can keep in motion and rapidly eliminate all targets. I tossed my assault rifle on top of the barricade protecting me and drew my sidearm. I remained motionless listening for foot falls. When I heard the nearest pair of feet right around the corner, I whipped around, pistol whipped him in the throat, and shot another a few yards away between the eyes.

There couldn't be too many left, could there?

I ran towards the second body I dropped and climbed onto the top of the container next to it. I spun around to locate as many foes as I could before, "There he is!" Before one of the brothers spotted me. I fired off a shot in the general direction of the shout and walked off the container. I figure it easier to let them come to me rather than me running around in this maze of a room to find them.

I started running towards the side of the room where the twins were first shouting from. Firing pot shots at enemies I spotted in my peripheral and only actually eliminating the two that stood in my way with a snap of the neck and a bullet to the head. I finally reached the other side of the room where a smaller room stretched along the length of the wall. There was a short clearing to cross from where I was, next to a crate, to the doors into the room I hoped the kids were in.

I whispered in an attempt not to break the eerie silence in the room, "Robert, I'm nearing the kids. Next check in will be when I secure them.

Copy?" There was no response. Just silence. What could that mean?

I stuck my head out and looked both ways before crossing the street, or in this case, an open range with me as the only target. I crossed the clearing and was one step away from the door when, "Stop right there Rahm." That was Isaiah to my left.

I reached for the door handle, "The door is rigged to blow when opened." And that was Eli to my right. He could be bluffing and I could probably make it inside before they can hit me but the risk was too great. If the door really was rigged to blow and I opened it, it would be game over and everything would have been for naught.

"Drop the gun and put your hands behind your head and interlock your fingers." Smart. Keeping my hands away from my sides where my weapons are but what they don't know is that I'm always prepared for every contingency. Stuck on my upper back underneath of my shirt I have two throwing knives ready for use. I remember from yesterday morning, at breakfast, Isaiah is right handed while Eli is left. If I can hit both of their dominant arms anywhere below the elbow I shouldn't have to worry about them shooting at me. "Turn around and kneel on the floor."

I did as Eli said, or was it Isaiah. Now that I see them I can't tell which is which. I hate twins, "Which one of you is Eli and which is Isaiah? Twins get me all messed up."

The one to the left stepped closer, "Do you think this is funny?"

"Yeah. Is this not supposed to be funny?"

They spoke in Russian, "Why don't we just shoot him in the head to make it easier?"

"Alexander said we get more money if we deliver him conscious."

"Hey I have an idea. I'll let you take me to Alexander. I'm looking for him anyway." The twins looked at each other as if to be terribly thrown off by my words, "Yeah. Just let me see the kids and make sure they're okay." The one nodded to the other. The one on the left walked past me and opened the door for me to see inside.

No explosion.

I saw two steel barred cages with a child in each, "Now that I see that the kids are safe, you can take me to Alexander." Robert wasn't responding but hopefully either he or Boris heard that and would send in the reinforcements to get the kids out of here. Having them escort me to my target is the best thing that could happen. Now I don't have to waste time searching the complex.

"Keep your hands behind your head and walk. We'll tell you where to go." I did as they said and they began leading me further into the complex.

"Hey Danny you there?" Howey's voice came in through my ear piece, "I don't know if you can hear me but something's happened at Robert's post. I can't get in touch with anyone over there. I'm sending a few agents there now to check it out. Just wanted to give you a heads up. I'll get back to you when my men arrive on the scene."

What was happening now? Could Hunt have gotten to them? If he did, what did he do? Who did he kill? Who did he take? I will soon find out. I'm being led right to him.

***

After a half dozen turns we finally entered a room with only a giant screen on the wall, "Where's Hunt?"

The twins looked around apparently having been deceived by Hunt. The screen came to life revealing an image of the man I was looking for, "Where are you Alexander? Where is our money?"

It was Hunt. His face covered the screen blocking the sight of anything behind him. He looked happy. Thrilled almost.

"Calm down. Your money is under the floor panel one yard in front of Mr. Silver." Hunt laughed, "Though I doubt you'll get to do anything with it." The twins looked at each other to see if the other knew what Hunt meant, "Isn't that right Daniel?"

Before they could register Hunt's words and ready their weapons I drew Bisha. On the withdraw I sliced through one twin's abdomen. I put my second hand on the tsuka (or handle), gripping Bisha with both hands then brought her back down, severing the other twin's head from his body. I flicked the Russian blood off of my katana and sheathed her.

Hunt clapped, "That looked fun. Was it fun? Feeling the rush of a kill, dirtying the blade of your weapon with the blood of your enemy. Must have been fun."

I hated being manipulated. Sure the twins deserved to die, but I wasn't going to kill them. Not yet anyway. Being forced to kill them when it wasn't necessary made me feel… uncomfortable, "Face me Hunt."

"In due time Daniel. There is much we must discuss. But first I'm sure you would like to know the status of your compatriots. By now I'm sure Howard's men have reached Robert and his van."

"Danny." Howey's voice echoed in my ear, "We found Robert and that's the only good news. Both of his legs have been broken below the knee. Steven's been bleeding out in the back of the van. Michael is gone and so is Sierra."

Howey paused long enough for me to have to prompt him, "What about Boris?"

"He's dead Danny."

Chapter Thirty-Two

My son. Dead. Murdered by Hunt no doubt.

"You son of a-!"

"Uh uh uh." Hunt raised his finger and wagged it back and forth, "You don't want to talk about your mother like that do you?"

What? My mother? Before I could piece together what he meant, he turned the camera to reveal Sierra, "Yes I broke Robert's legs, left Steven to die, killed Boris, and took Sierra. I only knocked the General unconscious since I foresee him playing a very interesting role in our story."

I turned around to leave the room when the door shut and locked me inside, "You need to stay and listen."

"Why can't we talk face to face?"

"We both know the answer to that. While you are a patient and composed individual, I have provoked and infuriated you far too much for a face to face conversation to even be remotely possible. You would attack me, unable to control yourself, so I'm afraid this is the only way to tell you what you need to hear."

I walked to the center of the room and stood, "Fine. Why? Why torment me? Why not somebody else?"

"Oh but it has been somebody else; so many times before. You see I've been around just a tad longer than you. And for the past couple hundred years I've been watching you, following you. When you walked into my bar a few decades back playing the role of the infamous killer Rahm, I knew who you really were, and I was expecting you."

"You see, our paths have crossed countless times throughout history, however indirectly. You have your stories of heroism and selflessness all the while I've been the one who wrote those stories. I can see the puzzled look on your face."

Hunt had to be lying, "You still haven't answered my question."

"The answer you're looking for comes at the end of this story. If I gave you your answer right away you wouldn't understand." He looked over his head at Sierra bound in a surgical chair, "Where was I? Ah yes, stories I've written starring you as the hero. Take the most notorious and infamous criminals in human history, in our lifetimes that is. Adolf Hitler,

Joseph Stalin, the so-called "Zodiac" killer, and Jack the Ripper. There are many more but I chose to name only the individuals I'm sure you're most familiar with. Each of them has their own story in a long series where the only two consistent characters, which remain behind the scenes, are you and I."

"You and I are the only ones that know what really happened to them for you were the one that brought about their demise. But what you've never known is who played the role of motivator, or inspirer if you will. Every major disastrous event or series of events, every psychopath that has long been dead but will never be forgotten, all of it was orchestrated by me."

Is it possible for what he says to be true? That he had influenced those men to do the heinous things that they did, "What motivates you?"

"Now you're asking the right question and the answer is quite simple: chaos. I enjoy chaos. Like watching stuff blow up or somebody kill somebody else, like you did just a few moments ago." He closed his eyes and inhaled deeply, "I enjoy it, thoroughly. Take any thrill-seeker and their thrill; nothing comes close to the exhilaration that I am filled with when chaos, suffering, and torment is loosed into this world."

"So you cause chaos for chaos' sake?"

Hunt leaned back in his chair in a sense of accomplishment, "Yes! Now you get it."

"There's only two reasons why the antagonist of a story confesses to the protagonist; he knows one of them is going to die."

"Hmmm. Sadly enough you're right, or only half right, but before either of us can die I need to tell you a very special story. Please remain silent while I share with you this very informative piece of history."

***

"Once upon a time there were two brothers. The first was born in October of 1669 while the other was born in June of 1667. They were both born in New York and at the young ages of fourteen and sixteen years they ran away from home in May of 1683. The two of them had an inseparable bond and would have died for each other."

"In August of 1687 they began a life of piracy and were very good at it, the best even. In February of 1693 they began to command a ship together, making the one brother twenty-four and the other twenty-six. They spent their lives pirating in the Pacific and by 1695 their names had become synonymous with piracy, and were infamous on an intercontinental level and for that era that was quite an accomplishment for word to travel that far."

"The next year they stepped up their game and began stealing from English ships then sinking them, making the two all the more wanted criminals. You can imagine how difficult it became to simply live once their ship was the most wanted in the Pacific. After eight years of fleeing, they were found, followed, and encircled by a fleet of ships over top of

Mariana's Trench; there was no way out. The ship was boarded and ironically it turned out they were hunters looking for revenge. They killed the crew and forced the two brothers to the edge of the ship with iron balls chained to their ankles. The two brothers looked into each other's eyes and smiled defiantly as they both walked off to their death. At the ages of forty and thirty-eight."

"Now this is when the story makes us legends."

"'Us'? What do you mean?"

"The answer to that is the same to your first question: you and I are the brothers in the story."

My stomach sank and my heart skipped a beat. I didn't know what to say, or which of my hundred questions to ask.

"Speechless huh? I thought you might be. I don't know why I retained my memory and you lost yours. That's been a question I've kept on the back burner. The more important one is *how*? I know you've been wondering the same thing, even if you can't remember. How are we alive? How do we remain healthy? How is it that we can't die? How do we regain missing limbs? How do our bodies rebuild when we've exploded into a million itty bitty pieces? How did the shackles and steel balls around our ankles come off? What is it in Mariana's Trench that has made us who we are?" Admittedly, he had grabbed my attention by this point.

"Now if you would put aside our differences and be open minded about something that isn't effected by our ideologies or right and wrong." I'm sensible enough to be able to do that.

"This is where the research and development section of this facility comes into use. Though technology has come a long way it is still too primitive to provide me with the answers I need and my lab here even surpasses your labs abilities at Acro. I've gathered the greatest minds in the world here. I have them experiment on me, test me. I have a room that I use specifically for blowing myself up so they can monitor how it is that I come back to life."

"Which brings me to my next point: what the hell is 'blacking out'? We don't go unconscious, we die. We become brain dead and we have no heartbeat, yet our consciousness is still there since we're able to think. You know what I'm talking about. But instead of remaining dead, there's something in our physiology that brings us back. You know about the SIRT1 gene and the extra Y chromosome which only explains our agelessness."

"Now what I have to say next is a bit of a stretch and before you dismiss it as science-fiction or some other nonsense, keep in mind, this is who we are, this is our life. I believe the truth lies within us at an atomic level, possibly even sub-atomic."

"A person weighing seventy kilograms has roughly seven octillion atoms in their body. As you know a majority of those atoms are hydrogen, oxygen, and carbon. I think that there is some number of atoms within us that have the designated role of putting us back together when we fall apart, so to speak. Whatever phenomenon that happened to make us this way happened when we sank into Mariana's Trench." We stared at each other, "Oh you can talk now."

"Yes I want to find and kill you but I'm not so ignorant that I would ignore such information no matter how much of a psychopath the source is. And yes, while all that you say is intriguing and deserving of more thought, none of it explains why we are here and now, in this situation."

"Oh why do you have to go back to that? Why can't we just brainstorm and work together. All of my trials have been unsuccessful but with your help-"

"Trials? What trials?"

"Oh did I? I did." Hunt bumped his palm to his forehead, "I forgot to mention the trials. I've dropped a few test subjects into Mariana's Trench whilst mimicking the circumstances in which we were dropped. I've kept records of everything: ocean tides, sea levels, time of day, exact coordinates, and time in which it would take the subject to sink to the bottom in said conditions."

I didn't want to encourage him but I needed to know, "What were your results?"

Hunt smiled, "I assigned pairs to camp sites along the coasts of all land masses within a one-hundred mile radius of the drop-site expecting a body to turn up somewhere." He lowered his head and a somber look fell on his face; certainly not in thought of the lost lives but because of his failures, "Fourteen trials with zero results."

He raised his head and narrowed his look on me, "I've shared all that I know which means this is where our story nears its conclusion." The door behind me unlocked, "Head to the R&D wing and follow the halls my personal guards are posted in. You'll find me at the end." I turned around and walked out, "Don't forget to enjoy yourself on the way here." I ran down the hall hearing Hunt's laughter behind me.

Chapter Thirty-Three

As I backtracked through the hall the Russian brothers brought me through I thought about all that Hunt told me. Is he really my brother or was his story of our early years as pirates just the incessant babbling of a psychopath? Could the secret to our regenerative abilities really lie at an atomic level? Have I really died so many times and just get "put back together"? What kind of phenomenon would account for something resulting in who Hunt and I are but then be unrepeatable? How did the shackles and weights get off of us after we sank into the ocean? It all seems too unreal and science-fictiony, but then again this is real life. And I can't forget the fact that Hunt is a psychopath and probably deranged.

I passed the stairs we took to get into the complex and raised my hand to my ear as I ran, "Howey, you still there?"

"Finally. Where have you been?"

"You telling me you didn't hear anything Hunt said?"

"You've been radio silent for the past few minutes. I was about to send some men down there to look for you."

"I'm on my way to Hunt now." I rounded a corner and was spotted by the first guard. I back peddled and waited for him to come to me, "Make sure Force Recon has the Dome on lockdown and keep the warehouse secured. No one in or out."

"Got it."

The room I was in must have started blocking all radios signals once Hunt started telling his stories. If Hunt wanted to keep what he was saying between us that could mean he plans on coming out on top when this is all over; keeping his secrets within the walls of his R&D facility.

I didn't have any more firearms on me so when the guard came around the corner I drew Bisha and cut through him. I saw a camera down the hall looking in my direction. Hunt was watching and no doubt enjoying what he was seeing.

I followed the halls that had guards posted in them and cameras watching. Hunt put these guards here not only to guide me but for the thrill of watching me kill them.

About ten halls later and an equal number of guards, I reached a highly secured door. I sheathed Bisha and approached it. It was a heavy looking iron door. It had a finger print scanner next to the door for authorized entry only. There was a square window in the door about head height. When I walked up to the door I peered through the window but before I could make anything out Hunt's head quickly appeared on the other side only barely startling me enough to make me blink.

"Glad to see you made it though I knew those guys wouldn't slow you down any." I could feel his closeness. I just wanted to reach out and grab him by the throat but with the door in the way, "Don't look at me like that. No greeting for your long lost brother? Oh that's right. You came here for her." He turned away from the window allowing me to see Sierra lying in the chair restrained and gagged.

Hunt walked around the chair so I could see him pick up a scalpel, "Chaos Danny. That's what I live for." He brandished the surgical tool as he spoke, "I'll give you thirty seconds to get in here and stop me from cutting away at poor little Sierra here."

How could I possibly get inside?

"I never tried it with Dimitri but I do wonder if my atom theory applies to those we gift with our blood, like her for example." He looked up at me, "Twenty-five seconds." Hunt started whistling the *Jeopardy* tune.

I took a step back and looked around the doorframe. I could break the glass and probably make a cut in the door with my katana but that wouldn't be enough to get me through the door.

"You might be able to totally ignore pain but others like Sierra and I haven't gone through the proper training to do that."

Damn it!

"Fifteen seconds Danny."

Could it be so easy? This all seems to be a game to him. He wouldn't give me a time limit that he didn't think I could complete the given task within. I leaned down to analyze the finger print scanner.

"Ten seconds."

But how could he have entered my prints into his security system? I placed my right thumb on the pad and the door buzzed.

"It's about time!"

The door slowly opened towards me. As soon as I was able to squeeze myself through, I quickly side stepped into the room. Hunt was right there waiting for me and plunged the scalpel into my right shoulder. I pushed his arm away, deflected an incoming punch from his left side and punched him back in the throat, "That's for Robert." He staggered backwards, reeling from my hit. He grabbed a large knife from the counter and raised it. I drew Bisha cutting his hand off and it fell to the floor with the knife, "That's for my son."

He yelled and stepped back. I gripped the katana with both hands and pointed the end of the blade at Hunt. I thrusted forward piercing his abdomen, "And this is for Sierra." I lifted him up and slammed him against the wall having Bisha penetrate it and now keeping Hunt suspended hanging on the blade.

Hunt smiled, "This isn't over brother." He coughed up blood and the life in his eyes dimmed then vanished. Is that what I look like when I black out? No. Having seen it so many times before, I know that's what death looks like. Actually seeing the life leave his body only adds to the mystery that is us.

Now for Sierra. If the answers do lie on an atomic level, do they lie within her too like my blood does? I never want to have to find out.

I removed the gag from her mouth, "Are you okay?"

She coughed as she worked to moisten her mouth. When I freed her wrists from their restraints she quickly leaned up, pulled out the scalpel I forgot was in my shoulder, and wrapped her arms around me. Through her sobbing I could barely make out the two words she wept, "Thank you."

"I'm sorry. Again." I pulled her off of me, "But it's all over now."

I began undoing the buckles around her ankles, "Was what he was saying the truth?"

"I've been trying to come up with a reasons to convince myself he was lying." I freed her legs and she spun to hang them over the chair and look into my eyes for an answer, "And I don't know."

I put my arm around her and reported in to Howey, "I've got Sierra and Hunt is incapacitated." I turned around before I told Howey to send a team to retrieve Hunt but was stopped when I saw who had found their way here.

"Thanks for leading me straight to him Daniel. I had gotten lost down here until I saw you run down a hall cutting a man in half."

It was Sierra's father Michael and he was aiming his sidearm right at me, "What are you doing here?"

Sierra cried out, "Put that away."

"Stay out of this Sierra!" He snarled at his daughter then turned his attention back to me, "I'm doing what's necessary to most assuredly make the United States the most feared and powerful country in the world."

"Are you serious? Everyone in human history and even in fiction with that mindset has ended up killed for believing they were helping when really all they were doing-"

Too quickly for me to react, he pulled the trigger, double tapping me in the heart.

No. This can't be happening. So close yet so far away. I finally got to Hunt only to have him slip through my fingers. He said Michael would play a critical part in our story. Did he know this would happen? How could he?

Michael fired a third round into Hunt's head, probably for good measure. I backed against the wall and slumped to the floor, and Sierra kneeling with me on the way down. She held my head in her hands and screamed at her father, "Why?"

I looked up at Sierra, still aware and conscious of the situation, but my body bleeding out and too weak to do anything about it. When her eyes met mine and Michael approached Hunt's body she yelled once more and ran to her father hitting, more in a fit of anguish than to cause pain, "Bastard!"

Without sparing a moment, with one arm, Michael threw Sierra off and she fell to the ground, sitting there, weeping and in shock.

"You take him and I'll kill you." They were the last words I could muster up but I'm sure they didn't sound very threatening from a man sitting on the floor bleeding out.

Michael put his shoulder in Hunt's chest and pulled Bisha out of him. Hunt's body laid on the General's shoulder and my katana dropped to the floor, "Have fun finding me."

As Michael walked out with his captive, Sierra sat on the floor next to me and rested my head on her chest. As I was fading in and out of consciousness I heard her say, "We'll find them Daniel. We'll find them."

Chapter Thirty-Four

"Give me an update Howey?"

"The transport unit is pulling onto the tarmac now and the plane is scheduled to depart in five. Looks like it might be sooner than that though."

It took a few days but with Acro backing him up, Howey was able to track down Michael and his hired transport team of mercenaries. General Morning had flown back to the States the same night he had taken Hunt. Howey's been tracking him since they landed in West Virginia and drove all the way onto a private runway in Atlanta Georgia where they have a jet fueled up and standing by to take them to a secure and isolated location in Kansas. I had an idea of the location they were going for, but I wasn't about to let them get away again.

Now I'm speeding down busy roads to get to them before they start boarding the plane. Sierra is with Howey in the command center, keeping an eye on the situation from there. Robert's in the hospital recovering from his broken legs while Stephen is in a coma after losing so much blood.

As for Boris, my son… Sierra helped me burry him in my private graveyard with all of my past friends and loved ones.

"I can see the airport now."

"Danny. I can see Michael getting out of the middle truck." After he shot me in front of her, Sierra hasn't called him dad or father, she's just called him Michael.

I drove onto the private area of the airport, going about eighty, and the gate guard jumped out of the way right before I rammed through it.

"Danny! They just opened up the back door of the middle truck and we have a visual confirmation on Hunt. It's him." I continued speeding along the runway and spotted the transport down at the opposite end, "What's the plan here Danny?"

"You know how I had the mechanics customize this car?" There was no response, "I'm going to kill them all."

I was about two hundred yards away when they saw me coming. The three trucks emptied out and all their passengers opened fire as bullets ricocheted off of the windshield.

"Danny what are you doing?!"

I took Bisha off of the passenger seat and held her against the steering wheel to brace myself for the impact. At twenty yards out I saw Michael standing on the other side of the middle vehicle, my target.

I rammed my armored car against the side of the truck and my neck whiplashed. I quickly pulled myself together and pushed my door open and dove out, rolling back up, and slicing the first mercenary in half. The others behind me had me in their sights so I moved around to the back of the rear truck and waited for them to stop shooting.

The heightened suspension on the truck made it possible for me to crawl underneath. When he was next to me I cut the mercenary down at his ankles and when he fell I pierced his throat. I rolled out towards his body and while on my back I threw a knife over my head into the face of a third mercenary. Before his body dropped I was already back on my feet.

I ran around the back of the truck and to the other side and stabbed through the fourth mercenary that had his back turned towards me. When I pulled the blade out, dropping his body, I threw another knife at another hostile's elbow, forcing his trigger arm to release his weapon. I dashed towards him and decapitated the fifth mercenary.

The sixth and last that I counted was on the other side of my car and its crinkled hood. Before he could get a shot off I vaulted the car and sliced him in half, from the head down. I swung the blood off and sheathed Bisha.

I walked around the front of the caved in prisoner transport vehicle with Hunt inside, "It's about time bro. I've been waiting for you." For the moment, I was ignoring him.

The General was lying on the ground with a broken leg from the truck impacting him. He drew his sidearm and pointed it at me, but I was too close to him now. I grabbed the weapon and turned it, breaking his finger in the trigger guard, "I told you I would find you."

"You won't kill me."

"I would but I know that even though Sierra hates you, I don't think she would forgive me for killing you."

He smiled as if he had beaten me, "You're weak."

I took his side arm and pressed it against his temple, "It's taking all the strength that's within me to not just do what comes naturally to me." I pushed the gun harder against his head and whispered, "Boom!" I stood up, "I'm not above disabling you." I shot him in each knee and he screamed, "Good luck trying to come after me."

I turned around and walked towards Hunt's vehicle where he had his head sticking out of the window watching me, "Oh come on! Why didn't you just kill him?"

I pointed the gun at him and he attempted a puppy-dog face, "This one's for me." I pulled the trigger shooting him in the head.

I opened the door and threw him over my shoulder, "I've got Hunt."

"Good work Danny. I have a recovery team on standby waiting to take him to the secure location we spoke of."

"I've already got a jet here waiting for me. I'll just relieve the pilots and fly it myself. Bring Sierra with you and meet me there."

"If you say so."

***

After landing on a very old and overgrown runway in a secure and extremely remote location in Alaska, "Oh where are we?" I shot Hunt in the head again and carried him on my shoulder for about a mile through the woods until we reached where we needed to go.

I searched for a specific tree that I had chosen three decades ago. Back then, I had cut into a tree and placed a remote device inside of it, allowing the tree to grow around it. Once I found the tree, I calculated the exact number of years and months since I was last here and the height in which the tree would have grown in that time. I took a knife out of my belt and carved into the tree where I approximated the remote would be.

When I carved out the remote I entered the five digit code and just a few yards away the ground began to move. The device opened up a circular hole in the ground five feet in diameter and went down fifteen feet.

Hunt had woken up again, "Oh what is that?" There was evidence of true curiosity in his voice.

"Do you really want to know?" I grabbed him by his bicep and walked him near the hole then tripped him so his head was hanging over the edge, "You asked."

"You'll regret this brother." I grabbed him by his feet and lifted him into the hole, head first.

I heard the crack of a twig and spun around with my gun up, ready to fire. The two of them stopped and quickly raised their arms, "It's just us Danny." I lowered my gun and Sierra looked happy to see me.

"I'm glad we waited to use this place. There's never been anyone else more deserving." Howey had walked past and looked down the hole.

"My thoughts exactly." Sierra and I joined Howey above the tunnel entrance, "Howey, I'll need you to stand watch while she and I go down. I'll close the hatch behind us, so here's the remote." I handed him the device and he turned around to start keeping look out.

"Can you tell me what this place is? Howey wouldn't tell me on the way here."

I took her hand and walked her around the hole to the top of the ladder leading down, "You'll see when we get down there." She looked hesitantly at me. "It's just a short tunnel that leads into a single room. I'll go down first to turn on the lights and you follow."

I looked over at Howey in the distance and he gave me the all clear. I began my decent into the black hole and once at the bottom I placed my hand on the wall activating the lights running along the floor on either side of the five-foot wide, twenty-foot long hall.

I checked Hunt's head and noticed his skull had already reshaped and didn't show any signs of having been dropped fifteen feet. I kicked his leg to check for life then looked up, "You can come down now." I shouted up to Sierra.

She reached the bottom and I hoisted Hunt onto my shoulder, "Just down the hall."

Sierra followed me to the six inch thick steel door at the end of the hall. I placed my hand on the wall and a tiny panel slid open at eye level and performed a retina scan on my eyes, "Howey did mention this place was thirty years old. How is there a palm and retina scanner down here?"

"Howey spoke the truth, but that doesn't mean this place is outdated. Acro had technology like this back then."

The iron bars in the doors creaked and receded into the walls, ceiling, and floor. Smaller latches and locks came undone also. Once the noise stopped I pushed the door open into the room. When Sierra stepped in behind me I closed the door.

I walked over to the surgical chair in the center of the room and laid Hunt on it, "Can you tell me what this place is now?"

While strapping Hunt down I explained, "Howey and I had this place built for one purpose: to hold a single captive for an indefinite period of time. In the past we agreed that the actions of the enemies we had faced didn't warrant the use of this location. The past week though, has made us realize this is the only place we can keep Hunt."

"What is this place used for besides just 'holding' somebody?" Sierra was looking around at the different cabinets, carts, chairs, and then at the door in the back of the room, "And I thought you said there was only one room."

"That's just a restroom and this room is fully equipped to extract information from whomever is being held here. Hunt has a wealth of information within his head. He mentioned to me Hitler, Stalin, the Zodiac Killer, and Jack the Ripper. He might have the keys to some of the world's biggest secrets and mysteries. He'll stay here forever, or at least until I come up with a way to permanently kill him."

Hunt's eyes opened, "Where am I?" He shook in his restraints, "What is this place?"

"You're in an undisclosed location that doesn't exist and you'll remain here forever."

I took a blindfold and wrapped it around his eyes and behind the chair, keeping his head down, "I'll get out of here. You know I will!" Next I took a gag and pushed it into his mouth, against his will of course. I then put a couple layers of duct tape over his mouth.

I turned to Sierra, "You ready to go?"

She looked at Hunt then back to me and smiled, "Let's."

I took Sierra's arm and walked her out, locking the heavy door behind us. We climbed the ladder, closed the hatch, met back up with Howey, and walked the mile back to the clearing I had landed the jet in.

Sierra grabbed my arm before we boarded, "What is it?" She looked around the side of my head and plucked a hair, "Ah! What was that for?"

She held a strand of hair just inches in front of my face, "When did you get a gray hair?"

I took the hair to examine it for myself. It was indeed a gray hair; one that I've never seen before. Am I actually aging? Does this hair mean that I've reached the halfway point in my life? Could it be an omen? Marking the end of an era plagued by my brother's evil? Or marking the beginning of a new one free of it?

Then again it could just be a gray hair that means absolutely nothing.

"Hello? Earth to Daniel."

Sierra broke me from my daze, "Huh. How bout that? And to think it took three-hundred and fifty years to get my first gray." I smiled and dropped it, letting the wind carry it away.

Her gaze followed it back into the forest, "Is it over now? For good?"

I pulled her attention back to me so I could look into her eyes, "It's all over. We never have to worry about him again. We can go away to a place where we won't be judged for who we are but instead welcomed. We won't have to look over our shoulders for anyone that might wish us harm. We can sit in our own little corner of the world."

"Can you two love birds wrap it up so I can get home to my wife, and more importantly, my bed?"

We laughed at Howey's impatient remark, "How about we go get started with that house on the beach we talked about?" She smiled, we kissed then we walked onto the plane, leaving the source of all our problems behind us.

END

Made in the USA
Middletown, DE
24 December 2016